# The Wrong Way Round

Road Dog Publications was formed in 2010 as an imprint of Lost Classics Book Company and is dedicated to publishing the best in books on motorcycling, motorsports, and adventure travel. Visit us at www.roaddogpub.com.

No part of this book may be reproduced by any means, nor transmitted, nor translated into a machine language, without the written permission of the publishers.

*The Wrong Way Round:*
*How* Not *to Travel to Burma by Motorcycle*
Copyright ©2019 Andy Benfield
All rights reserved.

ISBN 978-1-890623-68-5
Library of Congress Control Number: 2019932491

An Imprint of Lost Classics Book Company
This book also available in eBook format at online booksellers. ISBN 978-1-890623-69-2

# The Wrong Way Round

## How *Not* to Travel to Burma by Motorcycle

*by*

Andy Benfield

Publisher
Lake Wales, Florida

To Christopher Robin and Piglet—for inspiring me to venture beyond the Hundred Acre Wood.

# About the Author

Andy Benfield was born and raised in the UK but soon caught the travel bug, quitting his first proper job in an investment bank to go and live on a farm in Israel instead. He returned home to get a degree, feeling that might help sustain him overseas in future, and was off again the day he graduated. A variety of odd jobs followed, including teaching English in the Sudan, interning at the British Embassy in Spain, and most incongruously, showing people how to grow rice in rural Madagascar. A stint living in Hong Kong learning Tai Chi was followed by two years meandering around Africa, the Caribbean, and the Pacific advising small businesses on how to be more productive, while squeezing in as much adventure as possible on the weekends.

Andy eventually wound up living in India, working for a diplomatic mission, and took up riding Royal Enfield motorcycles, fast developing a love of two wheels and the open road. When he was forced to leave his bike behind and move to Ethiopia for work he took up flying instead, which he claims he had pretty much down, apart from the landing bit. Moving on to Namibia, his love of the African bush was firmly cemented as he off-roaded across some of its most remote parts, pretty much destroying an innocent two-wheel drive sedan in the process.

Asia beckoned again, and Andy wound up in Bali, where he bought a house in the jungle and resolved to settle down. But the bug wouldn't quite leave him alone, and he ended up turning the house into a boutique hotel and moving on again, this time to Kathmandu. The joys of motorcycling through the Himalayas kept him in one place for over a year, something of a record, before he heard tell of a secret Asian gem that had lain hidden from the world for the past five decades. And that's how he ended up in Burma and this story began.

(Andy is currently based in Singapore but may well have moved again by the time you read this.)

# Table of Contents

About the Author _____ v

1  The Big Idea _____ 1
2  Bitten by the Bullet _____ 9
3  Into the Frying Pan _____ 23
4  Wild Times _____ 45
5  Hell and Heaven _____ 61
6  Borderline _____ 83
7  Tea and Trains _____ 95
8  Shake, Rattle, and Roll _____ 113
9  Breaking Up and Down _____ 127
10  Meeting the Thunder Dragon _____ 141
11  Shangri Las _____ 157
12  Exit the Dragon _____ 175
13  Into the Wild _____ 187
14  Taming the Head-Hunters _____ 199
15  Bombs and Bikers _____ 221
16  The Golden Land _____ 237
17  Police State _____ 251
18  The Final Stretch _____ 267
19  Burma and Bust _____ 277

# 1
# THE BIG IDEA

"There's a good reason why they call it the Highway of Sorrows you know," the avuncular Indian diplomat raised a bushy eyebrow as he gazed at me with a mixture of bemusement and pity, "This is most certainly not being a tourist thoroughfare, sir." He reached up and indicated a dotted line on the map that was hanging on the wall of his office in the tranquil confines of the Indian Embassy in Rangoon. It snaked across north-east India and up to the Burmese border and was, he explained, in reality a stretch of broken tarmac and dirt that was unfortunately prone to highway robberies, kidnappings, army-rebel clashes, and general all-round skulduggery. "I wish you luck," he paused and raised his visa stamp over my passport, "What you are planning is most definitely not the usual nor, some might say, the advisable." He seemed to have resigned himself to my fate, however, and so completed the formalities then handed me back my passport as I started to wonder just how much I might look back and regret this moment in future.

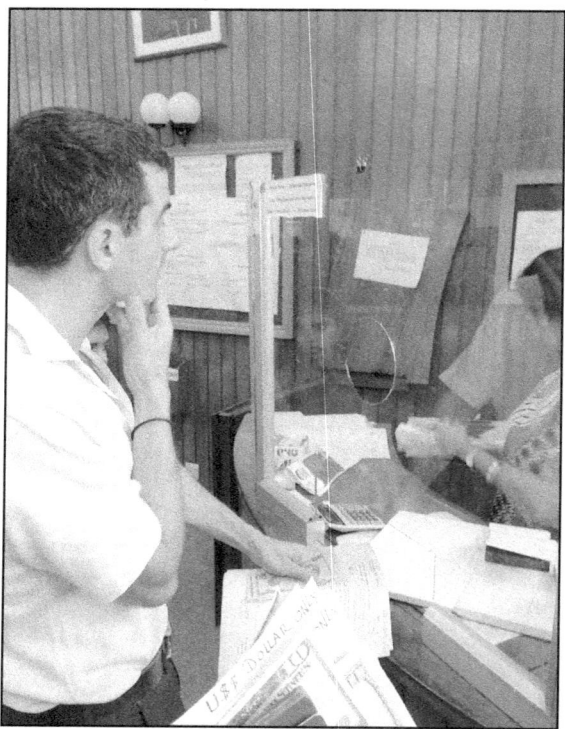

**Indian visa time**

Quite simply, or so I liked to think, my plan was to fly from Rangoon, the capital of Burma (or Yangon, the capital of Myanmar, as the military had renamed them, but I still liked the old titles better) where I currently lived, to Delhi, the capital of India, and then ride a motorcycle 4,000 miles all the way back to Rangoon. The initial motivation for what might seem like a rather pointless exercise was a practical one—my job as an aid worker had recently brought me to live in Burma, but I still had an old motorcycle stored in Delhi, where I'd lived a few years previously, that I thought would be just perfect for pootling around the backroads of Mandalay.

Riding it over from India seemed so much more romantic than shipping it in. Just the names of the places such a journey would see me pass through—Kathmandu, Sikkim, Bhutan, Nagaland—already had the goose bumps rising in an adventurous tingle up my arms. It was a route that offered some of the most stunning scenery in the world: the mighty Himalayas, the pristine wildernesses of Bhutan, and the wild jungles of Nagaland. I would be brushing shoulders with Nepalese Sherpas, Bhutanese yak herders, and Naga head-hunters as I travelled along old trade routes that have long fallen into disuse and decline as, after the military takeover in Burma in the 1960s, they became roads to nowhere, ending in an abrupt full stop at the now closed India-Burma border. But all that was about to change, Burma was opening up and would soon assume its rightful position as a vital link between the two regional titans, India and China. That meant that the forgotten lands I was dreaming of were about to be shaken from their long slumber, with all the blessings and curses that would entail. I wanted to see them before the magic was gone.

In addition, I had to admit that I wasn't getting any younger. Pushing thirty-eight, since finishing university in the UK I'd been fortunate enough to spend my time moving country every couple of years, eventually winding up doing consultancies for western embassies and aid agencies in the developing world, a vocation that had taken me from Namibia to Nepal and from India to Indonesia. But while I still had no intention of returning home just yet, the days of riding around on the roof of the bus or going out camping under the stars in the desert seemed rather far behind me. My "adventures" were becoming increasingly posh, pre-planned, and air-conditioned, even if the locales remained quite exotic. I couldn't remember the last time I had set off with a backpack or without a hotel reservation, let alone travelled with a fellow passenger's chicken in my lap. So perhaps this was all just a rather desperate attempt to prove something, cooked up by my insecure and rapidly approaching forty sub-conscious.

I should confess that there was one final motivation, somewhat of an elephant in the room. In a tradition that one may no doubt find paralleled in the origins of some of mankind's greatest undertakings, I was trying to impress a woman. I planned to take off on this adventure with my new girlfriend, Rebecca. Maybe I was only even seriously considering it because of her, as a way of holding the attention and admiration of a woman who, even when in my arms, always seemed to remain somehow outside of my grasp. She was, in fact, Lady Rebecca, progeny of a European aristocratic dynasty that had been ruling over peasantry like myself for several generations. Utterly fearless, precociously intelligent, somewhat emotionally unavailable, and unfeasibly tall and blonde, she had remained an enigma to me ever since we had met at a diplomatic reception in Rangoon six months earlier.

She was some twelve years younger than me, and so one might imagine she'd be the one trying to retain my attention rather than vice versa. But Lady R was a rather special case, which I guess is what had attracted me to her in the first place. There was that formidable brain to start with, displaying a degree of sharpness, insight, and reasoning ability that had led her to be an international chess champion before she was ten and the holder of masters degrees from three different top international universities by her early twenties. It made conversation with her in turns stimulating—as she immediately understood your point and could further develop it—and intimidating—as she sliced through your arguments with effortless panache to expose your shoddy thinking, all the while with a bemused expression on her face that seemed to ask how you could quite possibly be so dim-witted. She was also insatiably curious but always, it seemed, about things and people other than me.

Then there was the aristocracy issue. Being a member of a noble family and enjoying her own title, there was never a question of social insecurity or trying to prove oneself. Close friends included dukes and countesses from around Europe, and she had told me more than once that she was expected to marry into another such lineage. She would often describe an acquaintance in terms of whether they were from a "good family" or not, an expression I thought the rest of us had stopped using back in the 1850s. I was certainly up for a title myself, though, and so became somewhat disheartened when she informed me that, should we marry, the rules stated that I would not get one, however, any subsequent offspring would. That I felt could cause terrible resentment on the part of their father and lead to a whole host of domestic difficulties. But, then again, marriage and babies did not really seem to feature in her future plans, which instead included competing in a round-the-world yacht race, undertaking a PhD, doing a three-month long meditation retreat, and moving with a group of friends to a hippy colony in southern California. But I, sadly, didn't seem to feature in any of them.

On the upside then, I was never bored, nor was I likely to take her for granted, but on the downside, I was left with a nagging doubt that I just wasn't quite good enough, that I was merely a placeholder until someone better came along. Which was, I suppose, one of the reasons I'd pushed for us to move in together just a few months after we met, keen for a bit more security. As that still didn't seem to do the trick, well, what better way to finally convince her of my charms than a two-month odyssey across the wilds of South Asia, me in the starring role and her clinging to my back in an admiring swoon?

As far as I could make out, no-one had ever driven or ridden from Delhi to Rangoon before, and it wasn't too hard to work out why. Leaving Delhi, we'd need to plunge straight into the arid badlands of India's poorest and most populous state, Uttar Pradesh, to reach the border with Nepal. If we managed to cross over, the Terai would await us, a little visited swathe of the south of the country, infamous for its descent into semi-anarchy after the collapse of the Nepalese monarchy in 2006. Regular shootings and bombings marked the ebb and flow of power there between a heady mix of corrupt politicians and policemen, armed "liberation" movements, former Maoist rebels, and Mafiosi businessmen.

After Nepal, a traverse of the remote Himalayan kingdom of Bhutan would give a brief respite—a peaceful nation with a stunning mountain backdrop and the world's cleanest air and lowest crime, a place so enlightened that they had replaced Gross National Product with Gross National Happiness as a measure of how they were doing. The only real menace there would be a dose of altitude sickness on the high mountain passes. Or, come to think of it, sliding off an unpaved road and plummeting over a cliff. Oh, and then there were the yetis to look out for, of course, it being the only country in the world to have a national park dedicated to their protection.

Having run across the length of Bhutan, we would enter India once again, but a very different part of it this time. We would be riding into the country's north-east, a remote and restive land of hills and jungle. That was the part of the journey that Lady R was most excited about and that I was most dreading. Ever since independence in 1947, a kaleidoscope of armed ethnic groups have battled there against the paramilitary forces of what they refer to as the "mainland" for self-determination. While doing so, they have steadily fractured into a bewildering array of factions whose dislike of recent brothers-in-arms seems to rival even their disdain for Delhi. *Fronts* seemed to be their moniker of choice, and we could look forward to encountering the United Liberation Front of Assam, the National Democratic Front of Bodoland, The Karbi Longri Hills Liberation Front (absolutely not to be confused with the Karbi Longri North Cahar Hills Liberation Front, of course), the United National Liberation Front of Manipur, and the Mizo National Front. Even more exotic-sounding were the All Tripura Tiger Force, the Achik Mantric Liberation Army, and finally, the People's Revolutionary Party of Kangleipak, known more commonly by their delightful acronym *PREPAK*. In spite of their impressive names, in recent years some such organisations had moved away from their original independence struggles and towards the more lucrative pastimes of extortion, kidnapping, and smuggling drugs and guns over the Burmese border. To make our way across the north-east and reach that border, we'd need to ride through their heartlands on the infamous Highway of Sorrows. If we succeeded, then we would face the biggest challenge of the trip—crossing a frontier that has been officially closed to foreigners for the past fifty years. Should we somehow manage to convince them to let us pass, it would be terra incognita from there on in as we entered a remote area of Burma and tried to make our way back down to Rangoon.

My concerns didn't stop there, though. A good part of the route would be unpaved tracks through the mountains, and we would be using a standard road bike, rather than one of those, err, bouncy ones with the knobbly tyres. Getting a vehicle across five international borders was going to be anything but easy in that part of the world. And, finally, there was our complete lack of mechanical skills; on my side a shameful inability to fix anything beyond a flat tyre (and admittedly even that was a theoretical capability I felt I must possess as part of my Y chromosome, rather than something I had ever actually done in practice).

As I did some more research, I eventually discovered that someone had, in fact, driven the route previously. Back in the summer of 1955, a group of six plucky Oxbridge students kitted out with a couple of Land Rovers, a good supply of gin and tonic, and, no doubt, some damn stiff upper lips, set out to be the first people to drive from London to Singapore. Many had tried before them but had always fallen foul of the India to Burma section, given its lack of roads, formidable natural barriers of mountains and jungle, and less than friendly locals. These plucky Englishmen, however, were able to make use of some rough tracks that had recently been hacked through the hills by the Allies at the end of the Second World War in order to open a supply line from India to China. And so, to cut a very long and truly epic story short, they became the first ever motorised travellers to make it through from India to Burma and subsequently rumble victoriously into Singapore. Shortly after, though, Burma was taken over by the military and the border was closed, so any chance of other foreign travellers following in their footsteps was abruptly scuppered.

# 2
# Bitten by the Bullet

On a rainy Sunday morning a few weeks after the appointment at the Indian embassy, we stepped out of our apartment in Rangoon, and I wondered just what on earth we were going to go through before I again turned the key in this lock. We passed the open-fronted tea-shop at the bottom of the stairs, and I greeted the betel nut salesman, who was hawking his wares just opposite. A light drizzle drifted down through the palm trees that lined the street and pattered against the roof and walls of the beautiful old colonial town house across the way. This, like the rest of British-era Rangoon, was mouldering and crumbling rather attractively as Asian climate progressively triumphed over European architecture.

In a shaky old taxi on the way to the airport, Lady R fished a notebook out of her bag and started scribbling with fervid intensity. I turned to her curiously,

"What you got going on there, baby?"

"I'm planning a first article for our blog."

"Oh, great!" this was really the least of my concerns right then, but I tried to feign a little enthusiasm, "So, what's it about?"

She sighed a little impatiently, "Well, basically a treatise on the history of the Ghurkhas, examining the historical links between Burma and Nepal viewed through the prism of their colonial-era migratory patterns."

I gulped, "Well that sounds very, err, interesting; no doubt our readers will be delighted." Should we have any, I thought. We'd set up a fresh new shiny website and blog that we aimed to fill up as we went along, but I wondered how our rather different approaches to writing were going to gel together there. For example, my own plans for a first blog piece were at that moment finely balanced between (a) a reminiscence of how a music video by 1980s Norwegian pop sensation A-ha had made me want to ride classic motorcycles in order to become more like the lead singer, the oh-so-dashing Mr. Morten Harket, and (b) a featurette on the perils of the intimate chaffing that was likely to result from long hours in the saddle.

As the plane reached cruising altitude, I busied myself by running through the mental checklist that I had been incessantly re-hashing over the last few days. I desperately tried to remember the things that I had forgotten and nervously pulled at the loose ends of those that I remembered, watching with morbid fascination as the whole endeavour appeared to unravel before my eyes.

True, it wasn't like I'd never been on an adventure before, I'd had my fair share of scrapes and scares in various corners of Africa and Asia, where I'd been working and travelling. I'd been arrested in Sudan, caught malaria in Madagascar, been ambushed in Indonesia, and crashed a car into a goat in Ethiopia (it really was not my fault), for example. But, well, this trip seemed like it might take things to a whole new level of risk.

Granted, we did have a rough overall route planned out that looked sort of feasible on paper, though whether certain faint lines on the map corresponded to navigable roads on the ground, especially just after the monsoon, was another matter. And we had managed to get special permission to enter India three times during two months, which was normally a no-no (apparently to prevent foreigners getting involved in dodgy smuggling activities). This was a necessity for us, however, (the permission, not the dodgy smuggling activities) as we planned to travel through Nepal and Bhutan, and each country borders India on its west, south, and east sides, giving some idea of just how large India is. We had also secured special permission from the Bhutanese authorities to take a foreign-registered vehicle through their country. For Nepal, though, there had been no time in the end to get visas, and it was still not quite clear whether one was officially allowed to ride across the border from India or not. So the plan was to try and wing it through using a combination of charm, wit, bombast, and perhaps a little "tea money." Most worryingly, though, I had failed to secure any response whatsoever to my request to the Protocol Department of the Burmese Ministry of Foreign Affairs for a special exception to the usual ban on independent travellers crossing the India-Burma border. I naively let myself believe permission would somehow magically appear before we reached it (which I reckoned we only had a fifty-fifty chance of doing, in any case). It was the biggest longshot of the trip.

Then there was the serious question of whether we really had the requisite mental and physical resources for such an expedition. Our lack of mechanical knowledge was complemented by a notable absence of any first aid skills or local language ability. We had not a stick of professional motorcycling clothing between us and no camping gear, should we get stuck out in the open somewhere. Lady R's fearlessness, I feared, could get us into all sorts of trouble, and it didn't help that part of my strategy for wooing her was throwing my own habitual caution to the winds. I sighed and consoled myself with the thought of something I did have—a homemade survival kit that I had put together and stashed in my rucksack. This consisted of a Swiss Army knife, a hip flask of single malt, and a slab of Kendal Mint Cake. Here was one aspect of my preparations those Oxbridge chaps would definitely have approved of.

The five-hour flight from Rangoon to Delhi made rather a mockery of the two months it was going to take us to ride back. Just while eating our in-flight meal we had covered a distance that would take a week's worth of motorcycling. It was all rather surreal, suspended here at 30,000 feet, cocooned against climate and culture, trying to imagine what might lie beneath. As I leaned over to peer out of the window, I took the opportunity to snuggle up against Lady R and then tried to transpose my own worries onto her,

"Sweetie, I just want you to know that I realise it must seem quite scary what we're about to attempt but that, well, it's OK to feel like that."

She looked back at me nonplussed,

"You mean scary as in adventurous and fun?"

I paused, "Well, hopefully that too, yes, but of course there are, err, a whole bunch of potential hazards down there and so, you know, I want to reassure you that I'm here, I won't leave your side."

Her lips turned up into a wry smile as she patted me on the knee,

"Well that's good to know; it will make it much easier for mummy to protect you that way."

The seatbelt light pinged on, meaning I had to pull back into my seat and buckle up. I couldn't help noticing that she looked slightly relieved to no longer have my arm around her. The passionate side of our relationship left a little bit to be desired, to be honest, I mean, yes, it existed but only quite irregularly. Things had never quite been the same since the evening she had mused out loud as to whether she might be more sexually attracted to me if only I was just a little bit taller.

At nearly six foot, this was the first time I had experienced such criticism. But rather than file it away in the unreasonable category, I, instead, added it to the list of things that I felt I must do better in future in order to properly capture her heart, while starting to consider a new stretching regime or maybe some subtle shoe inserts.

A few minutes later, the nose of the plane pulled gently up, the engines sighed, and we bumped down onto the parched tarmac of Delhi's Indira Gandhi Airport. Arrival in Delhi has been very much sanitised in recent years with the construction of a shiny new terminal and a rather calm and quiet processing of incoming passengers. That is a nice change from the old days when the terminal was a seething, sweaty mass of humanity that you had to writhe your way through, but does absolutely nothing to prepare the innocent traveller for the noisy, colourful, and unpredictable city that, thankfully, still lurks intact right outside the doors of Arrivals.

I had always found India a tricky country to pin down, chiefly because most statements one makes about it tend to reveal their opposites to be true just a moment after. The flyover that thrust ambitiously skywards on the highway into town, cutting a path up between two glittering new skyscrapers of steel and smoked glass, sent a clear message of a country on the move, making money, firmly middle class. But as we drove under it, braking to avoid a lumbering cow, we passed a rickety shelter of bamboo sticks and old plastic sheeting clinging to the support pillars. This was home to the construction crew that had been working to build this symbol of the new India. Whole families were camped out there and would no doubt soon be moving on to the next building site, which would be the only place they had to call home. Two small children, barely covered by a few stained and threadbare pieces of clothing, played with left-over building materials next to a mound of rubbish that the curious cow was now languidly pushing her nose into.

The contrasts continued thick and fast: the Sikh temple next to the new shopping mall; the bullock cart stuck in the traffic jam alongside the Mercedes S-Class; the people donating food to the orange-clad, trident-wielding wandering holy man while stepping over their low-caste homeless brethren who were lying on the pavement next to him, seemingly viewing them as an entirely different species. Yes, India is rich and poor, spiritual and material, compassionate and heartless, timeless yet changing at breakneck speed. It is a country that will make you love it and hate it, laugh and cry, and fill you with inspiration and despair, normally all in the space of a single afternoon. But one thing you will certainly never be is bored.

Lady R was staring out of the window of the taxi at the chaotic traffic and frowning at a passing rickshaw that was sounding its horn incessantly and for no apparent reason. I saw my opportunity,

"There's a method in their madness, you know."

She turned to me and raised an eyebrow, which was her usual signal that one is permitted to proceed, and I started to relish one of the rare moments when I was going to be able to tell her something she didn't already know. "So, some of the more wily rickshaw-*wallahs* actually wire their horns to their metres so that every time they honk, the metre runs a little faster, and hey presto, the customer gets charged a little more. Pretty innovative, huh?"

She laughed and looked out of the window again with renewed interest. I decided to capitalise on my momentum,

"So, another thing you can check out—it looks pretty much likes chaos out there, right?"

She nodded, "It's certainly not Geneva."

"Quite, but actually there is a whole vehicular caste system in effect. So, you've got your buses and trucks at the top, cars in the middle, then motorcycles, and finally bicycles and anything flesh and blood powered at the bottom," I pointed out at the traffic, "so if you look at who gives way to who, you'll see that hierarchy is pretty strictly observed."

She peered intently across the lanes for a minute, "Dammit, you know you're actually right."

I was on a roll, as was our driver as we swerved to avoid another cow, and so I took the opportunity to add a final titbit.

"Oh, but I should add that cows trump all of the above and may sit in the middle of the highway all day long chewing unmolested as the rest of the sub-continent skids frantically around them."

She giggled, and I got the reward of a hand on my knee. Yes, this trip might just provide the rebalancing of our relationship that I yearned for. As I'd lived in both India and Nepal previously and also travelled in Bhutan, the journey was going to be full of such moments where I would be the one able to explain the places, people, and events, to arouse her interest and inquisitiveness. Bingo.

After another half hour of stopping, starting, dodging, and weaving, we edged our way into the northern reaches of Delhi and entered the enclave of Karol Bagh. A labyrinth of small streets greeted us, peppered with second-hand motorcycle shops and repair garages, the sidewalks strewn with fuel tanks, tyres, and various other pieces of motorcycle anatomy, the air thick with an exotic mix of sandalwood incense and exhaust fumes. With my head thrust out of the window, bravely risking decapitation by the oncoming traffic, I eventually spotted the landmark I was looking for; a gnarled old peepal tree growing straight out of the side of a cracked yellow wall. I signalled our taxi driver to pull over, thrust a wad of grimy rupees into his hand, and pulled Lady R out into the torpid afternoon heat.

The tree marked the entrance to a narrow alley that led off the main street. A few metres along it a faded sign above a dark doorway announced that we had arrived at our destination—Inder Motors. A concrete ramp descended directly from the doorway into the ominous gloom of a basement, giving no inkling of what might lie below. We slithered down into a dimly-lit workshop full of dismembered Royal Enfield Bullet motorcycles, spare parts, tools, and a handful of smiling greasy mechanics. At the end of the room, holding court behind his polished wooden desk, head wrapped in an immaculate dark blue turban, and long white whiskers tied neatly together beneath his chin, sat the inimitable Mr. Lalli Singh.

"*Namaste*, Lalli!"

**Lalli and me chat over** *chai*

"Ah is that you, Mr. Benfield? It's been quite some time, sir."

I smiled, "About six years by my count, how are things, *ji*?"

"Oh fine, fine, Andy, you know tickety-boo, now how about some *chai*?"

Lalli's welcome tended to be the same whether it had been ten days or ten years since you had last seen him, and whether you'd just been mooching around Delhi in the meantime or undertaken a heroic two-wheeled circumnavigation of the globe. Probably somewhere in his mid-fifties but never seeming to actually age, Lalli presided over perhaps the best motorcycle workshop in India and was the expert on both bikes and routes, not only throughout India but right across the region. His clientele were an adventurous bunch, and you would normally find a handful of long-haired, dusty overlanders sitting drinking tea in his workshop and

## Bitten by the Bullet

recounting their adventures while Lalli smiled gently at their tales, forever polite, calm, thoughtful, and sage.

"Lalli, let me introduce Rebecca."

He stretched out a hand towards Her Ladyship, "Ah pleasure to meet you, madam. So, you are latest model?"

I coughed and intervened quickly, "Forgive him, darling, his English is quite terrible; he has no idea what he is saying." He wobbled his head and laughed while Lady R did her other type of eyebrow raise. Introductions complete, we started to sip the sweet milky tea that one of the mechanics had brought over on an old silver tray, and I enquired as to the status of my beloved,

"Yes, yes, your bike is quite ready, tip-top condition only, just needing *puja* and exceedingly good to go."

I eyed Lalli quizzically, "We have to do a religious ceremony for the bike now? Well this is a first! Were the oil changes not bringing you in enough cash?"

He let out one of his impromptu and quite charming giggles, "Ceremony is only for very special VIP customer, Mr. Andy!" Then, just as I was thinking how much I must already be rising in Lady R's estimation, he added, "Or for non-sensible journeys that are really needing help from other side."

I laughed a little nervously, "Err, surely you must have had some other clients who've ridden to Burma, Lalli? It does neighbour India, after all."

He shook his head vigorously, "*Nahi*, you're the only one I've ever heard of to try. You know, closed border, that is what they are saying, and I suppose those head-hunters in the northeast are also scaring people off."

He gave Lady R a conspiratorial wink and then proceeded to light up some incense, string a garland of flowers around the motorcycle's headlight, and start reciting a prayer, soliciting Ganesh's protection for our travels.

The Royal Enfield motorcycles that surrounded us in the workshop are ubiquitous in India. Classic 1940s-style machines that can be found chugging along highways and byways across the country, piloted by moustachioed khaki-clad cops, turbaned young Sikhs, and anyone who wants a little piece of Bollywood machismo in their life. Years ago back in England, I'd seen an old photograph of one in a book and was pretty much hooked on the basis that (1) it looked like something Steve McQueen would break out of Second World War prison camps on (2) the Enfield company's slogan was "Made Like a Gun, Goes like a Bullet," and best of all, (3) it rhymed perfectly with my surname, thus presenting the tantalising prospect that, should I become the proud owner of one of these machines one day, people would start to call me "Benfield on the Enfield." Or perhaps just "The Royal Benfield."

When I moved to live and work in India years later, I became further entranced by the Enfields that rumbled past me on a daily basis. But it took a good few months before I plucked up the courage to look into buying one and braving the Indian traffic. Finally, a friend recommended Lalli, and I paid my first visit to the underground workshop where we now stood. In a couple of weeks, he'd found me a lovely old bike, negotiated the byzantine registration process for foreigners, and started to teach me how to ride. I was at first truly terrified by this noisy, growling beast but gradually managed to stop shaking while riding and then to successfully manoeuvre the bike up and down the piece of wasteland near the workshop that served as my training ground. Eventually, I even managed to change gear without it sounding too much like a mechanical disembowelment. But I was still feeling light years away from being able to navigate smoothly through the Delhi traffic on the day that Lalli softly but firmly informed me that I would be riding the bike back through town to the workshop that afternoon. The leg shaking started again as soon as I turned onto the road, and I promptly forgot how the gears worked and where the brakes were, then stalled the bike right in the middle of one of northern Delhi's busiest intersections. This led to an absolute cacophony of horning, hollering, and some choice Hindi phrases from my fellow motorists, which I managed to get the general gist of, thanks to the accompanying hand gestures.

But over the following days and weeks, the bike gradually metamorphosed from a fearsome and unwanted pet into one my most treasured possessions. The first venture out of Delhi, though, saw my riding confidence shattered again as I struggled to control a baggage-laden and hence very wobbly bike along the dusty, truck-infested highways that stretch out of the city into the state of Uttar Pradesh. Only some hours later, with a semblance of equilibrium and self-respect restored, could I finally start enjoying the freedom of cruising the back roads of India on that wonderful machine.

After several more cups of *chai*, we bid our goodbyes to Lalli, who gave me an unusually firm handshake, looked me square in the eye, and told me he was very much hoping that he would see me again. We rode up the ramp out of the workshop and into the smoky haze of Old Delhi, cutting between rickshaws and taxis, buses and street dogs. I sounded the new horn Lalli had fitted for me. This was a huge bright red monstrosity, basically a klaxon bolted to the bike frame, which had the very useful benefit of exaggerating our size to those in front. We soon had motorbikes, cars, and small trucks pulling to the side of the road to let us pass, then looking on indignantly as we overtook them, revealing our deception. This tactic works particularly well in India, as no-one uses the rear-view mirror, instead relying purely on sound to detect if anyone is behind them trying to get past, and if so, to gauge their position in the caste system and thus their eligibility for being let through. Lady R's arms were tight around me, and I heard her sigh with pleasure. She was no doubt enjoying the breeze through her hair, the freedom of being on the bike, and I liked to think, the press of my body against hers as we twisted and turned through the backstreets.

**Into the streets of Delhi**

We planned to leave town the next day, giving us time to pick up some last-minute provisions and also to pay a visit to the Delhi representative offices of Nagaland and Manipur, the two diciest north-eastern states that we were going to have to pass through. That also allowed us to have a first test run at navigation. Lady R swiped around on Google Maps on her phone and called out directions to me from the back of the bike. It worked rather well and I savoured the teamwork as we wound our way across town. After half an hour we pulled into a small leafy street in the embassy quarter and dismounted. We pushed open a pair of large iron gates and wandered across a courtyard and into a two-storey whitewashed concrete building. After waiting fruitlessly at an empty reception for ten minutes, we started to explore a series of dusty corridors, peeking into dimly-lit offices, where the odd person sat idly leafing through/eating lunch off/snoozing on a newspaper. It didn't appear there was much interest in Delhi for the north-east or vice versa.

"May I help you?"

Finally, we'd aroused someone's suspicion.

I put on my best poor-foreigner-in-need-of-aid smile as I addressed the middle-aged woman in a purple sari who had just appeared in the corridor behind us and was now looking at me expectantly,

"Thank you, yes, we are looking for some advice on safety in Nagaland while traversing the state on a motorcycle."

She opened her mouth in surprise and then closed it again, "Well. I see. That doesn't really sound like such a good idea I am thinking." She considered further. "But Rajive-*ji* should be able to tell you how the situation is up there this season."

She beckoned for us to follow her a few doors down the corridor and ushered us into an office, where a gentleman with freshly oiled hair, a finely waxed moustache, and a formidable pot belly sat looking out of the window.

Our guide coughed politely, "Sir, I am having two crazy foreigners for you."

With that, she turned on her heel and left. Despite this introduction, we were, after a moment's hesitation, invited to sit down, and *chai* was swiftly produced from the pantry. I felt I had better break the ice, "Yes, so, sir, in fact, we are planning to ride a motorcycle from Delhi to Burma and to cross Nagaland and Manipur on the way, and well, we were just wondering what the security situation is up there now?"

As he considered my question and I looked at him expectantly, I realised that a not inconsiderable part of me wanted him to reply that this was completely out of the question, thus giving me the perfect excuse to call the whole trip off. He twiddled the corner of his moustache for a moment before replying, "Nagaland, yes. Dangerous."

I waited for more, but he didn't continue.

"Right, thank you for your assessment," I paused for a second, "in fact, we were hoping for maybe just a little more precise information than that, if you could, possibly?"

He sighed, burped, pulled a half-eaten samosa out of a drawer, examined it somewhat longingly, then popped it back in.

"I am not being one hundred percent sure about present situation. But probably best you take armed escort."

"Oh, I see. And so how might we, err, organise such a thing?"

"You don't have?"

"Erm, no, we didn't bring one along, unfortunately. Terribly short-sighted of us." I smiled ruefully at my own stupidity, "Might the local authorities up there be able to oblige, do you think?"

"Possible," he waved his hand a little dismissively and started hungrily eyeing the drawer again, "Best you call on the chief of police in the first town you reach."

"Noted. And we should presumably mention that we are doing so under your recommendation?"

He looked at me like I was an idiot, "Of course not. Now, good day!"

With that, he opened the drawer again and made a full commitment to his samosa. Right then, we'd just roll up at the local police station once we got to Nagaland and ask if they might have some armed men available who wouldn't mind escorting us to the Burmese border. I couldn't imagine what could possibly go wrong.

As the sun approached the horizon, burning the sky a vivid blood orange (rather romantic if one ignored the fact that this was largely due to the substantial amount of Delhi pollution that the sunbeams were being filtered through), we drew up at the charming B Nineteen guest house, our home for the night. This enjoyed a spectacular location overlooking Humayun's Tomb, Delhi's answer to the Taj Mahal, and was surrounded by a series of beautifully manicured gardens, a welcome reminder that there are still parts of Delhi that are calm, green, and delightful. It was also owned by two old friends of mine who were only too pleased to welcome us into their city oasis; "a last bit of proper pampering before the madness starts" as they kindly put it. I killed the engine and pulled the bike up onto the stand, spending a moment running my eyes over this wonderful machine, silently apologising for what I was about to do to her. The poor old girl had simply no idea. But then neither, as it would turn out, did we.

# 3
# INTO THE FRYING PAN

While I was well aware of Lady R's voracious appetite for new knowledge, a mobile library had not been on my list of expedition essentials. I had just stepped back into our room at the guest house and was congratulating myself that, after much shoving and swearing, I had finally managed to wedge our rucksacks into the rather small wrought iron panniers that were welded to the back of the bike. But I was now presented with a stack of books that she had squirrelled away somewhere on the way over including *Where China Meets India*, *A History of Nagaland*, *Man-Eaters of Kumaon*, and rather inevitably, *Zen and the Art of Motorcycle Maintenance*. I decided to start by ignoring them.

"Well, I've managed to squeeze everything in baby; now we're just about ready to hit the road!" She looked up and smiled at me like I had been a really good puppy then kissed me on the forehead,

"That's great darling; you're my hero! Now we just need to find a little tiny space for a couple of booky wooks."

I smiled apologetically, "Err, look, seriously, there's really no space left; you should really go and see . . . " Her smile turned into a frown, and so I tried again, "I mean if I'd known before, maybe we could have left something out but now, well. Anyway, I guess books aren't the most essential item when push comes to shove, right?"

She looked at me with more than a little disdain, "Excuse me? What could possibly be more essential than books? What would be the point of continuing to exist if one did not have the stimulation of the written word?"

"Well yes, err, possibly, I suppose, but I guess there's always e-books that we could download?"

She scoffed. "Oh yes, if we were heathens, I mean the feel of the paper, the heft of the book in one's hand, are both of course essential parts of imbibing a great work, as you well know, Andrew. Now please stop being so ridiculous."

I considered how filthy everything on the bike was likely to become after a couple of days' riding and the effect this would have on that sacred feel and heft but decided that now was the pivot point where, before annoying her too much, I could instead back down and claim some of that affection that I prized so much in return. It was an approach that I knew would make me feel both better and worse at the same time; getting attention and validation but feeling this was just because I was giving in to what she wanted. I recalled some of the other points I'd conceded in a similar fashion over the last six months, including not having a TV in the apartment (it was just too low class), riding on the roof of a bus down a terrifying mountain road in Upper Burma (it will be so much more airy), eating fried larvae from a street stall (what does not kill you makes you stronger), and crossing into a restricted military area somewhere outside Rangoon (this looks like it might be quite interesting).

"Well, I suppose we could dump the jerry can we have with the emergency fuel supply?" I suggested reluctantly. Her face lit up in triumph combined with a modicum of affection. "What a wonderful idea; I knew I could count on you! And as an added bonus I'll have something to read if the tank runs dry and I'm waiting for you to fetch more petrol!"

I couldn't help but laugh, yes those blessed books were going to solve a problem that would not actually exist without them.

So, this was it, the bags (and books) were strapped in, our helmets were on, and the tank was full. I took a couple of deep breaths, squeezed Lady R's leg, and then kicked the bike into life and rolled my hand around the throttle a couple of times. The engine growled softly, a measured, comforting sound with a rather stoic air. I turned to kiss Lady R, but the open-faced helmets acted as a rather effective contraceptive, forcing us to settle with a light head-butt. Pulling in the clutch with my hand, I pressed my left foot down on the gear shifter to put us into first, revved the engine a couple of times, and then slowly let out the clutch and pulled away from the kerb. I wobbled a bit at first with the unaccustomed weight and balance of the loaded bike, but by the time we reached the main road I had it stable again. The bike that is—as for me, my hands were shaking, and my heart was beating way faster than normal. I really couldn't believe we were actually doing this. It seemed so ridiculous to even attempt it, and such an invitation to trouble. It was absolutely unfathomable that we were going to make it all the way through to Burma.

Lady R had managed to convince me, in spite of my better judgement and the map clearly showing that Burma lay to the east of India, that we should start our journey by heading south. This was because, as she declared with something of the air of a European noble on an eighteenth-century grand tour, one simply could not visit the subcontinent without taking in the architectural splendour of the Taj Mahal. I had asked her whether, in addition to quenching her cultural thirst, this might also be a romantic gesture, given the Taj's fame as the ultimate monument to love, and she had agreed. But, I felt, rather too quickly.

One advantage of this detour-before-we'd-even-started was the road quality, something that would come to be quite an obsession in the coming weeks. Once we'd cleared the Delhi traffic, we joined a brand-new highway, the Yamuna Expressway, that connects Delhi to Agra, and one that is virtually empty due to its high toll charge. As well as a nice and easy, dust and bovine free start to the journey, this also meant a lovely stretch of peaceful tarmac where Lady R could have her first try at riding a motorcycle. After an hour's cruise I pulled up by the side of the empty road and got off the bike to let her slide forward into the driver's seat.

The Yamuna Expressway

"Now, OK, so this is the throttle, and here's the clutch," I reached over to demonstrate both, "So, gear change is here; brakes are here," I indicated the brake lever on the handlebar that operated the front brake and the right-side foot pedal that was connected to the back one. Then I felt a little sermon might be in order,

"Look, you don't have to do this you know; I am quite happy to ride us all the way there."

She turned to look at me, "And be a knight in shining armour escorting the poor helpless lady who then falls into a swoon over his gallantry at the end of it all?"

Damn, I had been found out, "Of course not, darling! I just mean, you know, I've been riding these bikes for years, and it's not easy; they are big, heavy beasts and what with these roads and traffic, really it's a hell of a task and . . . "

I was interrupted by her pulling smoothly away and heading off up the highway into the distance. She was perfectly balanced and even changed from first up to second without a hitch. I started cursing. But then as she went to go up into third there was a cacophonous crunch of gears, the engine cut out, and she ground to a halt. I sprinted happily up the road to the rescue.

A hundred and fifty miles later, with me back at the helm, we came to the end of the highway and were unceremoniously ejected back into the real India. We entered a maelstrom of old Hindustan Ambassador cars (the staple transport for Indian civil servants and Aunties-who-lunch for the past half a century), ox-carts, bicycles, and roaring Tata trucks. The heat, noise, and smells were all-consuming. We were entering the town of Agra, and the traffic was only getting worse. Then, as we came out of a particularly messy intersection and up a small rise, we caught sight of what at first looked like a mirage in the distance; a huge, white marble, onion-shaped dome seemingly suspended in the sky. The Taj Mahal.

We parked the bike up next to the tour buses and chartered taxis and wandered in to the Taj complex with our helmets dangling nonchalantly from our arms. I was feeling quite superior to the mere tourists who were milling around snapping photos and getting fleeced by touts. After all, we were travellers, adventurers, explorers, a breed apart. Then it came back to me that we hadn't actually done anything yet; it was all just intentions, all plans.

**The Taj Mahal**

I was distracted at that point by the beauty of the building that revealed itself ahead of me. Expansive gardens led down to the riverbank, where the flawless white dome sat atop an octagonal base cut through with arches. The whole structure was on a raised platform, itself flanked by minarets and perfectly symmetrical. As we got closer, we found inner walls decorated with delicate mosaics and inlaid with jewels arranged in meticulous floral patterns. Verses of the Koran inscribed above them offered advice on love and death. The Indian poet, Tagore, described the Taj as "like a solitary tear suspended on the cheek of time." And given its history, that seemed rather apt. It was built 400 years ago by the emperor, Shah Jahan, to house the body of his deceased wife, Mumtaz Mahal. It took 20,000 labourers and 1,000 elephants twenty years to construct. But actually it was a job still unfinished, as the emperor's original plan had been to have a mirror-image Taj constructed on the opposite bank of the Yamuna river, in black rather than white, which would house his own tomb and be linked to his wife's by a bridge. Unfortunately, though, he was overthrown by his own son before that could happen and locked up in a fort, where he spent the rest of his days, presumably due to concerns that mausoleum construction was eating up all of the family inheritance.

After wandering round for an hour or so, we found a nearby café and settled in for some lunch. The waiter came up to check on the food and, rather satisfyingly, noted our helmets hung over the side of our seats,

"Ah, *namaste*, sir, madam, I see you are riding one another?"

I almost choked on my *roti*, "Err, well, we are on a motorcycle, yes, if that's what you mean."

"Oh yes, very good. Coming from Delhi only?"

"Yes, we rode down this morning; lovely bit of road!"

He smiled knowingly and wobbled his head, "Ah you foreign fellows are only ones with enough rupees for driving this road. And next going, I am guessing, to Jaipur?"

I shook my head emphatically, "No, actually to Burma."

He looked nonplussed, "I am sorry sir?"

"Burma, Rangoon, you know the country to the east of India?"

He thought for a minute,

"You are pulling your leg?"

I laughed, "No, not at all; today is the first day of our journey there."

He shook his head, "But firstly, you are going wrong direction sir. Burma this way." He pointed off towards the east before continuing, "And in any case, better you continue south, view beautiful India only. To Burma, you must be passing north-east India, and no security." He looked pointedly at Lady R and drew his finger across his throat. He was probably right on the mark, but I decided to change the subject and order some more drinks. It, anyway, seemed laughable to be claiming we were already on some epic trip and were going to ride all the way to Rangoon after a mere day's easy trot down a freshly-minted highway from Delhi. Maybe we should just head south and have a nice holiday in Goa instead.

When we got back to our hotel that evening, Lady R decided some meditation was in order, and I heartily agreed. We both settled into a cross-legged posture and closed our eyes. I then leant across and popped a quick peck on her cheek.

"What are you doing?"
"Mmmm, kissing you?"
"Why?"
"Because I love you?"
"Well don't, it's interrupting my meditation."
"Didn't Buddha preach compassion and loving kindness?"
"Shut up."

I laughed, and we got down to business. After twenty minutes of focusing on the breath the timer beeped and Lady R turned to me, "Are you not feeling a little bit scared about this whole thing?"

I breathed a sigh of relief, "Oh yes baby, absolutely, quite terrified to be honest, but I didn't want to say anything, as I didn't realise you felt the same."

She looked at me quizzically, "Well I don't really, I just asked because you looked a bit panicked. And you've been smoking in the morning, which by the way, you really need to stop. Anyway, don't worry, as I said, mummy will take care of you."

I threw a pillow at her and announced I was trading her in for a camel first thing in the morning, which finally got me my kiss.

The breakfast buffet was expansive and we took full advantage, unsure of when our next decent meal might be. Lady R even gave me a special dispensation to have a cigarette with my coffee, due to the historic circumstances. We hit the road just after 8AM, before the heat of the day had set in and while the traffic was still light, heading due east out of town into the vast, hot, arid plains of Uttar Pradesh. "U.P." as it is ubiquitously known, is India's most populous state, home to a mind-boggling 200 million people. If it were a country, it would be the sixth largest in the world. The state has produced over half of the country's prime ministers but doesn't seem to have benefited from any of the ensuing patronage that one might expect. It's one of the most conservative and poorest parts of India, with more than a quarter of its inhabitants scraping by on less than $1.25 a day.

We bumped along dusty roads that cut through swathes of dry farmland and small towns and villages, trying to avoid collisions with speeding Ambassadors, top-heavy lorries, and weaving motorcycles. We were the only foreigners there, and there were a lot of stares, whether out of curiosity or hostility we weren't quite sure. Lady R suddenly seemed very, very blonde.

But the buses were the scariest thing, driving at breakneck speed to reach their next stop and thus their next paying fare. The drivers rented them for a fixed daily fee from the owners and were dependent on ticket receipts to cover that cost and then make a profit. Margins were extremely slim, so you could understand the rush knowing that by saving a few minutes, taking on a few more passengers, it could make the difference between them having enough money to feed their families today or not. That understanding didn't make their driving any less terrifying however. You'd see them pull out from amongst the oncoming traffic to overtake and start flashing their lights and honking their horns as they bore down on you on your side of the road, as though you were the one at fault. Now, the vast majority of motorcycles on Indian roads can handle this situation, as they are slim, domestically-made, Bajaj models that can slip through narrow gaps or pull onto the verge without too much of a problem. But we didn't have a Bajaj, we had a fully-laden Enfield and so were very heavy and, with the baggage racks sticking out on each side, very wide. This meant we were much less manoeuvrable than a smaller bike and much less able to squeeze between small gaps or to run into the gravel by the roadside without crashing. The bus drivers, however, just saw a motorcycle that should be accepting the usual caste rules and getting the hell out of their way. So we played a deadly game of chicken each time a bus pulled out ahead and started barrelling towards us. I horned and flashed my lights while Lady R waved both hands frantically (while giggling delightedly at the prospect of an imminent collision) until the driver got the message that we really weren't pulling over or going to attempt to fit between him and the other traffic, and so accepted he was going to have to pull back on to his side of the road instead. But damn they left it very late.

Meanwhile, clouds of dust were constantly thrown up by the traffic, and the searing heat ensured a stream of sweat dripping incessantly into my eyes. A level-crossing barrier being lowered ahead provided a welcome opportunity to pull up for a minute. As I twisted my head to peer up the railway track that crossed the road and wound off into the haze, I heard the distant whistle and chug of a locomotive. The engine emerged out of the distance, a bright red locomotive that clanked past us towing behind it twenty odd carriages that jostled and rolled on the tracks. It was packed, and not only on the inside. The roof was a separate community in itself, covered with people sitting with their legs dangling over the sides of the carriages, heads swathed in scarves or T-shirts to give a little respite from the heat. Nimble hawkers picked their way among them selling snacks and tea. I just hoped there were no tunnels up ahead.

As we waited for the train to finish passing, I noticed that the traffic waiting along with us to cross the tracks had now spread over both sides of the road. When the last carriage finally rattled past, I saw the same had happened on the other side where there was likewise a solid mass of trucks, buses, cars, and bikes covering both lanes. As the level crossing barriers came up, these two mechanised armies advanced towards each other and then stopped, given neither could go any further. Everyone then simultaneously leant on their horns while refusing to budge. The noise was absolutely deafening. But this was where two wheels were better than four, as I was able to nudge and cajole a path through the masses, urging people to move a few centimetres here, a few centimetres there, until there was just enough space to squeeze through. While doing so, I inexplicably lapsed into a very plummy British accent and started coming out with such gems as "So terribly sorry old chap," "I say, would you mind awfully budging over a jiffy?," and "Oh, do come on my man, let's at least try to be a little civilised about this" and was dimly aware of Lady R tutting and apologising after each utterance. Maybe we did make quite a good pair after all.

Once free of the scrum, the miles started to tick by again, and small villages, fields, and tea stalls flowed past us as if on an eternal loop. We were aiming to cover a hundred and fifty miles by sundown, but it was becoming increasingly clear that this was going to be quite a tall order, given the state of the roads and the traffic that rendered riding at anything over fifty miles per hour practically suicidal. I therefore decided to radically restrict tea and toilet breaks in order to speed our progress. After two hours non-stop, I finally relented and pulled over so that we could take a breather next to a small river. A few minutes later, a passing motorcyclist spotted us lounging on the riverbank and pulled up. He didn't respond to my greeting, but instead just stood and stared blankly at Lady R. Then a colourfully painted truck ground and wheezed to a halt, and the driver hopped down and joined the first chap, who was by then on his phone, muttering in a conspiratorial fashion while casting furtive glances at my companion. A taxi then arrived, and the driver and passenger got out. It was becoming clear that the sole reason for everyone being here was to look at us. Or rather at Lady R, the likes of which were clearly not often seen around these parts. We soon had a semi-circle of staring, unsmiling men before us, and I was starting to feel quite uneasy. Once again, the glaring opposites of India revealed themselves—this was a country where, more often than not, I had been humbled by the most overwhelming hospitality and kindness I'd ever experienced, but on occasions like this a wholly opposite and menacing side appeared that instead had me fearing for my safety. Lady R seemed oblivious, though, and laughed off my whispered advice that we might want to get out of there ASAP. I decided to try some conversation with our new friends instead and walked up to the chap nearest to me flashing my best please-do-not-rob-and-rape-us smile,

"*Namaste*!"

He moved his head from side to side in reply.

"All OK?" I looked at him expectantly.

"OK." He gave me a curt nod then moistened his lips and resumed his appraisal of Lady R's chest.

I coughed, "I am from England, errr, India very good!"

He turned and looked me in the eye, "Here, dangerous."

"Sorry?"

"Here. Very dangerous. Very much crime."

Whether he meant U.P. in general or this spot in particular, I wasn't quite sure. But the hint of a sly smile at the corners of his mouth led me to fear the latter.

The facts weren't exactly reassuring. U.P. has about fifteen percent of India's population but witnesses half of its shootings and a third of its overall crimes. My trip prep had also uncovered the uncomfortable statistic that last year it had the highest rape rate in India, standing at more than five attacks per day. That, of course, was just the reported ones, and in this particularly conservative area where rape perversely carries an almost worse stigma for the victim than for the perpetrator, it means the real figure is certainly much higher. Even when cases are reported, the police are rumoured to refuse to register them in many instances, particularly if the victim is poor and powerless, in order to keep the official crime rates down and their political bosses happy.

As I was considering how we could make a swift and graceful exit, Lady R came up behind me and, without warning, started slathering suntan lotion onto my lightly roasted neck. As her hands worked the cream in and slipped under my shirt to rub my shoulders, there was a low murmuring from the crowd, their eyes following her every movement, accompanied by some adjusting of penises through trousers. It was really time to go. I pulled Lady R towards the bike, in spite of her protests, and thanked Ganesh when the kick start fired up the engine on the first try. As we were pulling away, Lady R gave one of her beautiful smiles to our admirers. One of them then reached out towards her. She took his hand and held it for a second. In an area where there is usually no physical contact between women and men who are not related, this caused a round of whooping from the others who then surged forward towards us to also try their luck. I lunged at the throttle and accelerated away with such aggression that Lady R nearly fell off the back of the bike, for which I got a sharp prod in the ribs and an agitated "Just what the hell is your problem?"

In the early afternoon we drew into the city of Bareilly and spotted some women riding mopeds, a sure sign that we were now back in a more cosmopolitan area of U.P.—such modern behaviour wouldn't be tolerated in the rural dust belt we'd just passed through. There were Internet cafés and shopping malls too along with the standard hustle and bustle of a typical Indian metropolis. We pulled up outside a cosy-looking restaurant and eased ourselves off the bike, stiff, aching, still vibrating, and absolutely filthy. The waiters inside, on the other hand, were immaculate in starched white shirts and smartly pressed grey trousers and showed wonderful self-control in treating two filthy foreigners as though they were actually worthy of the establishment. We collapsed into a booth and ordered half of the menu, gorging on *chapatti*, *dal*, *paneer tikka*, butter chicken, and mushroom *matar*, gulping down copious amounts of chilled mineral water, and bathing in the gloriously cool air conditioning.

Once fully stuffed and refrigerated, we considered our options for the couple of hours of daylight that we still had left. It was a toss-up between throwing in the towel and finding a place to stay in Bareilly for the night or continuing for what looked on the map like another hour or so up the road to the town of Pilibhit. That would put us within easy striking distance of the Nepali border the following morning. A quick bit of Googling revealed that this Pilibhit had but a single claim to fame, though it was a rather fine one—it was home to a man-eating tiger. To find out more I summoned the waiter,

"Sorry, I have a question that is not strictly food-related."

He gave me an impeccable smile, "Please be telling me only."

"We have read that there may be a man-eating tiger in these parts; is that true?"

"Oh yes sir, I'm afraid very much so."

"Right, OK. So this tiger then has actually really killed and eaten people in the area?"

He considered for a second, "Let's be saying, only fifty percent sir."

"I'm sorry?"

He gave me the kind of smile you offer a small child when trying to reassure them about something that's blindingly obvious to everyone else, "He has been attacking, you see, yes, but not eating whole people, no, only some certain pieces."

Well that certainly took the edge off the danger, I mean what was a missing limb or two after all? That settled it for me, I'd had enough adventure for one day, and I was more than happy to go and find a bed for the night, even more so as I knew (because Lady R had told me after starting on *Man-Eaters of Kumaon*) that a tiger's preferred hunting time is at dusk. Lady R, however, got very excited and insisted we leave immediately for precisely the same reason—the tiger's preferred hunting time was fast approaching, which would offer us the best possibility of a sighting, something we should absolutely relish, as they are such beautiful and rare animals, and it would be so terribly exciting, and anyway, who had ever heard of a tiger attacking a motorcycle?

Having lost the argument yet again, we set off out past the grubby outskirts of town and then down small rutted roads through thick forest in the gathering gloom. I saw tigers' eyes every time something glinted through the trees in our headlight and several times mistook the rumble of our engine for the growl of a big cat. However, much to Lady R's disappointment and to my great relief, we rolled into Pilibhit unscathed a couple of hours later. It turned out to really be a one-tiger town, not much more than a dilapidated main street with some muddy alleys leading off it that were littered with small shacks selling cigarettes and candles, interspersed with food stalls sagging under boiling vats of *dal* and large hot plates loaded with sizzling *roti*s.

The choice of accommodation was limited to a single faded hotel. But the broken floorboards of the lobby and the dusty, cracked chandelier were immediately compensated for by the warmth of the welcome we received. Tea and flower garlands emerged as if by magic, and we were then invited to sign our details into an enormous leather-and-cobweb bound ledger. This consisted of the Indian standard of Name, Country, Father's Name, and Religion. We were then led up a rotten wooden staircase and shown into a cavernous, dimly-lit room with an even larger bathroom, given some more tea and biscuits, and left to our own devices. I stripped off and spent a good half an hour trying to scrub off the caked filth while attempting to avoid the cockroaches scuttling across the floor. We'd survived our first real day on the road. But I was absolutely shattered, both physically and mentally. I realised I was going to have to toughen up pretty fast if we were ever going to make it through Nepal, let alone any further. Lady R, however, was in high spirits, busy writing a blog piece about the demographics of U.P., drivers of social change, and no doubt, the over-cautiousness of certain middle-aged Englishmen.

"Between 6AM and 7AM" is not the ideal time for anything in my opinion, least of all tackling an international border. But it was, we were informed, the only time that it's possible to cross from India to Nepal with a vehicle, which seemed very bizarre, and I was half-tempted to dismiss it out of hand, but then again, I didn't want to run even the slightest risk of losing a whole day right at the start of the journey. On the plus side, there's nothing like getting up at 4:30 in the morning and packing in the dark because the generator is off to add a real sense of adventure to a journey. Or so I told Lady R.

Traffic was practically non-existent as we rumbled through the half-light, leaving just the bumps and holes to contend with. Women (and it was only women who were out and about at this time) emerged wraith-like through the early morning mist, swathed in green and yellow saris with bundles of firewood balanced on their heads as they tramped homeward with their fuel for the day. I wondered what time they'd had to get out of bed. And I wondered what they thought of us, rich westerners who were, unlike them, in no way obliged to rise early because we had to get wood if we wanted to be able to make a fire and cook breakfast; no, we instead chose to do so for no ostensibly good reason. *Travel* derives from the French word *travail*, meaning work, which was quite apt in these parts where it was a hardship to be avoided if possible, and a sign of success was that you no longer had to do it as you could afford for things to be brought to you. But we had become so spoilt and coddled and bored back home that we actually romanticised this kind of thing. We had had everything brought to us all our lives but still not found true satisfaction, so we now actively sought out what our grandparents (well at least mine) had worked so hard to escape from. We went and created problems and strife for ourselves in the name of adventure. Perhaps, as the Buddhists would tell us, this was because we could never actually be happy, only strive for something else, something different, something new that we believed would

## Into the Frying Pan

make us so. Every single time we got it, we found ourselves immediately pining for something else. We were constantly falling in love with our imaginations and never learning our lessons. Presumably, these ladies thought we were absolutely crackers.

My thoughts were interrupted as we rounded a sharp corner and the road suddenly disappeared in front of us. It was replaced by a quagmire with three brightly-coloured Tata trucks entombed in the deep mud at various unnatural angles, having fallen foul of the less than optimal conditions. If we'd been in a car then we'd have been stuck for God knows how long. But it was two wheels good, four wheels bad, once again, as we were able to slither our way around, our smaller size enabling us to get through the gaps, and our lighter weight ensuring we didn't get bogged down. I got past the first slain Goliath, but as I was looking for the best way around the second, two headlights flared up ahead accompanied by the roar of a heavy diesel engine. Once my eyes had recovered from the initial blinding, I realised it was a bulldozer, and that it was coming straight for us. There seemed no question that he hadn't seen us, simply the driver seemed to be following the usual Indian vehicular caste rules and expecting such an inferior-sized vehicle as our own to cower out of his way. Motorbikes, however, for all their flexibility, lack a reverse gear, and this one was too heavy to push backwards through the mud using my feet alone. My efforts became increasingly frantic but no less impotent as the bulldozer closed in, until I finally gave up and started screaming and waving my arms as he crossed the final couple of metres between us. I had got to the point of closing my eyes and bracing for impact when, with a screech and an almighty puff of smoke, he finally applied the brakes. He was less than fifty centimetres away, and the sizeable mound of mud he was pushing in front of him was now touching my front wheel. We exchanged incredulous head wobbles. I then noticed that Lady R had already hopped off the back during his advance and was filming the whole thing excitedly from a few metres away. It was nice to know she was there when I needed her. With the help of some hand gestures, I made it clear I could not move, and the driver then kindly switched from trying to kill me to jumping down from his cab and helping me drag the bike backwards out of the mud. Lady R kindly filmed that too.

By the time we had extracted ourselves and got back on the road—which miraculously reformed itself around the next corner, leaving me wondering what kind of topographical and environmental conditions, or simple skimping on construction, allowed one section to be completely swallowed by the earth, while either side the tarmac was still putting up a decent fight—I had a growing sense that we were going to miss the border

# *Into the Frying Pan*

## Approaching the quagmire

crossing time window, so I started to speed up a bit. This naturally led to the ride becoming rather more bouncy. I felt a tap on my helmet and an accompanying poke in the ribs, which was fast becoming Lady R's standard way of attracting my attention over the noise of the engine. I twisted my head back so she could reach my ear, "Hey, what's wrong with your driving today?"

"What?"

"Stop being so jerky."

I turned my head around as far as I could, "It's the bloody road, thank you very much, not me!"

"Hmmm, it's like you are intentionally trying to hit every bump and pothole."

I started to get a little annoyed,

"That's because the whole road is full of them, sweetie."

"Well maybe you can try a little harder?"

I was about to retort but then thought better of it. I wanted it to be me and her together against adversity, not the two of us being driven apart by it. And it was true that you felt the bumps much more on the back. But it seemed she wasn't quite finished, "Do you even know where you're going?"

"Err, I thought you were navigating?"

Instead of waiting for a reply, I braked sharply as we came up to a man who was walking down the other side of the road, leading his goat on a string.

"*Namaste*! Excuse me sir, err, Nepal, Nepal?" I indicated with my hand the direction we were heading, and he nodded his head vigorously in reply. I turned to Lady R, "Well luckily it seems we're going in the right direction in any case."

She frowned and then called over to him again, "Nepal, Nepal?" while pointing in the opposite direction. He nodded his head vigorously.

We drove on more slowly and stopped the next five people

we passed, each time keeping our arms firmly to ourselves as we asked the question. Once we had four votes for the same direction we felt reassured. However, the road they had indicated soon became a single lane of broken tarmac that led us into a forest. I became rather doubtful. We passed a small village and again were told we were going in the right direction. But surely the route to an international frontier couldn't be this, well, provincial? We were then directed across a narrow bridge, wide enough only for a motorcycle.

**Heading to the Nepal border**

So now it had to be a border that could only be reached by foot or on two wheels. Distinctly peculiar. We reached the other side and bumped down a small incline into a copse of trees. And there, in complete tranquillity, we found a tiny one-storey yellow concrete building with "Immigration Office (India)" painted along the side next to a small barrier across the road.

Outside the building two gentlemen in tracksuits were sipping tea while nonchalantly perusing the morning newspapers. They greeted us with a smile and a yawn and rather reluctantly shuffled off to find some forms for us to fill in. The subject of us being accompanied by a vehicle—which we had presumed would lead to innumerable questions and delays given we had no official export licence—seemed to be of no interest to them whatsoever. International smugglers take note. They explained that most traffic in this area goes through another crossing, further to the south, which leaves them just to cope with the occasional pedestrian, dodgy biker or mule train. With papers signed and passports stamped, the gentlemen returned to their newspapers and indicated that we could raise the barrier ourselves and ride right out of India.

# 4
# Wild Times

We lowered the barrier behind us and drove slowly across no-man's land unobserved, other than by a nonchalant cow who looked up but then decided we were not worth stopping grazing for. After a couple of hundred metres we figured we must be in Nepal, despite the lack of any sign, gate, human being, or most importantly, immigration office. But tempting as it was to just ride off into the hinterland, the absence of a visa and an entry stamp on our passports would be bound to cause us problems later.

I pulled up by the side of the road, and we started to have a wander around. After a couple of minutes of peering this way and that I spotted it, down a bank to our left and across a muddy field, a crumbling one storey brick construction adorned with fading green, peeling paint and the word *Immigration* just visible above the door. We slithered down the bank, picked our way across the field, and entered the open doorway. Inside was a spindly table covered in plastic sheeting, two plastic chairs, and a filing cabinet that appeared to have been through both world wars. There was no sign of anyone who could issue a visa or stamp a passport however. I did the only thing an Englishman can in such situations and coughed, waited, then coughed again more loudly. I smiled to myself at the wisdom of my people when I heard the twang of a bed spring as someone stirred in the room next door, followed by a shuffling of feet, an almighty hawking of phlegm, and then a precise, hefty spit. The door to the next room creaked open. A plump, middle aged man with a tussle of brown hair, a formidable moustache, and thick tinted glasses emerged rubbing his hands over his stained white vest. We were instantly reassured as he broke into a broad grin,

"*Namaste*! Friends! Please sit!"

We smiled and did as we were told. He looked at us expectantly, "So, what may I be doing to you today?"

There was me thinking immigration was pretty much a one-fixed-service kind of business, but well, who knew what else he might be dabbling in. I took out my passport and placed it on the table, "We'd like to enter Nepal, please."

He raised an eyebrow, "Well, I see. And where might you be coming from today?"

Perhaps it was his first day on the job.

"Err, India?"

"Ah India, oh yes, incredible country." He looked at my passport wistfully, "Poor little Nepal; we are in between an India-China sandwich you know, squashed from either side." He squeezed his hands together on my passport and then seemed to drift into a silent, presumably geopolitical, reverie. I ventured another cough,

"So, would you be the right man to give us a visa and stamp our passports by any chance?"

He immediately brightened, "Oh absolutely, most certainly, with pleasure!"

He opened one of the drawers of the desk, rummaged around for a bit, pulled out a stamp, and then opened each of our passports without even looking at the pages that had our photos and personal details and slammed the stamp down in both. He then glanced with satisfaction at his handiwork for a few seconds and handed back the finished products to us before having another spit. I got up and gave him a little bow, "Thank you so much sir, it's very much appreciated."

"Very welcome, very welcome. And now I have done the needful, please you must be going, it is time for me to get on."

With that he shuffled back to the doorway, and a moment later we heard the bed springs creak again as he returned to the more important business of the day.

But we weren't quite done yet. Once back on the bike, we were flagged down on rounding the next corner and ushered towards a Customs hut. This time the bike had been noticed. We completed a number of forms in triplicate and were instructed that we must pay a small fee for each day we kept it in the country. But it all seemed quite reasonable and above board; there were no shady winks or requests for baksheesh, and in half an hour the paperwork was complete and we were free to be on our way. Perhaps this crossing international borders thing wasn't going to be so difficult after all.

A wave of exhilaration swept over me as we pulled away from the border town and out onto Nepal's East-West highway, which cuts through the Terai, the lowlands of the south of the country. Bright green paddy fields glistened with the morning dew, and beyond them, swathed in the early morning mist, rose the foothills of the Himalayas. The motorised traffic there was much lighter than in India, just the odd bus or tractor. Apart from that, other road users mainly consisted of old geezers on bicycles, school children in bright green and blue uniforms skipping along to class, women shuffling along determinedly with huge grass bales balanced precariously on their heads, and the odd creaking buffalo cart.

The road surface was also pretty good, and that meant

we could make decent speed. When there weren't men with guns barricading the way ahead, that was. We hit the first military checkpoint after a mile or so, with concrete barriers placed at intervals on alternating sides of the road, so you had to slow right down to weave around them, overlooked by machine gun posts swathed in razor wire. I smiled broadly as I belted out *namaste*s to the troops huddled in their foxholes but decided I wouldn't stop until actually instructed to do so. This worked quite well, as they seemed unsure of quite how to handle a noisy foreigner, and before they'd worked out what they should do, we were already gone.

This part of western Nepal has long been rather troubled and was one of the areas hardest hit by the decade-long civil war that besieged the country, pitching Maoist rebels against the state security forces. The war had ended several years ago, but it seemed that things hadn't really gotten that much better. The Maoists had demanded the abolition of the monarchy as a condition for laying down their arms, and this they had duly gotten, which saw peace nominally restored to the country. But it turned out that the king and his cohorts had been the lid on a pressure cooker. Over the years they'd spent considerable time and effort trying to assimilate the over one hundred ethnicities who call Nepal home but had done so with a heavy hand, for example, making it a jail-able offence to discuss differences between ethnic groups. At the same time, they had institutionalised special privileges for high caste Pahadis, who were the kind of people that turned their noses up at the very mention of the word *Terai*, seeing it as synonymous with low class, lawless, and not being a "real" Nepali. With the monarchy gone, those who felt they'd been unfairly treated had a chance to do something about it. And everyone wanted a piece of the pie in the new democratic Nepal. As a result, the drafting of a constitution that would set down who was actually legally entitled to what had been delayed interminably, deadline after deadline sailing past, as people struggled by means both fair and foul to influence its outcome. In the meantime, they tried to grab whatever they could to establish a fait accompli, and in the Terai violence was still regularly breaking out as different groups turned on one another.

After a couple more hours of riding, we pulled up at a small open-sided wooden shack for lunch. Ordering was easy, even if you didn't speak a word of Nepali, as there was one dish that was ubiquitous across the country—*momos*. These are small dumplings filled with vegetables or meat, normally buffalo, and a side of dipping sauce—bite-size, delicious and filling. As we were polishing off the last of them, we were surprised to see another foreigner wander in, dressed in a lumberjack shirt, grey slacks that had seen better days, and a Palestinian *keffiyeh* scarf draped around his neck. He received a friendly greeting from the owner and chatted for a couple of minutes with him in what sounded like fluent Nepali. He then looked over to us, "Hey bikers, mind if I join you? Where are you headed?"

For the first time it felt almost OK to reveal our plans to a stranger. I mean we had just crossed an international border, after all. I gave him a broad smile,

"Well, started in Delhi and planning on going through to Burma, if we can."

Dan, as he introduced himself, looked satisfyingly impressed. It turned out he was from Canada and had been working for an NGO in the area for the past couple of years, trying to help tackle local corruption.

"Wow, must be challenging; so how big of a problem is it?" I asked him.

"Well, Nepal's like 116th in the world in terms of clean government, ya know, so things ain't exactly rosy." He took a sip of *chai* and then continued, "And the thing is it's right across the board, from a couple rupees tea money any time you deal with officialdom to, well," he paused at this point and pointed to a field across the road, "That school for example."

"Err, what school?"

"Exactly, man. Local politician got paid for building one and just pocketed the whole budget. Then had the gall to claim for its operating expenses for the next couple of years until we exposed the scam."

"Wow, so he's in jail now, I guess?"

Dan tutted and shook his head, "Nah, got off with a slap on the wrist. Would have meant taking too many others down with him, and those guys had connections, if you know what I mean."

He explained that prosecutions for corruption are very rare, and so graft is just widely accepted as a fact of life. We'd read earlier that one MP, on being caught offering his vote on a piece of proposed legislation in return for a hearty sum, had protested that he should actually be praised for requesting only half the amount that his predecessor used to charge. Lady R wanted to know more, of course, "So what percentage of government funds around here would you say are, hmmm, how do you Anglo-Saxons put it, pilfered?"

He took the end of his *keffiyeh* and dabbed the sweat from his forehead, "Well a conservative estimate would be eighty percent."

I whistled in awe. He and his NGO must be treading on a lot of toes in that case. We wished him the very best of luck as we parted, and I gave him the same kind of look Lalli had given me in the motorcycle garage in Delhi as I told him I hoped to see him again. I wondered just how long Dan's maple leaf was going to protect him.

Lady R was now in the driver's seat, as these lightly travelled but decently surfaced roads seemed the ideal training ground. I was perched up behind, appreciating the view for a change and annoying her by shooting video of what I found to be her particularly amusing motorcycle face; brow furrowed, eyes squinting manically ahead, and ferociously biting her lip. I was also enjoying the surprised faces of those we passed on the roadside as they did a double-take on spotting a woman driving a motorcycle with a man on the back, something quite unimaginable in those parts. I liked to think we were doing our bit for female emancipation in the area. Though perhaps it was instead just giving the fellas the idea of yet another thing they could get their wives and sisters to do while they lazed around, adding to the list of gathering firewood, cooking, working the rice paddies, and taking care of the kids.

In the middle of the afternoon we crossed a large suspension bridge over a wide, fast flowing river, rushing impatiently down from the Himalayas on its long journey to the sea. On the other side the fields and villages began to make way for forest and jungle. We were entering the Baridya Nature Reserve and heading into a world of tigers, rhinos, and elephants. We'd heard of a nice lodge called "Tiger Tops" where we could spend the night, a retreat in the middle of the wilderness where one could reconnect with nature and, according to one website, "become intimate with elephants." I needed no more convincing.

But first we had to reach it. A sign pointing off the highway indicated the way sure enough but led down a track covered with loose stones, a motorcyclist's worst nightmare. I took over the driving again as we skidded into the jungle and gave Lady R strict instructions to look out for approaching large animals of questionable intent. We made fair, if somewhat wobbly, progress for half an hour, before the trees opened up ahead and presented us with the charming aspect of a beautiful wide river. On the other side we could see the track we were on continuing up from the bank. But there was no bridge or ferry in sight. We were unlikely to be able to reach any other place where we could stay the night before sundown, so it seemed we'd have to try to cross on our own. I pulled up and turned back to Lady R, "Well there seems nothing else for it but to try to ford it, baby."

She clapped her hands together excitedly, "Yes, let's go for it, go, go!"

I raised my hand, "Err, might a little preparation be in order, my dear?"

She pondered for a second, "OK, then why don't you try to wade across first, and if you don't drown, then we'll know it's all right."

My favoured course of action had rather been to wait for someone else to come along and see how they managed it, but Lady R's method at least had the benefit of making me look a little more manly and perhaps compensate for the rather obsessive fear of tigers that I'd developed over the last couple of days. So I rolled up my trousers and tottered down the bank. The water started quite shallow, then got a little deeper, and by mid-stream was well over my knees, but I reckoned that would still make it fordable, and the riverbed seemed fairly flat without any big rocks to throw us off. I sloshed my way back over to Lady R, "Well, I think it might be OK; shall we go for it?"

She looked at me quizzically, "You should go for it, yes."

"You're not coming?"

She grinned, "You know, I'm not sure I completely trust your ability to do this. Which also makes the prospect of staying here and videoing your attempt even more appealing." I couldn't help but admire the logic.

**River crossing**

I got back on the bike, engaged first gear, upped the revs, and went for it. I reckoned the key would be having enough speed to keep momentum going but not so much as to risk losing balance and falling off. Really scientific stuff. I entered the water and started bumping over the stones of the riverbed, lurching left and right. It was rather surreal not to be able to see the surface I was riding on, but I managed to maintain enough speed to stay upright as I pushed out mini tidal waves on either side. The bike slowed as I hit a larger rock, but some aggressive throttling got me over, and after a few more metres, I reached the opposite bank and made a triumphant exit, water streaming off me and the bike. I gave an involuntary and rather American "whoop!" and tooted my horn, to the amusement of an old lady who was washing some clothes a little further downstream. I waved to Lady R to wade across to join me. When she'd made it over, she pulled out her phone to show me the video, in which I admit I came off rather less elegantly than I had imagined; legs flailing out either side of me while screaming, as she put it, like a little girl.

We carried on into the jungle, and the afternoon sun soon had us dried off. An hour of gravel road and no large mammals later, we came to a small village of thatched huts and stopped to ask for directions from a group of elderly men sitting at the base of a gnarled old oak tree, smoking and watching the world go by. They indicated a muddy single-lane track leading off to the right. We dutifully bumped along that crossing a couple of single plank bridges as it narrowed into nothing more than a footpath. We were starting to have our doubts when a wooden archway came into view ahead with a carved sign hanging down from it, "Welcome to Tiger Tops."

The lodge sat in a peaceful grove, surrounded by the jungle, not a TV or Internet connection to be found. In fact, after turning off the engine, there were no man-made sounds at all. A handful of simple huts with small wooden terraces curved round the edge of the clearing, and in the middle a large thatched roof perched on top of a series of pillars providing an open-sided communal area with armchairs, tables, and a large fireplace in the centre to help with the chilly evenings. It was just about perfect.

We were planning to spend two nights there, and it was a great relief to know that we had a ride-free day ahead, with no dust, sore arses, navigation arguments, or near-death experiences to contend with. We unloaded the bike and washed up and then, as dusk fell, joined a couple of the guides sitting round the fire to hear their tales of tracking tigers, being charged by rhinoceroses, and taming elephants. They also shared a few drams of Bagpiper Highland Whiskey (Distilled in Bangalore), and as the evening got later, so the stories got taller.

Next morning, my plans of a risk-free day were abruptly dashed by Lady R over the breakfast table.

"So, safari?" she asked expectantly.

I nodded enthusiastically, "Absolutely! I think we have two options, they can either take us by jeep or on the elephant; which one shall I ask them to roll out?"

She pouted, "A safari should be made on foot, surely, otherwise really what's the point?"

I put my cup of tea back down on its saucer, "Yes, well I am all for purity of experiences, darling, naturally, but there are some pretty big and scary animals out there, and they've probably not had a blonde, mid-sized, mid-morning snack for quite a while."

She shook her head despairingly, "Well, I for one am going to do this properly!" She gave me a distinctly Hemmingway-esque look and banged her fist on the table. I laughed and sighed in resignation. There was clearly only one course of action possible. I called over to the guide and booked the walking safari plus a jeep for one. It was probably good to have a few hours apart, in any case.

In my open-topped 1950s olive green jeep I was accompanied by the amicable Jayaram, or Mr. J, as he insisted I call him—a wiry, yet chiselled man with a well-kept moustache, immaculate khakis, and a distinct military bearing, just the kind of chap I felt would be good to have around should we run into a spot of bother. Our first stop was to visit the domesticated elephants that live at the lodge and were indulging in their morning bath when we showed up, trumpeting and spurting water over one another in the river and rolling around blissfully in the mud. They were accompanied by their keepers, or *mahouts*, who Mr. J informed me are usually assigned to the elephant when both are very young and then stay bonded to each other for life.

"And they're pretty smart animals too, right?" I asked.

He nodded, "Oh yes, biggest brain of any land animal," he paused for a second, "Reading Pliny."

I looked at him in astonishment, "What? They can read?"

I got a bemused smile in return, "No sir, I was meaning you, maybe you have been reading Pliny, the Roman philosopher only? He was saying that elephant is the closest animal to the human."

"Ah, yes of course, right."

I was so glad Lady R wasn't around to see this. Mr. J went on to tell me that elephants demonstrate a number of what are normally thought to be exclusively human traits, such as grief, altruism, and self-awareness. And the story about them having very good memories turns out to be true too. They combine all these attributes in one particularly intriguing behavioural tendency, which is to regularly return to the site where a loved one has died, apparently to mourn them. As I watched them frolic (if something of such massive size can really be said to do that) and roll around, it struck me how much wiser they were than me, just enjoying the present, taking pleasure from simple joys. I was tempted to get in the river with them and abandon the bike trip all together.

**Jeep safari**

We drove on through a series of sleepy forest glades dissected by dusty shafts of sunlight where we spied some swamp deer eyeing us suspiciously from among the trees, ears twitching nervously. Deeper in the jungle the track started getting quite muddy and waterlogged, a delight now that it wasn't my problem and I could just sit back and watch Mr. J power expertly through. I also realised rather guiltily that it was a pleasant relief not to have a passenger that I was worrying about keeping happy. We drew up alongside another river, and Mr J. killed the engine and suggested we get out. On seeing the expression of mild terror on my face, he indicated a nearby observation tower. I relaxed as I realised I wasn't about to have a walking safari imposed on me against my will. We climbed up the rotten wooden staircase until we were at the level of the treetops, looking down over the river and mile upon mile of mottled green jungle beyond. Mr. J had inhumanly sharp eyes and indicated two grey boulders downstream that I'd briefly noticed then ignored, informing me that they were actually rhinoceroses. I looked unconvinced, so he handed me a small pair of binoculars from his pocket. Yes, he had a point. They looked like prehistoric tanks, with their low-slung angular bulk and battle-grey armour plating. Mr. J explained that, in spite of this indestructible appearance, they are actually quite vulnerable, as they suffer from particularly poor eyesight. This means that when they do think they might have seen something moving nearby, they have a tendency to charge, just in case it's a predator. That probably explained why a group of grazing black buck on the riverbank was eyeing them suspiciously while the rhesus macaques jumping through the canopy above hooted to one another in warning (I should note that these would have also just been deer and monkeys to me an hour ago before I'd met Mr. J).

As we descended the stairs of the observation tower again, my shoulder was suddenly grabbed from behind and the magical word *tiger* whispered in my ear. I stopped immediately and gripped the stair rail. I became aware of a low growling that was reverberating from the bushes about twenty metres away from bottom of the stairs. "Looking for his mate," murmured Mr. J. There was a cracking of twigs, a rustling of leaves, another growl, then silence. A few nervous minutes passed as I barely dared breathe, then there was another touch on my shoulder, "It's OK now, we can be going down." I felt both relieved and disappointed; it might actually have been quite nice to get a glance of striped orange fur, so long as it was moving away from us of course.

I was still thinking about the tiger as we bumped our way back to the lodge, and I decided to distract Mr. J's mind from the driving a little, "So, nothing much you can do, I guess, if you meet a tiger in the wild?"

He turned his head from the track for a moment and wobbled it in my direction, "Oh, they are not being that dangerous."

I wondered if he'd been drinking, "You mean one shouldn't feel scared to come across a 250-kilogram sabre-toothed carnivore in the middle of the jungle?"

There was a pause while he negotiated a particularly slithery section and then he continued, "Well, you see, tigers are confused by humans."

I laughed, "You mean, like, they just can't see the point of us?"

"Ha, maybe, yes, but tiger thinks other animals have same proportion like himself, so if he sees taller animal, he thinks it is also longer animal."

I was starting to cotton on, "So, you're saying that a tiger, approaching a human head on, kind of sees the height and figures that, as it's, like, at least twice the height of a tiger, it must be at least twice as long too?"

"Exactly Mr. Andy, you are being very quick."

There were now very few ways left in which Mr. J was not a better travelling companion than Lady R, "OK, right, so it imagines the human is much bigger than it really is and much bigger than a tiger, and so it doesn't attack; I get it. But, forgive me, what if the human turns or if the tiger has a little cheeky peek round the side to check its reasoning?"

Mr. J wrenched the steering wheel to the left to avoid a wild boar that had just run into our path out of the dense undergrowth, "Ah, well, then tiger is just confused you see, no horizontal back where there should be. So does not know what to do."

I furrowed my brow as I tried to take this in and then remembered something I'd read the night before after extracting one of Lady R's already well-weathered books from our mobile motorcycle library, "Mr. J, are you familiar by chance with the book *Man-Eaters of Kumaon*?"

He looked puzzled and shook his head then glanced at me expectantly.

"Well, this epic book," I could now safely talk like I'd read it several times and considered it a seminal classic, "tells the true story of the Champawat Tiger that, in the nineteenth century, seemed to quite successfully overcome his confusion about the proportions of the human form."

Mr. J raised an interested eyebrow, "Oh, and how so?"

I coughed, "Well, we can ascertain this, as the book recounts the tale of how said tiger went on to kill some 436 people in this very area. Before, I might add, being shot by an Englishman."

Mr. J turned to me laughing as I smiled in triumph, "Oh well, always with one rule is one exception Mr. Andy."

"Good to know—so now you understand exactly why I'm not going on a walking safari."

He laughed and slapped me on the knee, "Oh yes, I am very much seeing that it is your wife who is wearing the trousers."

I ended up being somewhat vindicated when Lady R returned to camp later that afternoon, breathless, shaken, and delightfully rosy. All had apparently being going well until they got, well, exactly what she had been hoping for—a very up close and personal encounter with the local wildlife. As they macheted their way through a dense bit of jungle, they had stumbled across one of the park's largest lone bull elephants grazing in a thicket. Like their human counterparts, big lone males of a certain age can get a bit unhinged. He'd started trumpeting when he saw them and then proceeded to push over a number of small to medium sized trees and seemed on the verge of charging. According to Lady R, the guide started to look very nervous and then whispered to them the rather priceless advice of "first keep fingers crossed, then if he comes, run like buggery." Which is exactly what they'd ended up doing, with the elephant in hot pursuit. Thankfully, all had somehow escaped unharmed, bar a few scrapes and scratches from dashing through the undergrowth.

Lady R spent the rest of the day writing a blog piece on tigers and how, with the destruction of their natural habitats across the world, their last chance might actually be the vast remote Burmese jungle reserves where they are still thought to thrive. The problem is that these are reserves in name only, with no practical protection for their feline inhabitants. Only a few poachers make the very arduous journey in to hunt them right now, as most don't seem to think it's worth their while. But that could change as soon as tiger populations elsewhere diminish and thus, the laws of supply and demand being what they are, the price for such questionable delicacies as tiger penis (sadly, a mistaken belief has grown up that it's a great aphrodisiac) in China and South East Asia rises. Plus, as Burma opens up and its infrastructure improves, those reserves are going to become a lot less remote. The only way to save these beautiful creatures, of which just 4,000 continue to live in the wild, may be to establish in Burma the kind of protections they enjoy today in Bardiya.

# 5
# Hell and Heaven

Eggs, bacon, sausage, even black pudding: Tiger Tops really weren't scrimping on the breakfast, and I quietly decided that there were some vestiges of the British presence in South Asia that I didn't mind too much. I dug in with gusto, explaining to Lady R over her muesli and yogurt that a man needed proper fuel to perform and that we had a long ride ahead. We both seemed to be looking forward to it though; a day off had been just what we needed, and we were ready to get on the move again.

We had to take the same way back to the main road, but this time I decided to take the river crossing at speed, no checking the path across or dismounting, just bosh and right in. This prompted Lady R to call me her "fierce little tiger" and thus kept me happy for most of the rest of the day. We got back to the East-West Highway (which we were travelling on west-east), and it took us out of the jungle and into rice fields and grazing land as we left the national park behind us.

After a few hours, we reached the small town of Butwal and diverted from our eastwards course to turn northwards, off the highway, heading up into the foothills of the Himalayas. The road started to hairpin up the steep sides of the Kaligandaki river valley, paved in some places but for the most part just rock and dust. We sent streams of pebbles plummeting over the precipice to their deaths at every corner. The riding was very different; there were no more long monotonous stretches, humming along straights, instead I was changing gear every few seconds and leaning the bike this way and that to make it round the tight switchbacks, my eyes glued to the road. Lady R nevertheless frequently pointed out things I should be looking at—a waterfall here, an interesting bird there—and not wanting to disappoint her, I would flick my gaze up for a second, mumble something appreciative, and then get back to business before the front wheel strayed too close to the edge.

In the late afternoon we approached Tansen, a little settlement that clings for dear life on to the slopes of the Mahabharat Range, or Lesser Himalaya. It had a certain medieval charm to it, a maze of narrow cobbled streets that snaked up and down at gradients which would make a San Franciscan blush, flanked by Newari shop-houses and Hindu temples. I would have no doubt greatly appreciated these aesthetic delights had I not been trying to navigate them on a fully-loaded Royal Enfield motorcycle. Going downhill was simply scary, as the brakes slowed you at first but then, with just a little too much squeezing, would lock up the wheels and put the bike into an uncontrolled slide across the cobbles. Uphill needed first gear at full revs plus a decent run up, and if you lost momentum, a backward downhill slide was inevitable. To guard against that, I resorted to frantic shouting and waving at any vehicle that showed signs of coming down a road as we tried to go up it. The lack of any street signs and the apparently circular nature of many of the roads meant I got quite a lot of practice at both ascending and descending before we eventually found the guest house we had been looking for, a good hour after we'd first arrived in the town.

We wearily climbed the stairs up to our room, which reception had told us was "on the roof." We took that to mean the top floor. But, no, it really was a little hut that had been erected right on top of the flat roof of the hotel. That meant we had a huge roof terrace all to ourselves, and laid out before us was row after row of steep-sided hills standing to attention, the closest ones displaying their forests and terraces in detail, the furthest mere phantoms lurking in the blue-grey ether. The clouds burned orange and pink as the sun slipped away. I spotted something above them and couldn't at first work out what it could possibly be, nothing should be higher than the clouds after all. An optical illusion perhaps. Then I felt an intense tingle run the length of my body as I realised what I was actually looking at. It was our first view of the high Himalayas in the far distance. Their rocky mid-sections were hidden by the clouds, but they were so unfathomably tall that their majestic white peaks were suspended above them, held somewhere between heaven and earth. The snows glowed golden for a moment in greeting and then, as the light faded, retreated again into their secret kingdom.

A couple of hours later I was still on the terrace enjoying my third bottle of Gurkha Ale when Lady R emerged out of the room looking purposeful. I slipped my arm round her as she came up to me, "How you doing baby? Have I been out here too long? Should I come in and cuddle up?"

She frowned, which was never a good start, "Actually, I wanted to talk to you about your blog article."

"Err, OK?"

The purposefulness got more intense. "We said we'd alternate in writing so that the website is balanced, and the fact is, to be frank, I've been waiting two days now for you to finish yours so that I can put my next one up, which is already finished and good to go."

I decided to go with a smile, "Oh right, well you know I've been a bit tired at the end of the days, what with the driving and all that, so let's just relax a bit, OK?"

Her eyes narrowed, and her mouth pursed. That didn't bode well.

"It's no excuse. You need to be serious about this, and we both agreed we wanted to record the trip as we went along, so it shouldn't exactly be any great surprise."

She was right that we'd agreed, and I knew that was important to her, but I was still starting to feel a little rankled. And before I could stop myself, that momentary emotion took control of my brain,

"Excuse me? What are you, my publisher now, hassling me for missing a deadline?"

She snorted, "Huh, well you obviously need someone to. So get it done, or I'll put my next one up anyway."

I banged my beer bottle onto the table, "Who the hell do you think you are? Just remember who brought you on this trip."

I knew I was being patronising, trying to sting her the way she had just stung me. I also knew that the half a second satisfaction I would get the moment my words bit home would be far exceeded by the longer-lasting damage I would cause. I should have just gently acknowledged her point of view then set mine out and tried to find a solution somewhere in the middle. Or gone with humour to defuse things. But I had, instead, just yielded to the immediate emotion like an idiot. Lady R didn't seem to want to take us back from the brink either,

"Oh, right, because I'm on your bike I'm now under your command, am I?"

This hit a different nerve, "Ha, well as you very well know it's exactly the opposite, it's me who's always trying to get your attention, always worrying if you are content or not, always seeking your validation, so I'd say you're the one with the power; no?"

I was now spitting out feelings I'd not even fully acknowledged to myself. It seemed I had only two speeds, either repression or hyper honesty. Lady R understandably looked a little taken aback.

"And do you know how I feel?" she shot back, "The one who's been brought along, on your bike, on your trip, the little girl dragged along by the man of the world, struggling for recognition in your shadow?"

It was my turn to be shocked. Could that really be true, that this woman I had been trying to get to notice me had, all along, been feeling the same way about me? It was a sweet and tempting thought. But did it really add up, given how she'd acted since we'd been together? Was she just trying to play me now to win the argument? Or was this really genuine, and actually it had all been a question of my own perception that had been warped by me projecting my own insecurities? I really didn't know, but in any case, this new turn of events had the effect of thoroughly dowsing my appetite for conflict.

"I'll come in and finish my article, baby. I'm sorry."

So she'd got what she wanted. Stop being so cynical, Andy.

*Lonely Planet* described it as "Nepal's finest motorcycling road," and we certainly weren't disappointed. We ducked and weaved through the hills, sweeping up and down, brushing past small villages perched on hillsides, descending into steep valleys to cross over rivers rushing down from the mountains, and negotiating hairpin after hairpin. Lady R had a go at driving again, but this was a rather different challenge now, no longer just a matter of pointing the bike straight and avoiding the livestock. Instead there was a corner every few metres, and with it came the need to change gear, brake, lean, then accelerate and change gear again. That was quite a lot to take on and did result in us drifting out onto the wrong side of the road on a number of turns and seriously close to the edge on others. But, as Lady R reminded me after one particularly close shave with an oncoming truck, "Remember again what Friedrich Nietzsche taught us—what doesn't kill you makes you stronger."

We rolled into the outskirts of the town of Pokhara, Nepal's premier backpackers' playground. We had to quickly reacclimatise to a world of chocolate lassis, dreadlocks, baggy trousers, and hundred-rupee T-shirts. Nestled cosily between the mighty Machhapuchhre, or Fishtail Mountain, and Phewa Lake, Pokhara serves as the setting off point for treks into the Annapurna mountain range that surrounds it, and is home to a plethora of cheap hostels, funky coffee shops, and overloaded outdoor equipment stores with either Bob Marley or *Om Shanti Om* chants ringing out from every other doorway.

We rode up and down the main tourist drag until we found the tiny alley we were looking for, squeezed between an alternative bookshop and an even more alternative café. I gingerly eased the bike along it, trying not to scrape the luggage carriers. About half way along, the engine gave a splutter, a clunk, and then cut out, absolutely refusing to restart. This was, however, not really too inconvenient, as our destination, some fifteen metres away, was a motorcycle workshop where we were heading for a check-up. Not just any workshop mind you, but one by the name of Hearts and Tears, by all accounts the best in Nepal. We pushed the bike out of the other end of the alley into a sunny courtyard where we were greeted by a jovial ginger-bearded Australian, "G'day mate, she givin' you a spot of trouble?"

I was about to pour my heart out to him when I realised he was asking about the bike and not Lady R.

"Hi there, yes, I'm afraid so, been fine all the way from Delhi but just conked out completely a couple of metres back."

"Ah that's karma for you," he broke into a warm grin, "Anyway, no worries, we'll get Raju on the case, best mechanic this side of Kathmandu. Now how about a nice cuppa tea?"

"That sounds just about perfect."

## *Hell and Heaven*

**Hearts and Tears to the rescue**

He reached his arm out to shake my hand, "Oh, me name's Matt, by the way, welcome to Hearts and Tears, mate."

We sat down to enjoy our tea, and after satisfying Matt's curiosity about our own adventure, we were keen to know about his. He'd graduated in his native Australia with degrees in chemical and environmental engineering and had come to Nepal a couple of years previously for work. After spending a year based in Kathmandu, he'd started to see the potential for the private sector to be giving something back to the community. And he'd also fallen in love with the Royal Enfield Bullet. So, he set up Hearts and Tears, not only as a motorcycle tour company and repair shop, but also as a social business, employing and training local people and providing benefits that were usually unheard of from an employer in Nepal, such as free health care and paid leave. He and his crew also sponsored a number of local schools and hospitals that they'd come across on their more remote rides. The Hells Angels they definitely were not.

We were happily grilling him on some of his latest philanthropic exploits when we were interrupted by Doctor Raju, who emerged from inside the workshop greasy and grinning, wobbling his head from side to side,

"Clutch is very much gone, boss."

Now even I knew that was a fairly important part of the bike. But it seemed that wasn't the only problem.

"And gearbox shot."

I laughed nervously, "Is that all?"

"Suspension buggered. Oh, and frame cracked."

I knew Lady R's driving had been a bit rough, but this was ridiculous. I turned to Matt, "So, any chance at all you can fix all that in less than, like, a few weeks?"

He grinned, "Ah no worries, mate, she'll be right, we'll have yer clutch and gearbox done by the time you're finishing your second beer this evening. But for the suspension and frame, though, we're gonna need a damn good welder."

I took another sip of *chai* and sighed, "Ah, I see, and I guess there's no chance of finding one in town?"

Matt turned to Raju, "Not in Pokhara, right? But how about old Rick from the hills; is he still up there?"

Raju wobbled his head in the affirmative.

"Great! So, let's send one of the chaps up for him."

Matt turned back to me and waved his hand vaguely in the direction of the mountains, "He lives up there you know, no bloody phone reception." I was intrigued.

While we waited, we went for a saunter along the lakeside, past Canadians comparing trekking routes and Israelis arguing about where one might buy the best ganga. We stopped at a waterfront café that offered seven different types of coffee and a rather disturbing paneer and pineapple pizza alongside a sign that proclaimed, "Relax, you are in Nepali time," which we discovered was actually there to explain the service. Well, it gave us time to watch the fishing boats on the lake, as well as the odd backpacker come flying down from the surrounding hills attached to a colourful oversized handkerchief, paragliding having recently become the new craze in the area. Lady R lamented we wouldn't have time to experience it, while I felt thankful that we didn't have to try one more way to die.

## *Hell and Heaven*

We were back at Hearts and Tears a couple of hours later, and as Matt and Raju updated us on progress, we heard the low rumble of an Enfield engine reverberating up the alley behind us. A rider drew up in the courtyard and stepped off his battered, dark green Bullet and pulled off his helmet. His deeply weathered face broke into a broad, childlike grin as he pushed his long, matted hair back over his shoulder, shaking it loose of the several beaded necklaces and trinkets that were hanging around his neck.

"How y'all doing?" he paused for a second to give another grin and offer his hand, "I'm Rick. From the hills."

Our saviour had arrived. The accent betrayed that Rick was American of origin, but it turned out he had left a good few decades before. He told us how one thing had somehow led to another until he'd ended up living outside a small village half-way up a mountain in the middle of Nepal. And far from putting his feet up and just enjoying the delightful views, Rick had, instead, set up a one-man welding shop where he turned out a range of affordable and environmentally-friendly cooking stoves for the local community. Matt later told us they'd pretty much revolutionised life for the local villagers, making cooking easier and safer while preserving the local forests. Rick cast his eye over the bike and then turned back to us, "So, where you guys headin'?"

This was getting to be my favourite question, "Well, Burma actually."

His rather bloodshot eyes lit up, and he moistened his lips, "Ah, the land of the rubies!"

Burma is, indeed, something of a gem capital, though that's not normally the first association people make with the country, so my interest was rather piqued, "Yes, indeed it is, have you been?"

Rick sighed, "Ah well, yes. I used to do a spot of work in the oil business, ya know, and we'd get regular R&R in Thailand. So, how to say, I kinda got to sneaking over the border into Burma and buying me some rubies on the black market. Then

I'd take 'em across to this sorta buyer in Hong Kong." He took a drag on his cigarette and started to look a little wistful, "Ah, that was good money man, easy money . . . and hardly any downside really."

I nodded in an understanding manner while trying to hide my surprise, "So, what, the only risk would be maybe fluctuations in global market prices?"

He shook his head, "Nah, mainly getting arrested and having the shit beaten out of me by the Burmese army for being in their country illegally, and sometimes a couple of nights in the can . . . ah, but man, it was good money." He sank into a reverie for a few moments and then shook his head briskly, as though sending some demons back to where they'd come from, "Anyway, let's have a proper look at this broken ride of yours, man, get you fixed up." I wasn't going to argue with that, despite how much I was tempted to take him for a beer and a thorough interrogation on his past life instead.

Thanks to Matt, Raju, and Rick, the bike was as good as new again by the next morning and we were ready to head to Kathmandu. We'd planned to set off from Pokhara early enough to reach our destination before sunset and thus stick to the "Never Drive in Nepal at Night" mantra that was chanted by both the British Foreign Office and the *Lonely Planet*, two of our guiding lights for the trip. But some early-morning, late-monsoon rain had set us back a few hours, as I had insisted we wait it out, which led to Lady R asking me whether I was, in fact, made of sugar. Our passage out of town was then delayed further by a band of flag-waving, drum-beating marchers, promoting their party for the upcoming elections. A bumpy detour down a couple of muddy side streets led us, with my infallible sense of direction, right into the path of another band, but marching to the tune of a different drummer. The third time that happened we decided to give up and accept that there were far more important things going on in Pokhara

## Hell and Heaven

than facilitating the passage of foreign motorcyclists, and so we just followed them at walking pace until we reached the turn off for the highway.

**Demonstration in Pokhara**

Well, it was called a highway, but it was blissfully almost empty, despite being the main road between the country's two most important towns. The surface was thoroughly decent and took us gently up and down the side of a broad river valley through green hills crosshatched with rice terraces. This very road had recently featured in the BBC series *The World's Most Dangerous Roads*, but I really couldn't see why. We motored along unhindered, enjoying the views and the easy riding. But the sun was getting lower in the sky, and it was clear we weren't going to make Nepal's capital by nightfall. And as the light went down so the traffic started to increase. We found out later that most sensible people start their car journey from Pokhara to Kathmandu or vice versa in the early morning. This means that by mid-afternoon they've nearly completed their ride, and so the middle stretch of the road becomes very quiet, just as we'd experienced. But then, an hour or so before sunset, another species of vehicle altogether sets out—the night trucks and buses. Hell-bent on reaching their destinations as fast as possible, those drivers have a penchant for keeping themselves awake with a variety of legal and less-legal stimulants that make their driving anything but safe and predictable.

**Pokhara to Kathmandu night riding**

We were about thirty miles from Kathmandu, and it was also at that point that the road became more "interesting," twisting and turning upwards, a precipitous drop to a turbulent river on one side and a sheer cliff rising up on the other. The surface had also suddenly become more pothole than tarmac. It seemed rather bizarre that the largely unused roads we'd ridden a few days back in the far west were perfectly maintained while this, the country's main artery, was left in such tatters. Buses and trucks came at us, careering downhill, horns blaring and with either full beam headlights on or none at all, throwing up choking clouds of dust as they swept past. I struggled to control the bike through the multitude of holes, some of them veritable gullies that led off either into the upcoming traffic or over the side of the ravine, threatening to trap the front wheel and guide us into one of two terminal fates. The mental strain of maintaining an acute level of alertness to cope with the road and the traffic combined with the physical toll of keeping the bike upright and trying desperately to make out what was up ahead made it the hardest couple of hours I'd ever ridden. At around 11PM, choking and filthy, we finally reached the ring road around Kathmandu. A few minutes later, I pulled out round a lorry and saw the small turn off we needed to take us to our hotel.

Life was instantly transformed. The deafening roar of the buses and trucks was gone, leaving just a light ringing in our ears. The clouds of dust had disappeared. A narrow, deserted road led us past traditional red brick buildings, their doors and windows covered with ornately carved wooden shutters, and their overhanging roofs loyally protecting their sleeping inhabitants. Every block or two on a corner we'd pass a small courtyard temple enclosed by a low stone wall, inside a statue of Ganesh or maybe the Buddha with some bells, a couple of flower garlands, and perhaps some prayer flags, Hinduism and Buddhism happily intermingling.

We wound on through the backstreets and then up a steep hill to find the Summit Hotel, a welcome and well-worn oasis nestled above the metropolis, its compound gates opening to reveal peaceful moonlit gardens and a friendly guard who looked us up and down and announced, "Don't worry, we are having hot water." Filthy, exhausted, and quite giddy, we checked in, ordered a bottle of red wine, and solemnly swore to always follow the Foreign Office's advice in future.

I slammed the door hard as I stormed out the next morning. It should have been an innocuous enough conversation about the best approach for getting the permission we needed to drive the bike out of eastern Nepal and back into India. Lady R felt she knew best, and I felt she didn't. But the real issue was the *how* of the conversation rather than the *what*. I felt she didn't take my opinion seriously and that there was an almost automatic assumption that she'd have the better plan. And it quickly degenerated into such helpful statements as "well you're just being ridiculous now" and "this is so typical of you" until I finally settled matters with a good old walking out. Firing up the bike and roaring off into the city way too fast gave me a minute or two of satisfaction. But by the time I got into central Kathmandu my anger had dissipated, and I fell into a rather melancholy mood, wondering why I never seemed to be able to feel fully secure, comfortable, equal, with Lady R. Was it really just her, or was it me?

Eventually, my rumbling stomach forced itself to the forefront of my brain, and I remembered that we'd been about to go for breakfast. I pulled up at a small and rickety roadside eatery. The dog-eared menu was only in Nepali, and I was about to order my default *momo*s when I noticed a small drawing of a fish at the top. I pointed at that instead, and half an hour later, a piece of tough, heavily fried, what might have once been cod, or mackerel, or even salmon, it was hard to say, was slapped down on a plate in front of me. It needed most of the salt and chilli sauce that was on the table to render it edible and washing down with a couple of cups of *chai* to get rid of the after-taste.

My re-entry into our hotel room was as dramatic as my exit had been a couple of hours before. I burst in and sprinted past a startled Lady R to dive into the bathroom, just in time to erupt into a simultaneous bout of vomiting and diarrhoea. It was a good half hour later before I emerged pale-faced and shaking and collapsed heavily onto the bed. Within a few minutes I had to rush back in again, and it continued like that for the rest of the day. Lady R—our earlier animosities put aside for the time being—kindly played nurse and coaxed me into swallowing down large quantities of rehydration salts. I complemented this with copious amounts of cola, as according to a tropical medicine specialist I once sat next to on a plane, this is one of the best remedies for a bad stomach, the various chemicals in the drink killing more or less everything they come into contact with, while the sugar and the caffeine give you a good old energy shot.

I figured a good night's sleep would sort me out, but next morning I was still extremely weak and nauseous. My bathroom visits had decreased in frequency somewhat, but that was probably because my stomach was by then entirely empty. I wasn't really in any condition to ride but convinced myself and Lady R that I could probably just about manage to get us to the small town of Dhulikhel, a couple of hours to the east of Kathmandu. That would at least put us a bit closer to Bhutan, the one hard deadline we had on the trip, as we'd had to give them a specific date when we'd be entering the country with the bike that couldn't subsequently be changed. I popped a few tabs of Imodium, just in case, and staggered out to load up.

I took it slow and steady through the heavy, smokey traffic out onto the highway heading east. There were no mountains visible, just grey, foreboding clouds. As we left Kathmandu behind us, the trucks and buses gradually thinned out, but the rain then started to fall. Riding became like a surreal video game, following the road, avoiding the obstacles, trying to stay balanced, but without any of the normal fear or concern, instead just a hazy, drug-induced, nonchalant numbness. Fortunately, we didn't have too far to go, and after an hour or so, a road sign directed us off the highway towards Dhulikhel. Looking for a nice hotel we'd heard about, we swung onto an unpaved road that started as fairly decent gravel but rapidly deteriorated into mud, and mud which the rain was making thicker and more treacherous by the minute. I started to think we must have missed a turn somewhere and was about to suggest to Lady R that we pull over and I collapse into the undergrowth for a little sleep when we spotted two security guards draped in waterproof ponchos looming out of the fog up ahead. Lady R gave me a pat on the back and a "well-done, you made it," which even in my drugged-up state, I lapped up appreciatively.

We pulled into a small garage by the side of the road and parked up as the guards looked at the bike admiringly. Very generous gold umbrellas were produced, and we were directed up a stairway cut into a steep rocky slope which rose up from the road. Up we climbed, me using my hands as well my feet, all sense of personal dignity having long-since been extinguished. At the top we found ourselves on a beautiful hillside populated by a variety of tasteful stone buildings with red-tiled roofs (which turned out to be the rooms) and small cobbled paths running between them. We were shown to our accommodation, and even in my dazed state, I was convinced there must have been a mistake; they had clearly put us in the Presidential Suite by accident. It was massive, bigger than most European apartments. The bathroom alone was the size of a standard hotel room. The "bedroom" housed an enormous bed, a lounge area, and a full dining table and opened onto a terrace giving a captivating 180-degree view of the Himalayas (or so we were told, rain for the time being having stopped play). My eyes took in the minibar that was really more of a maxibar, the three large jars stuffed with different types of sweets and cookies, the trouser press (which admittedly I probably wouldn't be using), and the Apple TV, and I resolved not to leave the room for at least three days. Then I felt my stomach churning and had to dash back to that magnificent bathroom. Perhaps I wouldn't actually have a choice.

Dwarika's Resort was clearly a labour of love for its owner, Sangita, who we met the next day. Her family owned Kathmandu's finest hotel of the same name, and now she, clearly not short of a rupee or two, had decided in her autumn years to set up the retreat of her dreams up there in the backwoods. Splayed over several acres of hillside, it offered, not only palatial rooms (ours apparently was far from the best), but also a variety of "wellness experiences," including the usual rub downs but also such intriguing offerings as Chakra Sound Chambers, Himalayan Salt Rooms, and a Meditation Maze. The restaurants (of which there were three) were supplied by the resort's very own organic farms (of which there were two).

But it looked like I was not going to enjoy any of that as I crawled between bed and bathroom. Sangita kindly arranged for the resident healer and spiritual adviser, known simply as *Guru-ji*, to come to the room to pay me a visit. He prescribed some special broth containing an assortment of mountain herbs that he hoped would put things right. I insisted he allow me to complement this with some western medicine, which he agreed to do on the condition that I permit him to cleanse my chakras. Along with his first-rate negotiation skills, I couldn't help but notice his smart appearance and distinctly military bearing, which I commented on to Sangita, who brightly informed me that there was a very good reason for this—this was *Guru-ji*'s second professional incarnation in this life-time; previously he'd been one of the legendary Gurkhas.

**Our terrace at Dwarika's Resort, Dhulikhel**

Back in the day, a Gurkha was just someone hailing from the Gorkha District of Nepal, near Pokhara. In the early nineteenth century, though, my British forefathers fought a war with Nepal and were mightily impressed with the military prowess of the soldiers that hailed from this part of the country. As a former Indian Army Chief of Staff later commented, "If a man says he is not afraid of dying, he is either lying or he is a Gurkha." And so, in the kind of classic two-faced U-turn that has made Britain famous, on winning the war we negotiated a peace treaty that, in return for giving back to the Nepalis all the weapons we'd captured from them, accorded us the right to recruit Gurkha soldiers into the British Army pretty much in perpetuity. Rather amazingly, given our usual distaste for foreign mercenaries, an annual recruitment drive continues to this day. It also seems to be welcomed by the Nepalese, with thousands of young men competing each year for one of the 300-odd available places. Lady R informed me that a less formal competition then ensues among the local female population seeking to marry one of the successful recruits. She noted with a sigh that this year's recruitment drive had been completed some time back, thus all the choice pickings would have already been taken.

I certainly couldn't compete on that front, as I was anything but fighting fit. For the next two days, when I was not on the lavatory, I lay propped up in bed, looking at the mountains, reading and watching trashy movies while receiving periodic visits from *Guru-ji*. Lady R, meanwhile, went hiking in the hills, worked her way through the various scrubs, chants, and contortions on offer, and wrote Buddha knows how many new blog articles. Despite the rest and medication, both eastern and western, my stomach just refused to get better and I seemed to be waking up weaker each morning. On the third day we decided I'd better get some serious medical attention. We informed Sangita when she made her morning round to check up on me, and she charmingly insisted that we use her car and driver to take us to the local hospital.

Lady R propped me up for the shuffle outside, where we found a rather battered Land Rover waiting for us that appeared to be at least fifty years old and in possibly worse shape than me.

"Looks like this has been in the family a while?" I offered as Sangita helped me in.

She smiled apologetically, "Oh yes, indeed, it's seen far better days I'm afraid."

I gave the solid-looking bodywork a pat, "Well, it still seems to run, that's what matters!"

She nodded, "Indeed, like a dream. Well, the king did take very good care of it over the years, you know."

I looked up, taken aback, "Err, the king?"

"Yes, I mean King Gyanendra, the last monarch of Nepal, my dear," she gave me a kindly smile as she helped me into the back seat. "He was a friend of the family and when, you know, the monarchy fell and whatnot, well he needed to get rid of it, so I took it off his hands."

I tried to pretend this was quite normal, "Oh, of course, naturally, well that's very good of you." I settled into the seat wishing that cars could talk and feeling rather chuffed that I was going out in such style.

Dhulikhel Hospital turned out to be a small establishment but the only one for many miles around, so there was a throng of people in the waiting room, many of whom had walked several hours though the hills to get there. To my great embarrassment, the nurse in charge at reception insisted I go to the front of the queue and wouldn't take no for an answer, telling me she was sure any hospital in my own country would extend the same courtesy to a foreigner. I hoped she never had the misfortune to visit London. This was also the hospital where nearly-qualified doctors and nurses from medical schools in the region went for their final training. Which explained why I soon found myself lying on a bed, an intravenous drip plugged into my arm, with six charming, giggling medical students crowding around in their white coats trying to guess what ailed me.

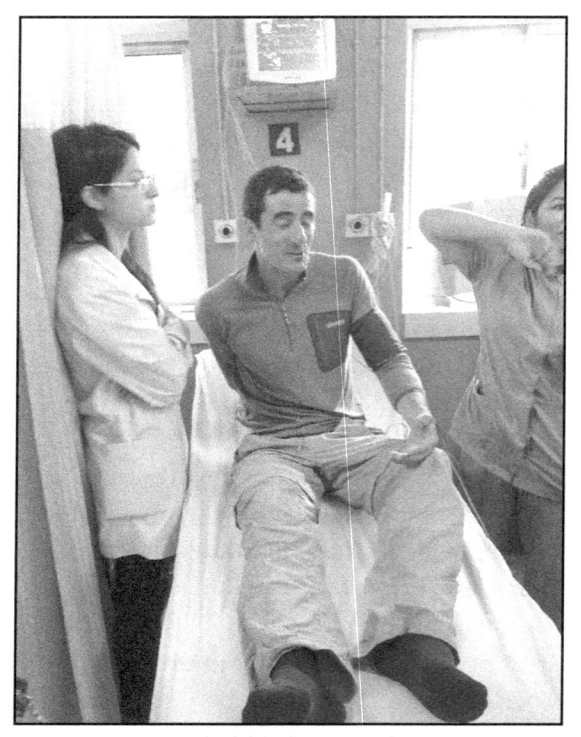

**Dhulikhel Hospital**

After some extensive prodding, questioning, and testing, this medical quorum surmised that the fish from a couple of days back was most likely to blame as the transmitter of a particularly vicious little tropical parasite that they had discovered in my gut. They reassured me that there was no cause for worry, however, as they had just the thing to put me right. I was then force-fed four large pills that tasted like a mixture of charcoal and rust, after which they pronounced me ready to be discharged. Though I doubted it could really be that easy, I quickly acquiesced, feeling very guilty for keeping the bed and their expertise from the people who really needed it.

But whatever it was they'd given me, the effects were amazingly fast. In a few hours my stomach had stabilised, I could eat without running to the bathroom straight after, and

I felt the strength flowing back into my limbs. I beamed at Lady R, "You know I think I'm finally over it."

She looked up from her book, "Well thank goodness. Mind you, it will teach you not to storm out in future."

I looked at her puzzled, "I'm sorry?"

She giggled, "I mean if this wasn't karma, then I don't know what is!"

Luckily, I had enough strength to lob a cushion in her direction.

# 6
# BORDERLINE

By the next morning I felt good enough to get back on the road. We did a poll of the waiters in the hotel before leaving to ask the best way of getting from Dhulikhel down south to re-join the East-West Highway that we had left a few days earlier. That would then take us up to the Indian border in the far eastern corner of Nepal, at which point we would have ridden across the entire country. After some debate, a consensus opinion was delivered that a new road of most excellent quality had just been finished and would provide us a direct route through the mountains to join the highway. An easy, smooth day's riding was just what I needed, so we eagerly went along with their suggestion. We bid a fond farewell to Sangita and Guru-*ji*, who generously deigned to bless the bike.

It felt great to be back in the saddle, and as promised, a perfect smooth, curving road led us out of Dhulikhel with hardly any other traffic on it. We spun down into a valley and rode alongside a river glittering in the morning sun. Orchards and small villages spread across the valley floor, and beyond them forested slopes climbed upwards towards a sky of unadulterated blue. We figured the completion of the road must have really been very recent and, thus, not yet widely known, as that was the only way to explain the almost complete lack of traffic during the first couple of hours. The surface was actually so perfect that it looked like it had just been laid down the previous day.

**The detour**

Five minutes later we discovered that it had. A barrier blocked the road ahead, beyond which the tarmac abruptly ended and we could see a bulldozer pressing gravel onto a roughly hewn dirt track in preparation for extending it. So, this was the end of the road and we were still a good fifty miles from where it would eventually join the East-West Highway, once it was finished. As I moved to turn the bike around and prepare for a very lengthy detour, I heard an engine fire into life above us. I looked up and saw a bus struggling up the hillside on a steep track of sand and rock. All the passengers had already been ejected to give it a fighting chance, and the old girl was now puffing and wheezing in an effort to make it up, accompanied by encouraging shouts from those trudging along behind. I called over to a nearby roadworker, and with some drawing

**Road hazards**

in the dirt and my five words of Nepali and his ten words of English, managed to establish that they had already started building the other end of the road coming up from the East-West Highway and that the two would eventually meet somewhere in the middle. For the time being, though, the track the bus was attempting served to bridge the gap, although after how many miles we were not quite clear. As the alternative was a diversion of over a hundred miles, we decided we'd better give it a go.

It was the steepest bit of "road" we'd encountered, and scanning up it, I could see it was full of bumps and gullies with a liberal sprinkling of loose rocks. I gently removed Lady R from the back to lighten the load then revved the throttle, stamped the gearbox into first, and went for it. The bike jumped up the first few metres with the front wheel rising alarmingly off the ground and then crashing back down. As it did so I started losing traction, and the engine sputtered and threatened to die. I squeezed the brakes, which locked up the wheels and led to me sliding backwards. It was not starting well. I lunged back for the throttle with my right hand as I flayed out manically with my feet to try and push myself forward. The tyres started to grip again, and I was back in business but now convinced that the only language this terrain understood was speed. That made the hairpin bend that appeared after I crested the top of the hill a little more challenging to negotiate as the back slid out alarmingly, but I motored on. I was getting very focused on the task in hand and so ignored the sound of an engine coming from around the next corner. Unfortunately, it turned out to be an oncoming bus, which left no room for me on the track. I swerved into the neighbouring bushes and just managed to wedge my foot down and prevent a nasty tumble as I skidded to a stop. I decided it was time to take a breath. Which also led to me remembering Lady R.

A few minutes later, she appeared around the corner chewing a stalk of grass—I had still not quite managed to work out the rationale she used to distinguish between things she looked down on as too uncivilised and others that, though they might appear to me to be equally gauche, she had somehow reinvented as cool. Thus, chewing grass, carrying luggage in plastic shopping bags, and sitting on the floor pretty much anywhere were all OK in her book, but T-shirts with V-necks, American fast food joints, and well, several other of my own predilections were viewed quite firmly as things one simply didn't do.

"Oh, what a lovely view!" She surveyed what was indeed quite a stunning landscape, while seemingly completely overlooking my heroic ascent. I decided some prompting was needed, "Yes, delightful isn't it? But, phew, that was a close call, did you see the state of the track back there?"

She carried on, blissfully ignoring my need for validation, "And the air is so fresh. I'd simply adore to hike through these hills."

I nodded, "Yeah, right. Well unfortunately, we have to shepherd this old girl through instead," I patted the fuel tank, "But seriously, did you see how tough that was? Can hardly believe I kept it upright."

She smiled at me and stroked my helmet, "Yes, dear, positively Herculean."

For the next couple of hours we wound along a dirt track that pitched perilously up and down barrier-less hillsides and occasionally took us along a dried-up riverbed. It was serious off-road riding using a machine that was really not built for the task. But the Bullet performed admirably, showing remarkable stability and agility for its size, and I started to get a bit more used to that kind of riding too, working out just when was the right time for a little brake, a touch of throttle, or repositioning my weight a bit to keep us moving forward.

Nevertheless, as we rounded a sharp bend and saw tarmac reappear up ahead again I breathed a grateful sigh of relief. Back on a decent surface, we made rapid progress down into the Terai and in the late afternoon came up to a T-junction and re-joined the East-West Highway. We pulled up at a roadside eatery that seduced us with its sign proposing a "Non-beatable Coca-Cola and Momo Combo."

On inspecting the menu, though, the *momos* were given a close run for their money by the "Boil" section, which included "Mutton Boil," "Chicken Boil," and most intriguingly, "Head Boil." It felt good that we had been moving again, making progress, and I guess we were also rather emboldened by having made it through the dirt road and reaching the highway. In any case, after eating our fill, we somehow agreed we should push on to the next major town, convincing ourselves we'd surely make it by nightfall, which would put us within striking distance of the Indian border the next morning.

```
Bhatmas Chiura Sandheko .................................. 30

                      BOIL ITEM

Mutton Boil ............................................. 250
Chicken Boil ............................................ 200
Head Boil ............................................... 200
Veg. Boil ................................................ 50
Aalu Boil ................................................ 40


        That calls for a Carlsberg
```

**Boil and Carlsberg?**

Four hours later I was struggling and we were still far from that elusive town. It was pitch black and the headlight almost made things worse, as the shadows it threw across the road made it hard to correctly judge the potholes ahead, plus it attracted a multitude of bugs that smacked into my face and eyes, making it increasingly difficult to see anything at all. Yes, we'd done it again; we were in the middle of nowhere in the pitch dark riding a motorcycle, something we'd sworn never to repeat after the hellish ride from Pokhara to Kathmandu, and this time we were doing it through the Terai, prime bandit country.

Suddenly, I saw a shape rush out from the side of the road up ahead. I realised it was a dog and that we were going to hit it unless I did something very fast. I slammed on the brakes as hard as I could and managed to slide to a halt a couple of centimetres away from its flank. It turned around nonchalantly and gave me a low growl, reproaching me for trespassing on its territory. It was at that point that I heard tyres screeching behind me. The next second a pick-up truck careered wildly around us—it must have been right behind when I braked and had just managed to swerve to avoid rear-ending us. He disappeared into the night blaring his horn.

"Jesus, that was bloody . . . "—my exclamation of relief was interrupted by a loud metallic crunch and the feeling of being taken firmly from behind as the bike was shunted a good metre or so forward. It was accompanied by the sound of breaking glass and plastic, along with what were presumably some choice expletives in Nepali. A motorbike and its two riders had driven straight into the back of us following our abrupt halt. They must have been right behind the pick-up truck but not shared the former's lightning fast reactions. The rider and his passenger were now lying splayed on the ground with bits of wing mirror and headlight scattered around them. My first concern was, of course, for their well-being,

"Oh my God, are you OK; are you hurt?"

The answer came quickly as they jumped to their feet and started yelling in my face. So not too seriously injured it seemed.

Having previously spent a couple of years living and driving in South Asia, I had learned to be particularly fearful of ever getting into a traffic accident. Firstly, as the foreigner, it was a little too easily assumed that it was your fault, and if you were idiotic enough not to have learned the local language like I was, you had little chance of convincing anyone otherwise. Secondly, your foreignness also made the occasion a bit of an event, so crowds tended to quickly gather. The combination of the two meant that mob justice could easily result.

The driver was getting increasingly worked up and started jabbing a finger into my chest. Clearly he felt the blame lay squarely at my door. I raised my hands, palms open in apology,

"I am very sorry, really, but it was an accident; there was a dog, a dog, right here; it ran right out in front of us!"

"*Kya* dog *panchoot*!" he screamed in reply. I had just enough Nepali to know that this translated as "what dog" followed by a rather uncharitable allegation about the nature of the relationship I maintained with my sister. I gestured to the road, "Right here, there was a dog! I braked because of the dog, the dog! I'm not crazy!" The dog was now nowhere to be seen, the little bastard.

"Yes, crazy, crazy!" He shouted, getting increasingly incensed. Then he gave me a push, grabbed my shirt, and started waving his fist. I gently removed his hand from my collar and tried to calm him down, but I knew we'd crossed a line and that violence was imminent. I pointed to the side of the road, "OK, OK, first let me park and then we can talk, OK?"

I started the bike again and made as if to pull over to the side of the road so that we could properly sort things out while whispering to Lady R to hang on. As I reached the verge instead I let the clutch out and gunned the throttle as hard as I could. We exploded forward, way too fast, and I prayed no nasty pothole was going to take us down. I kept the speed dangerously high as we shot away from them, straining to make out the fast-changing road surface ahead. Behind I could hear shouting and the sound of a revving engine. I just hoped the crash had messed up their bike enough to limit their speed.

Lady R was holding onto me tight and seemed nervous, constantly turning back to check if they were behind. Even though I was anything but calm myself, this gave me a certain pleasure; finally she was showing some vulnerability. When they hadn't caught up after a few minutes I knew I had to change tactics. If I maintained that speed I was going to crash into something sooner or later. But if I went any slower I risked them catching us. I started looking for a place to pull over and hide. As we came into a small village, I spotted a little side street and skidded the bike round into it, then pulled up behind a parked truck and killed the lights. I tucked the bike out of sight, sandwiched between the truck and a wall, and we scuttled into the back of a nearby teashop where we couldn't be seen from the street.

We were both out of breath and a little shaken as we collapsed onto a pair of rickety wooden stools and ordered some *chai*. I dug into my pocket for a packet of cigarettes and lit two up, passing one to Lady R, who took it gratefully. She slid her hand on to my knee as she took a drag, "God, that was close, they really looked like they wanted to kill us."

I exhaled a long puff of smoke, "Yeah, I think they did, that could have got quite nasty. I reckon we did the right thing to make a dash for it."

She squeezed my knee, "I think you're right, wow. I would have just frozen if I was on my own and then . . . well, I dread to think what could have happened . . . thank God I was with you."

Things were looking up. My fear of all the bad things that might occur over the coming weeks was now nicely balanced with the prospect of me being perceived as a saviour when they did. As long as I could keep branding running away as bravery, of course.

We waited half an hour and then emerged cautiously out of our hiding place and back to the bike. There was no sign of our adversaries/victims, so we decided to carry on. We pulled back out onto the highway and continued east, heartbeats still accelerating every time we heard another motorbike behind us. After another hour we reached the outskirts of the town of Itahari, about fifty miles from the Indian border. We cruised through empty streets, looking for any signs of accommodation, and eventually spotted a dilapidated sign half hanging off a wall that directed us to what was by far the worst, but most welcome, lodging of the trip. It was a filthy dive of a place, where we were offered a room with deeply stained carpet, bed linen that looked like it had not been washed for a couple of years, and a toilet that would shame a prison. It could not have been more different from the previous night's quarters. But we were off the bike and all in one piece after sixteen hours on the road, and that was all that really mattered.

I positively creaked out of bed the next morning, feeling at least ten years older. Everything ached; my head, arms, chest, legs, and I looked like a convict on the run. While I was shaving, Lady R kindly informed me that I should also consider ironing my face on a daily basis, and as I examined my grimy, deeply lined brow in the mirror I realised she might be right.

**In Itahari—not the best hotel**

We breakfasted lavishly on vegetable soup, *roti*, and fried eggs dripping with oil, washed down with lashings of hot sweet *chai*. I then set about what was by then the well-rehearsed routine of loading up the bike. As I manhandled the first backpack into the rear luggage carrier though, it refused to fit no matter how much I shoved, which was strange. I bent down to examine the frame and saw that it had been warped out of shape from the previous night's collision. I realised that I had, of course, not checked the bike for damage after the crash, so I stopped to give it a good looking over. Amazingly, the bent carrier seemed to be the only injury, quite a testament to the Enfield's sturdiness, especially given how the other bike had fared. I wandered out into the street and found a garage nearby that kindly agreed to lend me a crowbar. A little energetic levering later and the frame was back into shape, well, more or less. The Indian border awaited, according to the map just a couple of hours' drive away. Which in reality could mean, as Lady R perceptively observed, anywhere between one and six.

# 7

# TEA AND TRAINS

"Excuse me, sir, you are being aware that this is India only?"

I looked at the police officer, who had just pulled us over, in confusion, "What? Really? Oh God, I'm so terribly sorry!"

I felt a rising panic as I realised we had somehow sailed straight out of Nepal and into India without passing through immigration or customs, which was most definitely very illegal. The Indian border guards were, however, very gracious, and after we apologised profusely, they allowed us to head back over the bridge to return to Nepal without further ado. We eventually found the Nepali immigration office hidden behind a tree on the other side. Really, the Nepalese didn't make it easy. We got ourselves processed and stamped then headed back into India for the second time that morning. Sometimes borders fade almost into invisibility as you draw closer to them; the people, the buildings, the language, and the culture virtually indistinguishable on either side, throwing up a stark challenge to the artificial separation imposed by a fence and a handful of uniformed officials. But not so this time. As we cleared Indian immigration and set off again, the roads became smoother and wider, there were more multi-storey buildings, more mirrored glass, lots more advertising hoardings, more cars on the road, definitely more rushing and honking, and well, just a fair bit more craziness. There was simply no mistaking that we were back in incredible India.

We were heading up to Siliguri, which is one of those Indian cities you've never heard of that turns out to be home to more than a million people. If it can be said to have a claim to fame, Siliguri's would be that it is the gateway connecting the rest of India to the wild north-eastern provinces. Heading east out of the city you will soon find yourself in the "chicken's neck," where mighty India is crushed into a narrow strip of land between Bhutan to the north and Bangladesh to the south before ballooning out again a hundred miles or so later into a different world that is Indian only in name, as we would later discover. To the north of Siliguri, yet another balloon of Indian territory stretches upwards between Nepal and Bhutan, expanding until it is abruptly cut off by China. This is where we were heading, to the state of Sikkim, an ancient Buddhist kingdom that became part of India only in 1975 and remains in many respects a world apart.

But first we would overnight in Siliguri. As we came into town things still looked pretty mainstream Indian, teeming with people, trucks, cows, hawkers, and the odd elephant, shopping malls jostling for space with temples. We headed straight to the nearest Enfield garage for a much-needed service. We had some serious rattles; that bumpy ride over the hills must have shaken a few things loose, plus the engine sounded a bit weird, and it felt like we were losing power. I was also starting to feel that the steering was going a little off.

We left the bike at the garage, and they promised to "do the needful." This was one of the many Indian English phrases I

## Tea and Trains

had adopted and now wondered how I ever got along without, another fine example being *preponing*, the opposite of *postponing*. I mean why hadn't the rest of the English-speaking world already come up with that? And then, for example, we could be described at present as being "out of station" and thus in search of somewhere to "put up" for the night. We did exactly that, and half an hour later, we came across a small hotel set back from the road in tropical gardens. It was simple but clean and about seven stars up from our accommodation of the previous evening. We checked in, and after unpacking, I started doing a little exercise in the room to try to shake off the aches and pains from the day's riding. As I went through my routine of press-ups and sit-ups, Lady R decided to start briefing me on the political economy of the tea estates, which we would soon be riding through near Darjeeling. Once that was completed to her satisfaction, she took a rather different tack, "So, I've been thinking…"

I stopped mid-crunch and gave her a wink, "It's why I love you, baby."

She broke into a surprising smile at my interruption, which immediately made me suspect there was something bad coming next that she was trying to pre-placate me for. She paused for a second and then continued, "So, how would you feel about an open relationship?"

Bang, and there we had it. I could feel my face involuntarily contorting into a distinctly unattractive pastiche of anger, fear, and disbelief.

I sat back on my knees, "What? What the hell are you talking about?"

I saw her hesitate slightly as she realised she'd perhaps gone too far,

"No, no, please don't be angry. I'm just asking what you think about open relationships, that's all."

I quickly mopped my brow then threw the towel to the floor, "You said an open relationship, meaning us, not open relationships in general!"

She went to take my hand, "Well, I meant in general, I mean for anyone, and you know, like, hypothetically maybe for us, but in the future?"

I pulled my hand away, "So you do mean us! Right, and presumably because you think I'm actually not good enough for you?"

She laughed a little, "No, of course not, well, I mean, you know, is anyone really good enough for anyone? I mean isn't an open relationship just so much more honest, rather than trying to kind of hide and repress things?"

That really was not helping with my insecurities, but for once I decided to go with the honest and vulnerable response, instead of lashing out,

"Well, not if you have nothing to hide! You want to know what I think? I think I'd hate to share you with anyone; it would simply break my heart."

I'd been hoping to get through to her warmer, more empathetic core, but as I saw a blank face staring back at me, I was quickly overcome instead by a childish desire to hurt her in revenge, despite already knowing exactly where this approach would lead, and so I went for the jugular,

"I just don't understand how you can be so cold, so uncaring, to, to even think something like that, not to mention being so damn emotionally unintelligent as to actually say it," I was building up a nice head of steam now, "Jesus, you're so bloody young, so bloody immature, I mean you don't even appreciate what you've got right in front of you, what a rare thing it is to have another human being love you and connect with you like I do!"

This was admittedly pushing it a bit, given our recent interactions, but I ploughed on regardless, "Or do we actually already have an open relationship, and you were just trying to let me know?"

Which was a pretty ridiculous question, given that we lived together—logistically it would have been nigh-on impossible for her to pull it off. So now, of course, I'd discredited myself entirely. It was clearly best to take a breath, apologise, and attempt to discuss things calmly. Instead I stormed out of yet another hotel room, slamming the door behind me, already feeling like a petulant six-year-old as I did so.

Off I huffed into the backstreets of Siliguri, trying to walk off the swirling cauldron of emotions inside me. Women squatted in saris next to small fires roasting corn on the cob or making flat breads for sale on the side of the street. A truck full of musicians and ornately costumed dancers swept past on the way to some religious celebration—as usual I wasn't quite sure which it might be or even what religion they adhered to, India having such a pantheon of different faiths. In the main, these rub along quite nicely, with everyone respecting one another's beliefs. A handy by-product of that is that citing "religious reasons" can let you get away with just about anything, even walking naked down a main road at 2AM covered in crematorium ash in an attempt to transcend the duality of life and death, as I had previously discovered. To be clear, that wasn't me but rather an Aghori practitioner I'd almost crashed into in Delhi one night when I was living there, who had clearly been following his sect's mantra of rolling around in cremation grounds in an attempt to reach nirvana. I added that to my list of options if things didn't work out with Lady R.

I stopped in for a cup of *chai* and some samosas at a small street stall and then decided to head up to the workshop, where the guys had stayed in late to work on the bike. They were just finishing up and looked tired but satisfied. They gleefully informed me that they had given us a new clutch, a new steering bearing (no, not a clue), and even a new seat, as well as tightening up and adjusting numerous other bits and bobs. I thanked them profusely and handed over a large fistful of grubby rupees.

As I accelerated out into the street, the bike definitely felt more stable and had a little extra oomph, and I was confident that the mechanical problems were behind us. It was quite wonderful to ride into the night on my own, a sense of immense freedom. Like a lone wolf. Or maybe a stray dog. I considered just continuing right past the hotel and out into the hills but then remembered my passport was back in the room. I wondered if real adventurers got scuppered by such banalities. So instead I pulled over at a corner shop to buy some chocolate to take back to Lady R to accompany the apology I had decided to make. I'd finally properly calmed down and convinced myself that one should be more understanding of one's partner's views, and that I must also take into account that she was twelve years younger than me. That such questioning was purely natural. Well, almost.

A train track that crosses a road is not uncommon anywhere in the world of course. Normally, there will be warning signs as you approach it and barriers that block the way when a train is coming. What is rarer is a track that runs parallel to the road then suddenly lurches across it with no warning whatsoever nor any apparent system to prevent collisions, then continues more or less parallel on the other side, then crosses it again after another 200 metres and carries on in a similar fashion as road and track intertwine their way up into the hills. This was the reality of driving up the old Hill Cart Road to Darjeeling. It was the fault of the British, of course, who'd built the narrow-gauge track for the rather romantically named Darjeeling Himalayan Railway that ran from the railhead in Siliguri up to what was one of their favourite "hill stations," some 2,000 metres above the plains and thus an ideal place to escape the summer heat. The railway once ferried tea down from the hills on the first stage of its journey to drawing rooms across the world. Today that tea is trucked out, and only one train a day runs all the way down from Darjeeling to Siliguri, which is a great pity as it must be one of the most beautiful train rides in the world, though it did make our journey this morning considerably less hair-raising as there were no locomotives cutting across the road. Private investors have offered to buy the line and pour in money to set up a regular tourist service that would undoubtedly be enormously popular, but the state-owned Indian Railways, a huge beast that controls over 50,000 miles of track and employs a staggering 1.4 million people, has given them a firm thumbs down. Even selling off what is a minute tributary of their massive network elicits fierce opposition from their trade unions, which are fundamentally opposed to even the slightest whiff of privatisation. The result of that is that in a few years' time the train will simply run no more.

We were not actually supposed to be here at all, but thanks to Lady R's unique navigational skills, we'd ended up completely missing the normal road up from Siliguri and found ourselves instead on this little-known back way. However, as she happily observed, this was turning out to have been rather fortuitous, as we were treated to an almost empty road that led up through peaceful pine forests that shielded us from the midday sun. In the early afternoon we came back out into the open, high above the plains, and were greeted with sweeping views down over steep hillsides mottled with tea bushes and brightly-sari'd women moving slowly among them plucking the leaves, wicker collection baskets strapped to their backs. As we got higher still the road began to deteriorate, then the tarmac disappeared altogether, and finally it tapered into a walking path that was too narrow for us to continue on. I pulled up and caught the eye of a nearby tea picker who had turned from her bushes to inspect us,

"*Namaste*! Err, road no good? No Darjeeling?" I was stating the absolute obvious as I pointed at the vegetation growing over the footpath in front of us. She smiled and shook her head, "No sir, this one old road!" She had a twinkle in her eye as she called over to one of her co-workers in Nepali, the lingua franca around there, who started laughing. Well at least we were spreading a bit of joy.

**Tea plantations**

We turned back and stopped at the next village for consultations, praying for some way to avoid having to drive all the way back to Siliguri, which was now a good three hours away downhill. It seemed we were in luck. We were directed around the back of the village school and onto a near vertical single track of tarmac. This corkscrewed upwards through the tea plantations, requiring first gear all the way with the engine constantly threatening to splutter out. Thankfully, there was no other traffic to contend with—I doubted any truck or bus could make it up there in any case—and the recent bike repairs seemed to have given us just enough extra power to maintain momentum up to the top.

A couple of miles and a considerable increase in altitude later, we came to a small junction where the road finally levelled out.

**Darjeeling bound**

There was a sign for Darjeeling pointing off to the left, and I let out a sigh of relief. Next to it was another sign announcing that the tiny unassuming hamlet scattered around the crossroads had once been the home of Subas Chandra Bose. Mr. Bose had played a colourful, if ultimately rather futile, role in the Indian independence struggle. Though a Cambridge man and a former member of the (British-run) Indian Civil Service, he was understandably keen to get the Brits out of his country as soon as possible. But in contrast to his contemporary, Gandhi, he felt that words and non-violence just weren't going to quite cut it. So during the Second World War he made a secret alliance with the Germans and the Japanese, who promised that if he mobilised his country people to help the Axis against the Allies then they'd ensure a free India once they had won the war. The British, though lacking hard evidence, became suspicious of him and put him under house arrest.

And there the story might have ended, had one been dealing with someone a little less resourceful than Mr. Bose. Instead, he managed to disguise himself and slip out of home, right under their noses. He then commenced an epic journey that took him to Peshawar then Kabul then Moscow then Rome and finally Berlin. It made our own little trip look distinctly like a walk in the park. Once in Germany, he schemed with the Nazis to plan a German invasion of India that would kick out the Brits. But as time passed, he started doubting that German forces would ever get close enough to the sub-continent to execute the plan. In the meantime, though, the Japanese were making serious inroads into South East Asia, and so Mr. Bose convinced Mr. Hitler to let him go and join them instead.

A la James Bond, he boarded a German submarine that took him down to Madagascar where, somewhere off its southern coast, he surfaced and transferred to a Japanese vessel that took him back to Asia. Tokyo had by then seized a good deal of territory from the British in South East Asia and in the process captured plenty of Indian soldiers who'd been fighting there under British command. Mr. Bose took those men and started to mould them into a new "Indian National Army," which would accompany the Japanese on their march westwards and help liberate India. But, damn his luck, by the time he was ready to go the Allies had already rallied and were pushing the Japanese back from the border of India into Burma. Seeing the tide was turning, and man of international mystery that he was, he decided he'd make a dash for the Soviet Union via Taiwan. Who knows what further adventures might have then ensued had his plane not crashed on the way there and killed all on board. And that, well, was that.

As we continued towards Darjeeling the scenery became increasingly alpine and we passed orchards and wooden board houses that could almost have been Swiss chalets. The taxis cutting us up were four-wheel drive jeeps instead of the usual jalopies, the advertisements on the roadside billboards were for tea instead of *ghee*, and every now and again we were treated to a glimpse of the snow-capped peak of Kanchenjunga in the distance, the world's third highest mountain, as it shone a delightful pale yellow in the late afternoon sun.

**Kanchenjunga**

There were train tracks zig-zagging across the road again, but they were the least of my driving worries with all of the honking, jostling traffic around us and everyone trying to squeeze up this narrow mountain road to the old summer resort of the British Raj. That was until a piercing whistle followed by a bellowing horn sounded behind me and very nearly caused me to fall off the bike. I had failed to notice that the train track was now simply running right up the middle of the road. This road was narrow enough in the first place and already crowded with cars, motorbikes, people, and the odd group of animals. But as I looked over my shoulder, I saw we also had a massive blue locomotive engine with "Indian Railways" proudly stencilled on the front fighting for space, and much more persuasively and less flexibly than any of the other punters. It had a huge round headlight anchored to its roof and a bright red triangular metal plate bolted to the bottom of its frontage that gave it the air of a bloodthirsty cyclops intent on gobbling us up. It seemed we had finally met the Brahmin who sat at the very apex of the Indian traffic hierarchy.

Other vehicles grudgingly swerved off the tracks at the last minute as the locomotive came up behind them and sounded its ear-splitting horn. I went to do the same thing as it got closer and closer behind us but found that the traffic was chock-a-block on both sides, so there was nothing for it but to try to outrun her. I changed down a gear and hit the throttle. Lady R whooped with delight. We were doing OK for a bit, but then she started gaining on us again and showed no signs of any willingness to slow down, the horning and whistling just becoming more insistent the closer she got. I started to get bulldozer flashbacks. It was somewhere between comical and horrific as I made repeated rapid glances back and eventually found the front of the engine just half a metre from the rear mudguard. But just when a collision seemed inevitable, I spotted an opening in the traffic to my right ahead and managed to dart into it. The locomotive immediately came alongside, and the carriages brushed against our knees as they swept past. As the last of them went by, I cut in and fell in right behind, back on the tracks again, and let the larger iron horse do the work of cutting a path through the chaos for us. Lady R squeezed me tight from behind. This was motorcycling rock and roll.

**Train in the road**

Up until the early eighteenth century, Darjeeling was part of Sikkim, which was then an independent Buddhist kingdom. But then the town had the misfortune, shared in many corners of the world, of catching the eye of the British. They thought it would make a simply delightful place to retreat to in the summer months when they were desperate to escape from the bristling heat of Delhi. A few years later they'd pretty much taken over, firmly entrenching themselves with bungalows, churches, and gentlemen's clubs. They also built a number of boarding schools, which quickly gained a very good reputation and today remain the educational establishment of choice for the elite, not only of India but also of neighbouring Nepal and Bhutan. But it was tea that came to really define the town. The British "planters" came in droves, and as we'd seen on the drive up, the tea estates are still thriving today, so much so that most people outside of India are rather surprised to hear that Darjeeling is actually a real place in addition to being the name of one of their favourite brews.

We pulled up on the outskirts of town to stop for a cuppa and rest our aching backsides. I looked around with satisfaction; not only was the town looking rather charming but, now that we were off of the main road, the streets were also lovely and quiet, a real rarity in India. I turned to Lady R, "What a delightful place. You know it could almost be an English village in the 1950s. And hardly anyone on the streets; amazing."

She looked at me nonplussed, "Well, it is like that for a reason, of course."

It was a tone that led me to believe there was something she thought I should know but was pretty sure I didn't. I was quite familiar with it. I took another sip of tea before indulging her, "Which you are no doubt now going to educate me on, my dear?"

She rolled her eyes, "The general strike, man! You do appreciate there's a rebellion going on up here?"

This I hadn't expected, "What? Really? Here? Are you sure?"

She looked at me with a mixture of amusement and resignation, "Does the name *Gorkhaland* ring a bell?"

I considered for a moment, "Well, not super immediately, no."

This was enough to lock in school teacher mode, "Well, Andrew, most of the population here are in fact of Nepali descent, as opposed to the Bengalis on the plains we've just left. And they'd like their own state to live in, which they want to call Gorkhaland, as opposed to being lumped in with West Bengal."

"Ah, I see."

"So, there's a general strike on at the moment with the aim of putting pressure on Delhi to take their demands for autonomy seriously. Now this would presumably explain the lack of people on the streets and the shuttered shops; what do you think, hmmm?"

I nodded obediently and bit sheepishly into my biscuit.

As it turned out, things had actually been rather quiet for the past couple of years on this issue, but a recent agreement to allow a new Indian state to be carved out of an existing one thousands of miles to the south had reignited demands for similar treatment up here. In the past the Government had responded to strikes in Darjeeling by sending in paramilitary forces and arresting the leaders. That had a very tangible effect, but not quite the desired one—it had served to unite the various, previously bickering, factions that were calling for some kind of secession into a cohesive force set firmly against Delhi. This time round things had stayed calm so far, as the authorities had not yet taken any action in response to the strike, but it was anyone's guess how the situation was going to evolve in the next few days. People were as friendly to us as ever, though, even if one could quite reasonably argue that the current situation was all ultimately the fault of the British, as Lady R helpfully pointed out.

We checked into a rather decent old hotel for the night, all polished wood, overstuffed armchairs, and roaring log fires. The *pièce de résistance* was the welcome sherry offered to guests at check-in. Over dinner I set out my plans for a nice lay in the next day, but Lady R insisted we must instead set the alarm very, very early in order to be able to ride to a local vantage point and see the sunrise over the mountains. When I protested she reminded me how much time I had already cost us by getting sick, which as she helpfully reiterated, was definitely my fault for having argued with her and stormed off in Kathmandu, meaning I had missed out on the nice, parasite-free breakfast offered by the hotel. I called for another sherry.

At 3AM in the cold and dark we dragged ourselves out of bed and self-mummified, pulling on just about every item of clothing we had. The rise in altitude had been mirrored by a fall in temperature, and it was now only a couple of degrees above freezing outside. Like me, the bike protested at being asked to perform under such conditions and took a good dozen kicks before coming grumpily to life. Any sense of adventure that might have partially eased the suffering was quickly extinguished, as just after leaving the hotel, we entered a traffic jam of jeeps, all ferrying tourists up to enjoy that same sunrise from that same vantage point.

After a few miles the road lapsed into a rough stony track on which the jeeps all tried to overtake each other and we got squeezed in between. Much jolting and jarring and a few near misses later, we arrived at the vantage point, which was an absolute circus. Vehicles kicked up clouds of dust, tourists jostled and shouted, and *chai* hawkers clamoured for business. We huddled in next to a group of Indian soldiers taking selfies and waited for the magic to start. In the end it wasn't a bad sunrise, to be honest; the weather was clear and the peaks transformed from a dark grey in the pre-dawn gloom through to orange to pink to yellow to white as the day broke. I just objected to having to share it with 500 other people.

Back at the hotel I insisted on a hearty, full English breakfast in compensation as Lady R started to plan a walking tour of the town's principal attractions. As I finished off my black pudding, though, I felt an all too familiar churning in my stomach. I made a dash for the bathroom. It wasn't as bad as what I'd experienced in Nepal, but after needing three visits in the next fifteen minutes, it seemed clear I was going to be hotel-bound for the rest of the day. I wondered if maybe I had subconsciously induced it, as I realised I rather liked the idea of not going out. I didn't really fancy slogging round town being lectured on Indian history; no, what I wanted was a day off, to just lounge around the hotel grounds, drink some tea, read, and enjoy the view. But Lady R's youthful enthusiasm, restless mind, and higher energy levels (which I put down to her not having to suffer the rigours of driving, as opposed to me just being old and past it) meant that proposals of that kind were hardly ever entertained. So I started to plan my day off, first Googling for the potential positive effects of sherry on stomach bugs.

It turned into a rather perfect day. I wasn't bed-ridden; I just needed to be fairly near a loo, so I spent my time lounging around the beautifully manicured hotel grounds, reading, writing, daydreaming, looking at the mountains, and very much enjoying my own company. Lady R went out to do her sightseeing and returned in the early evening a little breathless and rosy-cheeked,

"Well, better?" The tone was, I felt, a little more accusatory than compassionate.

I rubbed my stomach, "Getting there, still a bit too weak to drive though, I reckon."

She frowned. "Hmmm. You do remember we have a fixed date that we have to get to the Bhutanese border by, right?"

I nodded, "Yes, of course, but I can't help being sick you know!"

She sighed, "Well, it is the second time in two weeks; I mean once I can put down to carelessness but twice, hmmm."

I considered various possible comebacks but then took a deep breath instead and told her that one would do one's very best to heal oneself as soon as possible.

# 8

# SHAKE, RATTLE, AND ROLL

After another day's slightly guilty rest, I was feeling much more perky and everything seemed to have stabilised, so it was time to get back into the fray. We headed out of Darjeeling on a steep hairpin road that would take us towards the heart of Sikkim. For three hundred years this state was a country in its own right, ruled over by a lineage of Tibetan Buddhist kings. When India threw off the British colonial yoke in 1947, its new government invited Sikkim to become part of the freshly-minted country, but they decided to take a middle path instead, becoming a protectorate of India and allowing her to look after such pesky issues as defence and diplomacy while they continued to manage their own internal affairs. The new king, who took over in 1973, changed all that however. He made himself so unpopular with his erratic rule that his people started rioting against him and then asked India to protect them from their very own leader. In 1975 all agreed that a referendum should be held, which was how Sikkim ended up becoming India's twenty-second state.

But what it didn't become was very typically Indian. The people and the culture were still very distinct from the plains, a kind of mix of Tibetan and South East Asian. Cementing this feeling of a land apart was the requirement that all foreigners need a special permit to enter the state; a standard Indian visa just doesn't cut it. That's partly because this is also a sensitive area geographically, forming as it does a little exposed pinkie finger poking cheekily up between Nepal and Bhutan to tickle the belly of China.

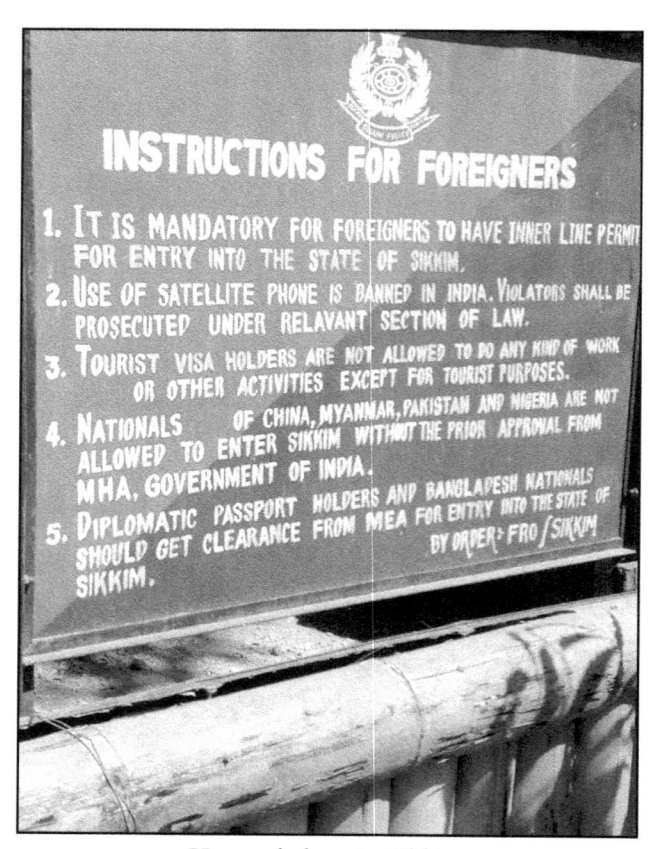

**How to behave in Sikkim**

## Shake, Rattle, and Roll

We'd summited a ridge and started descending a ridiculously steep and narrow switchback road towards a river, the wheels of the bike frequently locking up as I squeezed on the brakes, putting us into a slide until I could regain control. The old girl seemed to be juddering a bit too, but I put that down to the strain of the steep incline. When we eventually reached the valley bottom, a suspension bridge took us across to a police checkpoint. We pulled up and produced our papers and, after a little stamping and scribbling, were pronounced fit to enter Sikkim.

The road then took us up away from the river, twisting through pristine conifer forests that threw mesmerising patterns of dappled sunlight across the road. We were only seeing another vehicle every half an hour or so, thus it seemed a good time for Lady R to have another bash at driving. The winding road called for frequent gear changes, and when the engine spluttered and died after a couple of missed shifts, I presumed the bike had just stalled as she had mis-timed pulling the clutch in. She tried to kick it alive again without success, so I did the patronising alpha male thing and, with a glib smile, suggested she might want to step aside. It was with no small amount of glee that she then watched me repeatedly fail to do any better. She smiled triumphantly as I gave up after my twentieth unsuccessful attempt. I dropped the facade of competence, and we both laughed at my ineptitude until the implications sunk in of being broken down in the middle of nowhere with not a clue as to what the problem might be. Lady R looked at me sceptically as I started poking around in the engine,

"So, what exactly are you looking for?"

I glanced up, "Well just, you know, anything that looks kinda, err, wrong."

She placed a hand on my shoulder, "And would you have any idea of what looks kinda, err, right?"

That was a valid point. But as I was fumbling around for a witty comeback I actually spotted something,

"Aha! There we go!" I held up a wire in triumph that was attached to the engine at one end and dangling loose at the other. "Now that can't possibly be good."

**That can't be good**

I was rather pleased with myself, but I couldn't actually see where the wire had been attached before. So I just tried shoving it into various openings and against different bits of metal that looked like they might have something to do with it and then tried to start the bike again, but not too surprisingly, that made no difference whatsoever.

We hadn't passed a house, let alone a town, in miles, and the bike was too heavy to push for any serious distance. Thus it seemed that one of us would need to go for help while the other waited with the bike. The question was which one.

## *Shake, Rattle, and Roll*

Lady R seemed unconcerned, but I figured that leaving her alone on the roadside in the middle of nowhere was really a no-no. Better we wait for a passing vehicle, I flag it down and vet the passengers for any obvious signs of psychosis, and once cleared, she'd hop in. Then, on reaching the next town, she would find a mechanic and bring him back (*him* as the prospect of finding a female mechanic in rural India was unfortunately still infinitesimal), and then he'd do the needful. Lady R agreed to the plan, helpfully adding that it would, in effect, make her my knight in shining armour.

It was a good three-quarters of an hour before we heard a low rumbling from the valley below. A few minutes later a truck appeared, hauling itself spluttering and panting around the steep turns. I put on my best damsel in distress smile and waved it down. A bit of sign language explained our predicament and request for a ride, and the driver wobbled his head in acquiescence. An old Auntie among the five passengers already in the cab seemed to offer insurance against any funny business. I waved Lady R off and wondered how believable all this was going to seem on the police report if she never came back.

It was quite peaceful there alone in the forest. I lit a cigarette and sat on the verge, back against the bike, watching some bright green birds flitting from branch to branch above me. I dozed off for a while then woke up hungry so rummaged round in the packs. I found some broken biscuits but also some electrical tape, so I decided to have another go at fixing the bike myself. I tried taping that loose end of wire to just about everywhere it would reach on the engine, but it still made absolutely no difference. I leant back against the bike again. The birds had flown off and I was out of cigarettes. Then I remembered our mobile library. What a damn fine idea that had been. I prised out a very dirty and creased copy of *Ghurka!* and settled in.

It was two hours later when a horn sounding woke me up with the book in my lap. A pick-up truck was approaching, and to my great relief, I saw Lady R in the cab, accompanied by a gentleman who definitely looked dirty enough to know how to fix a motorcycle. She hopped out and triumphantly informed me that she'd got into the nearest town, which had turned out to be about forty-five minutes away, acquired directions to a workshop, succeeded in explaining the situation, promised we would pay a king's ransom for any assistance, and then managed to direct the mechanic back. I felt like quite a lucky little damsel.

The mechanic lumbered over to the bike and immediately homed in on the errant wire. I was hoping for some head shaking, perhaps followed by a declaration of the need for welding or a delicate replacement of the tappets, really anything that confirmed it was something far more serious than I could ever have been able to hope to fix alone. I turned to Lady R and asked her what the town was like, but as she started to reply we were interrupted, "OK, is now working, sir."

I turned to see the mechanic grinning and bobbing his head from side to side.

"I'm sorry?"

"Done, all finish, I am fixing wobbly wire only."

I noticed the engine was now running. He had spent all of twenty seconds with the bike, and I hadn't even seen him use any tools. Lady R shook her head in resignation. I paid our friend the equivalent of a week's wages for possibly the easiest work he'd ever had.

We decided we could probably still make it up to the town of Pelling by dusk, which we had read had a stunning view of the Himalayas. That was presuming the roads remained decent and nothing went wrong. Admittedly, such presumptions had not served us particularly well in the past, but then again, the road squiggle on Google Maps didn't have any dashed sections, which was always a good sign, and two mechanical incidents in a single day seemed very unlikely. We pulled in at the next town for a quick round of samosas and tea and a top up of petrol. With all three of us refuelled, we pushed onwards and upwards. Traffic was light, the bike sounded good, and we were soon out of town and back into the countryside, cruising along very nicely. After a couple of miles the road entered a long, unlit tunnel, burrowing into the side of a mountain. I flicked on the headlight and saw there was water streaming from the ceiling and the walls were bare stone. The tunnel lasted for about half a mile but was like the border between two different worlds. As we exited on the other side the friendly coniferous forests had disappeared, replaced by barren grey rock. On one side of the road a sheer granite wall rose up, on the other a steep scree slope swept down to a river a couple of hundred metres below. The tarmac had gone for good and there was not a crash barrier in sight as we bumped along close to the edge of the chasm. It then started to rain, something that most definitely wasn't supposed to happen at that time of year.

As we came around a hairpin bend a couple of miles on, the engine misfired and cut out momentarily. I gunned the throttle hard, and it came stutteringly back to life. Just a little blip, nothing to worry about. A couple of minutes later it happened again, dying and then coming back to life when I wrenched on the throttle. But the third time there was no resuscitation, and we rolled to a halt at the side of the road. I worked on the kick start to try to get her going again. Once, twice, ten times, but not even a splutter, she was completely dead. I checked the repaired wire, but that was fine, so the problem must lie elsewhere. Surely this couldn't be happening again, not twice in one day? We were tired, it was soon going to be dark, it was getting cold, we were wet, and we were in the most remote area of the trip so far. Really, what had we done to deserve this? I was starting to get quite annoyed, though I didn't really have a target. Lady R did, however, as she stood hovering over me with her arms crossed as I bent down to check nothing had got wedged inside the exhaust (which seemed particularly unlikely), "Really, I mean attempting this trip without any maintenance know-how whatsoever, it's pretty ridiculous, isn't it?"

I replied without looking up, "Yeah, well I guess we both knew our limitations when we decided to go for it."

But she wasn't going to let it go, "I'm not talking about 'us.' I'm talking about you."

I straightened up and looked her square in the eyes, "Right, OK, we both could have read up on bike repairs or whatever beforehand but, well, we didn't, did we?"

She gave a dismissive wave of her hand, "Well it's your bloody bike, you've been riding these things for years, how can you possibly not know how to fix them?"

This was essentially a good point, and to tell the truth, I did feel rather stupid, but I gave a sarcastic laugh, "I told you before we started out that I'm not really a grease monkey. I thought that's why you loved me." I kicked a nearby stone over the edge down to the river far below. She switched to a different tack, "You also told me it would be no problem, as in India there's always someone around who can fix an Enfield," she gestured at the moonscape around us, which showed not a single sign of human life in any direction, "Well?"

"Oh, bugger off."

I walked off a little way up the road to think. I was quite worried this time. We hadn't passed another vehicle in a long while, and people tended not to travel at night in those parts for the good reason that the roads were just too bloody dangerous. Even if someone did come along sometime soon and we could hitch a ride, there was no question of one of us staying with the bike in the dark, cold, and wet waiting for the other to return with help. Nope, we'd have to leave our ride on this desolate mountain road for the night and hope she was still there the next day. I realised I was already starting to shiver, and the sun hadn't even fully set yet. I walked back down to where Lady R was standing by the bike biting her lip. As she looked up at me I got right to the point, "OK that's it, we have to move, we'll leave the bike here, come back for it in the morning. Let's get the packs off, shoulder them, and start walking. At least that way we'll get warm. Then, hopefully, someone comes by at some point and we can hitch a ride."

I was surprised as she immediately nodded and started to unfasten the bungee chords that were holding our bags onto the bike. Maybe a more commanding, in control, me was what she really wanted.

As we trudged away from the bike, an icy wind blew up from the valley, hammering the rain into our faces. We rounded a corner and found the road winding further upwards into the gloom, our eyes squinting for any sign of a light to indicate an approaching vehicle or a house, but there was nothing. We slipped and stumbled on the wet stones, and the packs dug painfully into our shoulders—we'd never intended to carry them for more than a couple of metres and so hadn't invested in anything that would be suitable for backpacking. After a long hour of steadily mounting desperation, I stopped suddenly in my tracks. Yes, that was the low chugging and gear changing of a jeep somewhere further down the valley making its way uphill. A few minutes later a pair of headlights picked us out through the rain, and we waved the driver down. But as he pulled up and we looked into the back of the vehicle our hearts sank, it was already jam-packed with passengers and luggage and there was scarcely even space for a cat, let alone two lumbering white bikers and their gear.

Thinking about it, this was quite understandable, as there are few jeeps plying those roads in the first place and they rarely set out until they have more passengers and cargo than they can safely carry. The area is so sparsely inhabited that there's no point to leave room for picking people up along the way, as it's very unlikely there will be any. The jeeps also don't set out after dark, so this one was going to be one of the last we'd see that evening. The driver smiled apologetically and shrugged his shoulders before pulling off again, and we resigned ourselves to carrying on walking. Another forty minutes passed, by which time it was pitch dark and the wind and the rain were really picking up. Then, without warning, a set of headlights momentarily lit up the rock face ahead. We hadn't heard the engine this time due to the roar of the storm. Another jeep. But, again, it was full to bursting. We waved them on and continued. I was on autopilot by then, just placing one foot in front of the other and trying to stay upright, my mind all but switched off. I had to walk, that's all.

I'd lost all sense of time passing when Lady R grabbed onto my arm. I turned to see a vehicle pulling up behind us. We trudged over, resigned to it being already full. But as I looked into the back I had to do a double take as I realised that, no, it was actually completely empty. The driver, who also spoke decent English, told us we were very lucky, as he'd dropped off some passengers a while back at a remote farm and his vehicle was the last jeep that would be travelling the road that day. We offered him whatever he wanted to get us up to Pelling, and he gladly accepted. I offered a silent prayer to all the Indian gods I could think of.

Pulling the jeep door shut behind us and feeling the cosy blast of the heater, all my notions about the freedom of travel by motorcycle, the romance of the wind in your hair, the joy of being in the great outdoors, were firmly banished in favour of the warmth, comfort, and protection of a fully closed-in vehicle, and I swore to myself to only travel by car in future. The driver, who'd now introduced himself as Atul, turned back to us with a quizzical look on his face, "So, I am thinking, why you are going out walking at such late time?"

I laughed, "Well we didn't actually mean to. Err, do you remember maybe passing a motorcycle parked at the roadside some time back?"

He paused for a second and looked puzzled, and I started to think our ride had already been pinched, but then his face brightened,

"Ah yes! I am passing one Royal Enfield Bullet, wondering where is rider."

"Well, here we are! It broke down, unfortunately."

"Oh dear me, that is troubling. And you cannot fix?"

Lady R snorted, and I gave her a dirty look, "Well no, not quite sure what the trouble is. So, we'll try to go back and sort it out tomorrow. Do you think it will be safe there overnight?"

He considered for a moment, "I would say fifty-fifty."

"And that would be due to?"

"Well, maybe rockfall, maybe bandits, who can say?"

Oh well, I was resigned to whatever fate brought. And in any case, we could just hire a nice warm jeep to make the rest of our trip in if it got pinched. I had one last question, "Would you maybe know a mechanic that could go with us in the morning to help fix it; I mean presuming it's still there?"

Atul twiddled his moustache and smiled, "You are being very lucky; my brother is motorcycle repair *wallah*. He can have you tip-top by morning tea time; I am sure of it."

I looked triumphantly at Lady R as Atul continued, "You give me keys, tomorrow my brother go and fix bike, then deliver to where you are putting up in Pelling."

Wow, this was service, indeed, and the kind one only found in India. So we could just stay in bed in our hotel and have the bike brought to us the next day all ready to go. And if it didn't turn up, well, we could just stay in bed. Of course, there was the question of the wisdom of handing over the bike keys to a complete stranger, with no idea who he was or where he lived, if he actually had a brother, if he'd steal the bike and disappear, or just steal it and then tell us it had not been there when he got there. On the other hand, it meant I wouldn't have to do anything myself in the morning, apart from maybe file a police report. I smiled and sighed, "That would be absolutely fantastic. Thank you so very much."

We carried on twisting higher and higher for the next hour, and I realised just how wrong we'd been in our calculations. Even with the bike working perfectly we'd have been riding in the dark and rain on dirt roads with a huge unguarded precipice on one side. So overall one could perhaps argue that the breakdown had turned out to be a bit of a blessing.

I tentatively proposed that line of thought to Lady R and received a slap on the thigh in return.

We eventually found the hotel tucked high up in the hills, a crumbling old manor house approached through massive wrought iron gates and a wide gravel drive that was overhung with the tentacles of some unknown tree, as if seeking to reach down and probe arriving visitors. With the wind howling around the eaves it all felt rather Byronic, as Lady R pointed out, or a bit like a scene from the *Rocky Horror Picture Show*, as I offered. We drew up by the stone steps leading up to the front door and said our goodbyes to Atul, with me handing him the bike keys and vaguely wondering what the hell I was doing. But really, I was too tired to care.

I pushed open the two heavy wooden doors and entered a world of colonial-era abandonment, dark teak panelling, worn leather sofas, threadbare rugs, mouldering animal heads, and paintings of fat, uniformed white people on horses. The place looked like it hadn't been cleaned in a good decade, and the two staff sitting sprawled behind the reception desk in their faded, forty-years-out-of-date uniforms appeared distinctly shocked to see living, breathing guests. There was some nervous muttering, and then we were motioned to sit down on one of the sofas. After a couple of minutes, a butler emerged with a decanter of port on an old silver tray. OK, five stars on TripAdvisor.

"It is a very severe cyclonic storm; over one million people evacuated, Sahib."

I paused with my forkful of scrambled eggs halfway to my mouth as I tried to process what the waiter had just told me. We'd woken up to grey skies and more rain with not a snowy peak in sight, so I'd just enquired, in that indignant manner of the traveller who feels his host should be in control of absolutely all aspects of his stay, whether it wasn't rather unusual for the time of the year, given the monsoon was well past. It turned out that a cyclone had made landfall some 600 miles to our south and brought with it a blanket of unseasonable weather, the edge of which had reached all the way up to Sikkim. No view of the Himalayas today then. But the eggs really were rather good. I started considering an after-breakfast sherry.

"Walkies?" Lady R looked at me across the table expectantly and immediately shattered my hopes.

"Oh, well OK, yes, I guess we could, though it does look a little damp out?"

"Are we really going to do the sugar thing again?"

We clomped up the drive and onto the small road, which led into a forest. After a few hundred metres we came to a small side turning where some prayer flags tied to a post fluttered in the breeze, small coloured triangles of cloth printed with devotional text that Buddhists believe send their prayers heavenwards when the wind blows. A handy labour-saving automation of worship if ever there was one. We could see a monastery through the trees. We walked up the path and found some steps leading up to a large, square building, its bottom half whitewashed, its top half dark brown wood, with an elegant carved roof overhanging its walls. Ornate designs of red, gold, and green decorated each doorway and window. Inside we found the esoteric symbols of Tibetan Buddhism, a world away from its stripped-down Zen cousin, with paintings and statues commemorating a whole pantheon of gods and demons. That reflected how the religion in Tibet had merged and flowed with the older local traditions of Bon, an arcane folk belief that saw angels and devils in every valley and mountain top that needed to be feared and appeased. Butter lamps flickered, throwing dancing shadows onto the walls, and the low chanting of monks reciting their sacred texts echoed around the building. I felt the worries of the road melting gently away.

Back outside, the cool and the rain were actually rather invigorating, and so we walked on through a modest village, past a number of smallholdings, and eventually round and back to the hotel through a fragrant pine forest. As we strolled back up the drive the sounds of birdsong and cow bells tinkling somewhere down in the valley were complemented, quite beautifully I thought, by the unmistakable put-put-put of a Royal Enfield engine. It seemed Atul had been true to his word.

# 9
# BREAKING UP AND DOWN

An hour later we were saddled up and ready to go. I had a good feeling it really would be the last of our mechanical difficulties, leaving us free to enjoy the mountain roads of Sikkim over the next few days without a care in the world, just so long as that pesky cyclone cleared off.

We decided to aim for the town of Ravangla, which looked to be three or four hours away. Leaving the hotel, we started a winding descent down to a river, and I was enjoying the twisting and turning when, as I changed gear on one of the bends, the engine stuttered slightly. I dismissed it, but then at the next corner it happened again, accompanied by a loud clunk and the sound of metal bouncing on tarmac. Something seemed to have fallen off the bike. I stopped and looked back to see the exhaust laying in the middle of the road. It couldn't be happening. Lady R went back and picked it up. We then coasted further downhill towards a village and managed to find a mechanic's yard. There was no language issue in trying to explain the problem, I just held the exhaust up and shrugged my shoulders.

**An easy problem to explain**

It was getting harder to see the funny side. That wasn't what the trip was supposed to be about. It was the third time in twenty-four hours we had broken down. It was really unbelievable. But after an hour of banging and welding, the mechanic put us back on our way, and though we'd have to make a decent pace to reach Ravangla by nightfall, I reckoned we'd just about manage. We rode to the bottom of the valley and crossed a bridge to the other side of the river. It was back to climbing, tight curves taking us up foggy, forested slopes with not a soul in sight, just the occasional bleat of an unseen goat somewhere through the trees. I half turned my head to speak to Lady R, "So, it seems like they fixed the exhaust OK then, lucky for . . . " I was interrupted by another loud clank. It had bloody well fallen off again.

I pulled over and we both dismounted. I kicked the bike hard and swore. Lady R looked really pissed off too but vented her frustration in a rather different way, going to sit down in the middle of the road and repeatedly thumping the tarmac. It started to rain. I looked up at the sky in despair, "Oh God help us!"

A rumble of thunder echoed across the valley and duly humbled me for my impertinence in requesting divine intervention for such trifles. At that moment, a small motorcycle rounded the corner, narrowly missed Lady R, and then pulled over to park up next to our stricken Enfield. The two passengers dismounted and removed their helmets. They were both wearing priests' dog collars and positively beamed at us, "Good afternoon! You are in need of some assistance?"

I was speechless for a couple of seconds, "Wow, I mean, Jesus, oh I mean, no, sorry, but really? Oh, Good Lord!"

"Excuse me?" the driver looked at me, understandably a little confused, and I struggled to regain my composure.

"I mean, hi, err, good afternoon, so you really are priests?"

"Oh yes, indeed!" He smiled beatifically back at me, "Please let me introduce. I am Father Samuel, and this is Father Peter. We're stationed at Saint Mary's in Delhi but have come up country to visit some of the more remote congregations."

I couldn't help but laugh, "Wonderful, so it looks like our prayers have been answered."

He giggled infectiously, "Well now, we cannot see a brother and sister stranded on the road without offering assistance! You are both churchgoers, I assume?"

He looked at me with a friendly yet schoolmasterly inquisitiveness. Lady R and I both nodded vigorously. For my part, I was ready to get ordained right then if they could fix the bike. Father Samuel looked satisfied and then started poking around the former exhaust area, while Father Peter continued smiling at us radiantly. Having completed his investigation, Father Samuel then picked up the exhaust with one hand, took a large rock from the side of the road with the other, and proceeded to smash it back into place, finishing the job with a couple of very vigorous and distinctly un-Christian kicks. With it firmly reattached, he looked up and beckoned us to join hands with him and his colleague, "And now, let us pray."

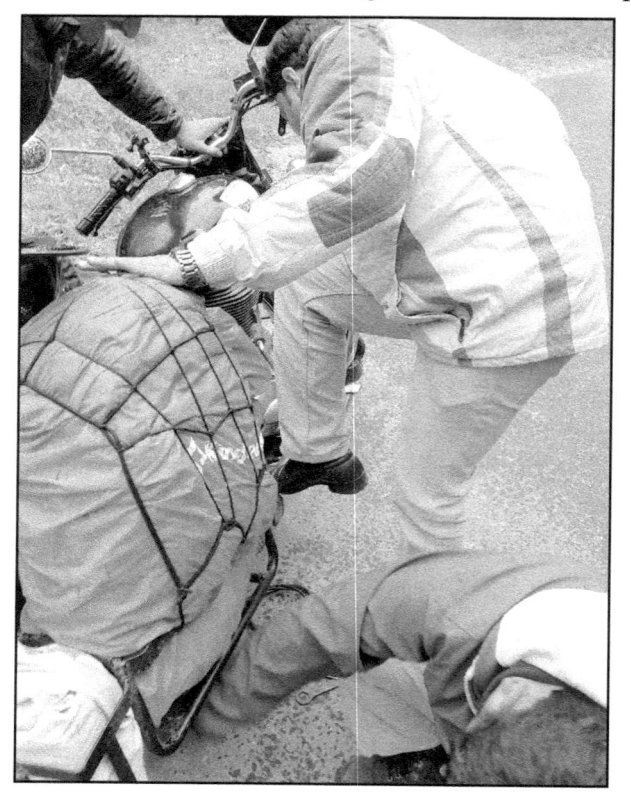

**Saved by the priests**

We linked hands in a circle over the bike and bowed our heads. I caught Lady R's eye, and we both started to smirk, biting our lips to stop ourselves laughing.

"Holy Father, we ask you to bless this couple and their errant motorcycle," I let out an involuntarily sputter, but it was all too true; she'd been a right sinful bitch, "and wish them Godspeed on their journey. May they be driven by your Word, and may the Holy Spirit fill their tank." We both had to cough outrageously to overcome our laughter that time. That would certainly cut the petrol bills.

"Amen!"

We thanked the priests wholeheartedly, gave them a donation for their parishioners, and hoped that now with both Ganesh and Jesus watching over us, we might have a bit of a smoother ride.

We continued our climb up through the rain. There were neither views nor traffic. It was just us, the fog, the ghostly shapes of trees occasionally looming through it, and the black mirror of the drenched tarmac. But the bike held steady, and a couple of hours later we arrived in Ravangla, a small town clinging to a hillside that allegedly also had absolutely stunning views of the Himalayas under normal circumstances. In addition, it boasted a couple of basic restaurants and guesthouses. We found one that looked slightly less downtrodden than the rest and hunkered down for the night.

Next morning the rain had still not abated. It was bitingly cold and low clouds clung to the surrounding hills. It was certainly not the weather for riding a motorcycle through the mountains, but we were on a ticking clock to reach Bhutan, so there really wasn't much choice. As we chugged out of town, already soaked to the skin (it not being monsoon season, we had not bothered to bring any wet weather gear along on the trip), a sign greeted us with the words "Caution, Road Damaged Ahead." In truth, the road wasn't damaged so much as it never seemed to have actually existed. It was just slippery rocks heading down a sharp incline with an unsecured drop off on one side. It was very steep indeed, and we slipped frequently, me shoving my feet down each time to act as a brake. I also couldn't stop shaking, whether from cold or fear I wasn't quite sure. When the mist occasionally lifted, we had glimpses of the gaping chasm that swept down to an angry white river far below. I stamped on the back brake once again as we rounded a corner into a sharp descent, and it made an almighty clanging sound and then locked up the wheel completely. I eased my foot off, and the wheel freed up. I then gently tried to apply it again. Nothing; it was shot. So, we were now down to just one brake. I wasn't sure if it was related, but the bike also seemed a lot less rigid, with the front and the back feeling like they wanted to go in different directions. I forced myself not to think about it further, switched on my newly discovered survival mode, and pushed on; there was nothing else for it.

Two hard, wet hours later we finally joined a tarmac road. The rain was still blowing down in sheets, but we could make much quicker progress and it was a hell of a lot less dangerous. Another twenty miles brought us to a small town, where we pulled up outside a bakery. The smell of fresh bread wafted out onto the street. We quickly shook ourselves off like a couple of dogs who'd just waded through a river, emptied our shoes of a pint or so of water each, and then ducked into the warm, snug interior. We were both shivering uncontrollably and eagerly clasped the glasses of hot, sweet tea that were immediately offered along with a plate of sweet buns. God bless them.

Once we were fed and pretty much dry and warm, we dragged ourselves back outside into the rain and cold to do it all again. The road, thankfully, stayed tarmac, and three soaking hours later we rolled into the town of Gangtok. We took refuge in the poshest hotel in town, another glorious colonial relic, and as I dripped onto the polished oak reception desk and searched for my sodden passport, a glass of sherry was proffered, what wonderful traditions hoteliers seemed to have adopted in the mountains. Up in the room we took hot showers then huddled around the electric heater, still shivering, sipping mugs of hot chocolate that room service had thoughtfully provided. But time was really ticking by. We were due to be at the Bhutanese border the next day, and it was about two hundred miles away, mostly through the mountains

## Breaking Up and Down

and, by the look of it, torrential rain. One thing we absolutely could not afford was another breakdown. This meant the bike needed to be fixed, properly, today. And that, of course, was my job. I reluctantly set down my steaming mug, pulled on some dry clothes, and headed out again.

Gangtok is spread across several hillsides, and thus most of its roads are rather steep. They were also drenched, of course, and I only had one working brake, though at least the bike was a lot lighter with one less person and no luggage. But that did seem to make the back swing out even more when I cornered, and I had a nasty feeling that, cartoon-like, she was about to split in two at any moment. I roved up and down and round and round, peering increasingly desperately through the rain. Eventually, I found it, a small placard hanging off the side of a low building up ahead, "Royal Enfield—Maintenance & Spares," and let out a heavy sigh of relief.

As I pulled up, a genial mechanic emerged from the depths of his workshop, wiping his hands on an oily cloth and offering me a gap-toothed grin. With some signalling and a very, very light smattering of Hindi, I managed to explain that the bike was buggered. He took it for a quick run round the block and came back grinning and nodding, "Yes, berry berry bad." I pulled out my phone to show him the route of our journey and pointed at Bhutan, "tomorrow, tomorrow!" He got the gist immediately, nodded vigorously, picked up a large spanner, and gave the side of the engine a whack, "Today, today, OK, OK." He then rolled up his sleeves and started dismantling the suspension.

I wandered out to the forecourt, where a small corrugated iron overhang provided shelter from the rain. A couple of lads were sitting on an old wooden bench watching the rain fall. I asked one of them for a light and sat down. It turned out they were fellow bikers, friends of the mechanic, and we were soon swapping stories of the road and smoking together like old friends. I felt a wave of guilty relaxation sweeping over me at being alone, away from Lady R, away from a situation that had become increasingly adversarial. After just five minutes I was more relaxed with those guys than I ever really had been with her. There just seemed to be no camaraderie, no "us against the world" feeling, instead we were each fighting from our own corner. We were both sick of breakdowns, sick of the cold and the rain, and sick of the constant pressure to get to the Bhutanese border. But we should have been helping each other through that, not adding to the frustration by lashing out.

After a couple of hours and quite a litany of new parts, the bike was pronounced as good as new. My new friends helped translate as the mechanic confirmed that the suspension had indeed been shot and the bike had been at risk of splitting in two. Perhaps she really was starting to mirror our relationship. I thanked and compensated him profusely then headed back towards the hotel, in love with India and its unbeatable levels of kindness and compassion. The bike, indeed, felt much more sturdy and responsive, and there was hardly anything left to replace now, so I prayed we really could continue the trip breakdown-free. That thought put me in a much better mood as I parked and then headed up to our room, determined to do the very same thing for my relationship with Lady R.

"All sorted!" I beamed as I opened the door triumphantly.

"You mean back to normal?"

"Well, yes, I guess, but feels great to know the mechanical problems should be behind us now!"

"You know, we'd never have had all this trouble at all if you'd known even the first thing about how to maintain your own bloody motorcycle."

"Right, well we've already talked about that," I smiled and pretended to have a thick skin, "and you're welcome, by the way, for me going out in the rain again and getting it all fixed."

This she summarily ignored, "Really, and I've been thinking, the cause of all these parts failing could well have something to do with your driving, I mean it's just not natural."

"Oh, but of course." My smile was becoming sarcastic now, "Nothing to do with the atrocious state of the roads."

"Hmmm. Well again, if you had just one iota of mechanical knowledge, then we'd have been able to fix most of this stuff ourselves, rather than being handicapped for days."

I took a deep breath and decided to change the subject, "Still pouring down out there mind you."

"We really should have brought rain gear with us too."

"Yes, you're right, but then again, we couldn't have known we'd be hit by the edge of a cyclone, could we? It'd certainly never normally rain here at this time of year, so I really don't think we should blame ourselves."

She shook her head, "You should have been better prepared. I mean I've never been on a bike trip before, but you have. Anyway, what about buying some plastic ponchos from the market here?"

I knew she was just venting, frustrated, didn't mean everything she said; God knows I often did exactly the same thing, so I resolved not to react, "Sure, great idea."

"Do I need to come with you?"

OK, I'd had enough, "Well, sweetie, as I have just been out in the cold for the last couple of hours getting the bike fixed and am still dripping wet and chilled to the bone, how about you take on this one?" I started emptying my pockets to make it clear I wasn't leaving the toasty sanctuary of our room anytime soon, "I mean, you know, in the interests of actually contributing something constructive for once?"

This was mean and unfair. But it did do the trick. As I walked over to the fire to warm my hands, I heard the door open, accompanied by a loud sigh, and then close firmly behind her as she headed out. So much for my attempts at relationship maintenance.

Next morning it was still belting down, which was kind of good, as it meant that Lady R's reluctant trip to the market had not been in vain. We loaded up, pulled on the rain gear, and got ready for a long day ahead. We had to get to the Bhutanese border that day, and I had calculated that to do so meant we would only be able to stop for breaks of about ten minutes every two hours. As I started up the bike outside the hotel, Lady R tapped me on the shoulder, "Oh, by the way, there's a monastery I'd like to visit on the outskirts of town."

"Well, that's nice, but you know we have to get to the border by nightfall, right?"

"Yes, yes, I know, but this journey has no point at all if we're doing it just to get it done, now does it?"

I opened my mouth to reply but thought better of it. I really couldn't handle another row right then, and she did have a rather good point.

"OK, but express visit then."

"Yes sir."

I really liked when she called me sir. And yes, it was true that we were starting to miss the trip in order to get the trip done, scurrying breathlessly from place to place concerned only with reaching the next stop and keeping the bike going. If we weren't actually appreciating and enjoying the places we were passing through, then what on earth was the point?

Just outside of Gangtok we swung off the main road and down a crumbling waterlogged byway, across which a number of trees had been blown down during the night and were now in the process of being removed. The five minutes Lady R had estimated it would take from the highway soon turned into forty-five. When we eventually reached it, the monastery turned out to be fairly uninspiring, but I heroically resisted pointing that out. We had a little walk round, noted the chanting monks and the Buddha statues (which were certainly beautiful, but pretty much identical from one establishment to the next), and then notably didn't admire the view that the place was famous for, due to the five-metre visibility.

But from then on we made good progress, circling down out of the hills, with the rain getting lighter the lower we went. There were various bits of tree and mountain strewn across the road at frequent intervals, witnesses to the last twenty-four hours' harsh weather.

"Good job they've got all that cleared," I shouted back as we passed a particularly large pile of rock and mud that had just been pushed off the tarmac.

"You're so right," called back Lady R, "and thank goodness we didn't get here half an hour earlier when it was still blocked—you see what a good idea my monastery visit was now?"

I couldn't help but laugh at that and reached back to playfully slap her thigh. She affectionately head-butted me from behind with her helmet. And then the sun started to peek through the clouds. Maybe the worst really was behind us.

**Indian Army, No Better Friend**

As we finally came back out onto the plains, we rode past a waterfall plunging downwards out of the glistening jungle into a turbulent river, both particularly feisty after the recent rains. We crossed the river on an old suspension bridge and on the other side were greeted by a huge billboard proclaiming "Indian Army—No Better Friend, No Worse Enemy" beneath a photo of some particularly fearsome-looking soldiers, faces contorted in rage, charging forward with bayonets. A mile or so later a more simple sign showed just the profile of a man's head wearing a hat at a jaunty angle and in large capital letters beneath it shouted out, "Gurkha—Blood and Guts!" and I started to wonder whether relations between India and (now nearby) Bhutan were really as smooth as we'd previously been led to believe.

Amazingly, it looked like we were actually going to reach the Bhutanese border by sundown. Back on the flat and with dry roads and good visibility, we purred along at a great clip through dusty brown villages and green paddy fields. I slowed down a little as we came up to a sign warning, "Elephants Have Right of Way, Do Not Obstruct," and reflected that the obstruction was more likely to be the other way around. Lady R, as navigator-in-chief, then informed me that we only had fifteen miles to go until we reached the frontier. I must have been getting tired though, because that last push seemed to take an age. Eventually, I suggested we stop for a break and, not wanting to publicly challenge my co-pilot's navigational skills, had a furtive peek at Google Maps. It confirmed what I had started to suspect. I approached Lady R, brandishing my phone in my hand, "Sweetheart, with all due respect, Google is showing me that our destination is now actually ten miles behind us." I showed her the map and smiled, "Might I suggest that there are few navigators in the world so deficient that they could actually miss a whole country?" She burst out laughing and blushed quite charmingly before regaining some composure,

"Well then, I make a lovely match for probably the only transcontinental biker who doesn't know how a motorcycle works."

I giggled and leaned in to kiss her, "We're quite a team, aren't we?"

We had a long, warm hug, and I promptly ceased caring about geography.

We turned back and reached the bustling border town of Jaigaon just before nightfall. That was, by far, the most exciting border, as beyond it lay Bhutan, or the Land of the Thunder Dragon, as it was more romantically known, a hermit fairy kingdom full of myth and legend, closed to outsiders for centuries, and ruled over by a benevolent monarch whose official title was The Dragon King.

But first we had to get in. We already had permission from the Bhutanese to enter with the bike, secured some weeks earlier after supplying a raft of documents to them, including an emissions certificate to make sure we weren't going to pollute their Himalayan Shangri-La. But on the Indian side we had no permission to take the bike out. After some consideration, I settled on the strategy of stuffing a large wad of rupees and a packet of cigarettes into my jacket pocket, ready to palm them off to the Immigration officials at the first sniff of trouble. First though, we had to find the actual border. We rode around the backstreets of the town shouting, "Bhutan?" at passers-by, and after a while were directed along a wide street, at the end of which was a massive carved wooden gateway. A double set of pillars on each side supported a huge three-tiered arch, painted ornately in red and gold and green, dragons curling up the pillars and demon heads adorning the roof. There were smartly turned out Bhutanese guards in pressed black trousers, short-sleeved shirts, and black berets under the gateway, but no visible Indian barrier or checkpoint before you reached them. This was definitely the entrance to Bhutan then, but where was the exit from India? We started asking around again and got directed down a small street a few hundred metres away, where a squat, mouldering grey building sported a threadbare Indian flag and a flaking sign announced, "Frontier Checkpost," even though it wasn't actually on the frontier—presumably it had been scared away by the grandeur and beauty of the Bhutanese border architecture and retreated back here in shame.

I suddenly realised, though, that the physical separation of border posts was just about perfect for us. I parked the bike around the corner, and we walked into the Indian post as normal tourists on foot wanting an exit stamp before entering Bhutan. A few minutes later, stamped passports in hand and having conveniently not mentioned the motorcycle, we were good to go. We walked out of sight around the corner, picked up the bike again, and rode through the backstreets to the Bhutanese gate with our Indian friends none the wiser. I felt a surge of anticipation and excitement sweep through me as we came up to the ornate arch. I knew it wasn't going to be one of those borders that just dissolve as you approach and cross over. There was a whole different world on the other side this time.

**The Bhutanese border**

# 10
# MEETING THE THUNDER DRAGON

It was the penises that really got me. They were everywhere. And not discreet, stylised *objets d'art* but rather massive, anatomically impeccable Technicolor paintings on the side of houses in nearly every village. Some were even in *flagrante delicto*, ejaculating triumphantly up to the second storey. This orgy of phalluses was all thanks to the Divine Madman, a fifteenth century wandering holy man whose interpretation of the Buddhist maxim to free yourself from desire was to embrace it rather than trying to resist it; he saw resistance as just another kind of attachment. In line with this philosophy, he drank and fornicated his way across the whole country, always moving on to show just how unattached he was. He is also said to have scared off a number of nasty demons in remote valleys by flashing his "thunderbolt of flaming wisdom" at them, otherwise known as his penis. And thus the cult of the Bhutanese protective phallus was born, one of the many things we were already loving about this country after our first morning's riding.

**Bhutanese phallus in *flagrante delicto***

When we had drawn up at the Bhutanese border arch the night before, the officials had been professional and polite, briskly checked our paperwork, and then waved us on through. As we pulled away, though, I heard a shout from the roadside, "Sir Andy?" I looked round to see a forty-something Bhutanese sporting a black leather jacket, slicked back hair, and an expectant smile with his hand up in greeting, "Hey! I'm Tashi; I'm your guide, man!"

I stopped the bike, and we dismounted to greet him.

"Great to meet you, Tashi; so we finally got here!"

"Yeah, I'm happy to see you! So, no worries along the way from Delhi, all smooth, yes?"

I looked at Lady R with a wry smile, "Oh yes, it's been plain sailing."

He gestured to a chap who was leaning against a nearby lamp post chewing on a tooth pick, "And this is Sonam; he'll be driving the pick-up truck."

I held up my hand in greeting, "Hi, nice to meet you Sonam."

"He doesn't really speak much English," whispered Tashi.

What he lacked in language skills, though, Sonam more than made up for in looks. He was a Bhutanese Adonis, chiselled jaw, tall athletic frame, long jet-black hair, and an extremely charming smile. And he knew it. We were soon to discover that any time that he wasn't driving, and even some of the time when he was, he could be found either preening himself in the mirror or chasing after a young maiden he'd just spotted.

"My God, he's stunning," whispered Lady R. This cemented my dislike of him while heightening my inferiority complex, given that the highest attraction rank she had ever accorded me to date as far as I could recall was "not bad looking."

Tashi and Sonam were there because the Bhutanese, while having granted us special permission to drive our own vehicle through their country, were not going to let us do so unaccompanied. No, like all other foreign visitors to the kingdom, we were obliged to be accompanied by a guide for our whole trip. And in this case they'd decided we required a guide on a motorcycle, Tashi, plus a pick-up truck driving along behind to provide back up. It was a strange feeling that we were going to be escorted 24/7 after the extreme independence of the last weeks when we'd had only ourselves to depend on. For the next fortnight there would be no fear of losing the way, no question of where we'd stay for the night or even where we'd eat, and no break-down worries, as Sonam also happened to be a professional mechanic, the bastard. In short, we'd have nothing to do but sit back and enjoy the ride.

Tashi led us to our hotel, and we attempted to celebrate our arrival in our third country with a beer. However, it was now Tuesday, and we were politely informed at the bar that there's no alcohol sold in Bhutan on Tuesdays because, well, no-one seemed really sure where this had come from, but it was put to us that we must surely see the wisdom of having a weekly day of abstinence. The smokers have it far worse than the drinkers though, as Bhutan is the first country in the world to completely ban the sale of cigarettes. Nursing a cup of tea and chewing a stick of gum instead, we sat and watched the news. After the weather forecast came the lovely surprise of an astrological forecast informing us what activities it would be auspicious to carry out the next day. Cleaning the house and visiting relatives were both good bets for Wednesday while getting engaged or purchasing land were likely to meet with less success. I discovered that nominating days for things was something of a national pastime as I leafed through the calendar that hung from the wall of our room. There were a whole series of specially assigned days that were marked throughout the year such as the "Commemoration of the First Sermon of Lord Buddha" and the "Death Anniversary of the Third King," though my firm favourite was the one that celebrated the end of the monsoon in September known simply, but oh so sweetly, as "Blessed Rainy Day."

Such charming discoveries confirmed my feeling that Bhutan was really unlike any other place on earth. It is a tiny kingdom, home to less than a million people, a David sandwiched between the Goliaths of China and India, and a country that came up with the concept of Gross National Happiness to measure its people's well-being (as opposed to Gross National Product), a place where no tree can be cut down nor any animal killed, where male skirt wearing is positively encouraged, and where an entire national park has been created purely to protect the natural habitat of the yeti.

Though only a stone's throw away from its Indian counterpart of Jaigaon, which we had crossed over from the day before, the contrasts in the border town of Phuentsholing were stark. The streets were quieter and cleaner, the buildings were adorned with colourful depictions of Buddhist folklore, people were ambling around chanting under their breath and spinning handheld prayer wheels, and overall there was a sense of reserved order that had been distinctly absent over on the Indian side.

While the citizens of its neighbouring countries have struggled to free themselves from rule by monarchy and military, the King of Bhutan actually had to force democracy onto his subjects in 2008 against their will, in a move that caused widespread national distress. They were, rather amazingly in this day and age, actually very happy with the way things had been going under the rule of a succession of benevolent monarchs who had overseen the introduction of universal education and healthcare, the maintenance of peace and stability, and steady economic growth. While Bhutan now has a civilian Prime Minister, the royal family remain very highly revered. Wandering around town we found photos of the king and queen—both stunningly attractive, His Highness being felt by Lady R to be even on a par with Sonam—on display in nearly every shop and tea house. Even the colourful Tata trucks rumbling past had "Long Live Our Benevolent King" painted on the back, as opposed to the more playful slogans we'd come to know and love in India, my favourites being, "No Girlfriend No Problem" and the rather wonderful "Use Diaper at Night."

Despite all these changes, it seemed we had not fully crossed into the fairy kingdom just yet. As our little convoy left the border town to make our way northwards to Paro, Bhutan's second city (well, hamlet really, having a population of just 15,000), with Tashi on his bike in front and Sonam in the pick-up behind, we realised that the real border between Bhutan and India was still in front of us and that it was a geographical one. The road rose steeply from the plains, painstakingly tracing a series of ninety-degree turns up through the mountains. We spent the next two hours climbing until eventually we entered the clouds, the final barrier, which reduced visibility to a couple of metres. The road then levelled out, but we could still see nothing ahead. Finally, the gods decided to grant us entry, the clouds parted, and we were presented with a view of what lay beyond the pass we had just blindly crossed over. A series of thickly forested ridges cascaded away before us, and beyond them rose the ethereal snow-capped peaks of the Himalayas glinting in the late morning sun. A valley stretched out below us dotted with small villages and whitewashed stupas with lines of prayer flags strung from the ground up to their pinnacles, sending up their praises in the breeze.

The road took us gently down to introduce us to the kingdom. We passed through a small settlement of whitewashed houses, nearly all adorned with colourful motifs of animals and, of course, those large colourful phalluses. People looked up as we passed, smiled warmly, and waved. The women sported brightly coloured blouses and smart, tightly fitting jackets accompanied by long skirts. The men were dressed in robes coming down to their knee, tied with a belt at the waist, and complemented with leather dress shoes and knee-length socks, making them look vaguely like transvestite English prep school boys.

**The Paro Valley**

## *Meeting the Thunder Dragon*

In the late afternoon we reached Paro, snuggled in a valley alongside a fast-flowing river, sheltering itself from the surrounding mountains. The valley is also home to the country's main, but minuscule, airport. It is one of the very few places in Bhutan where there is enough of a gap in the peaks for a decent-sized aircraft to get through and then trace a descent path onto a piece of flat land. But only just, as pilots still have to squeeze through a pass in the mountains into the valley and then follow its tight meandering path, wingtips almost brushing hillsides, until they find the town and airstrip tucked around one of its corners. There they have to dive sharply down and land on a runway with only just enough length to accommodate their aircraft. That explains why only eight pilots in the world are certified to fly in there. We watched with bated breath as one of this elite club swooped in and seemed sure to run straight into the hillside but then wrenched his craft round, lined up with the runway at the very last minute, and finally touched down and came to a halt a moment before the tarmac expired.

**Paro Airfield**

One advantage of our newly-acquired status as escorted travellers was that we had rather more sensible daily itineraries. We actually had time to stop and look at stuff and to diversify our range of pastimes beyond riding motorcycles and fixing motorcycles. On our second morning in Paro we set off on foot to visit the Tiger's Nest Monastery. From down in the valley we at first saw nothing, just a sheer wall of rock rising up in the distance. But as we trekked nearer we realised that a discolouration half way up was actually a series of roofs. Somehow there was a monastery wedged in a fissure in the rock face hundreds of feet above the ground with no visible way to reach it from either above or below. Tashi told us that it had been founded by one of the patron saints of Bhutan, Guru Rinpoche, who arrived there from Tibet on the back of a flying tiger. Given the location, it didn't seem that far-fetched. We followed a winding path that ascended through the forest. Now and again we came to a vantage point, and each time the monastery became a little clearer. There were actually several, multi-level, buildings clinging to the rock face that were built in the traditional Bhutanese style; whitewashed brick fortress-like structures tapering towards multi-gabled roofs of red and gold. Each window and door frame sported ornate paintings and carvings depicting Bhutanese folklore and Buddhist legends. As we got higher and closer we spotted a tiny bridge leading across a chasm that enabled one to get to the outer edge of the rock face, and from there a little path had been carved through it to reach the monastery. How they had ever got all the materials up there and actually built the thing, though, I had no idea.

The Tiger's Nest was also the first place that we'd reached on our trip that had a real connection with Burma. Before Aung San Suu Kyi became the de facto leader of the Burmese opposition to the military dictatorship in the late 1980s and then a household name across the world, she had received a proposal of marriage on that very spot. It was not, however,

**The Tiger's Nest**

from some errant monk following the precepts of the Divine Madman, but rather a fellow Englishman, Michael Aris, one of Britain's finest scholars of this region. He and The Lady, as she later became known, had met at Oxford, but Michael then moved to Bhutan to accept an invitation to become the official tutor of the children of the royal family, and she later popped over to visit. After accepting his proposal, she spent a year in the country living with him and is said to remain in close touch with the Bhutanese royal family to this day. The story of their marriage, though, is a sad one. Aung San Suu Kyi had gone back to Burma to visit her sick mother in 1988 and accidentally became the leader of the opposition to military rule overnight (the fact that her father had been the national independence hero who'd liberated the country from both the British and the Japanese helped a little). So she decided to stay on for a bit. It was the first time the generals had seen organised opposition of that calibre fronted by such a charismatic leader, and she soon wound up under house arrest at her family's crumbling lakeside villa. Michael and their two sons were based back in Oxford but visited regularly. But as her influence grew, so the military became keener to contain her. They stopped issuing Michael and the children visas to visit, however, when Michael became ill with cancer they told her she was free to leave Burma to return to the UK to see him. But she believed that if she did so they would never let her back in the country, and so she made the painful decision to stay. He died without ever seeing her again.

It was the kind of impossible choice one cannot imagine ever having to make. I shook my head as I recalled the story to Lady R while we sat on the steps of the monastery, a sheer drop just in front of us and the valley laid out far below, "Wow, can you imagine ever having to choose between your family and your country like that? I mean she was really noble and everything but choosing to not see your terminally ill husband?"

Lady R was resolute, "Well maybe she felt the future of sixty million of her country people was more important than one person."

I nodded, "Yeah, OK, in one sense, but that one person was her husband. I mean isn't that what love is all about, one person meaning more than everyone else?" I tossed a small pebble into the abyss, "And, well, at the end of the day she may have still been able to lead the opposition movement, even if she hadn't been able to get back to Burma; who can say?"

Lady R sniffed, "Well I actually think it's very admirable what she did for the cause. It's the kind of sacrifice that is in the best traditions of public service, something I hold in very high regard."

I laughed, "OK, but that aristocratic tradition of public service you have is maybe more to tackle the guilt that comes from stealing peasants' land, livestock, and money over the past few centuries. I mean that's basically how one gets into the aristocracy after all, isn't it?"

She giggled, "If you carry on like that, young man, I shall be demanding an extra cow each month from now on."

On the hike back down we stopped at a small teashop that had a stall nearby selling a variety of rustic Bhutanese jewellery. As Lady R went off to refresh herself, I had a little browse and found a charming old bronze ring with three green stones delicately embedded in it. I picked it up and had a crazy thought—wouldn't this just be the perfect place to propose? On a beautiful mountainside in Bhutan in the middle of our big adventure, what a great story it would make and what a promising start to a lifetime together. I decided to buy it. When Lady R returned and we were sitting alone sipping our tea, I turned it over in my pocket and started to compose what I was going to say. I opened my mouth and she looked at me expectantly, but somehow the words just wouldn't come. There was something deep inside me preventing it, I wasn't quite sure what. At that moment Tashi reappeared and the moment was gone. I patted my pocket and decided I might need a little more time to think it over.

From Paro to Thimpu, Bhutan's pint-sized capital that is home to a little over 90,000 people, it was a peaceful ride of a couple of hours along a meandering river valley. There was little traffic, the road was decent, the sun was shining, and everything looked and sounded and smelt fresh and crisp and pure. Thimpu could hardly be described as hectic, but the streets had the feel of a bustling medieval market town. The archaic air was reinforced by the absence of any traffic lights. One had, in fact, been installed a few years back at the main intersection but was met with indignation by the good citizens of the town. They much preferred the elegant, white gloved policemen who had, up until then, flawlessly directed what little traffic there was with Tai Chi like grace. Their kindly king promptly responded to their wishes and banished the mechanical devil a few months after it first made its appearance. And finally, as if determined to affirm their identity and counter the risk of being forgotten in their hidden corner of the world, each and every shop had "Thimpu, BHUTAN" written after its name on its sign board.

Ambling around the backstreets and seeking an escape from an imminent downpour, we found shelter in the entrance of a traditional arts school. We then ventured inside and discovered earnest young students learning drawing, scroll painting, carving, sculpture, weaving, and embroidery, all according to traditional Bhutanese methods. Their skill and quiet dedication were remarkable.

**Art school**

But I couldn't help but notice that a learning-by-rote approach was very much entrenched. This was art yes, but art by prescription. Displayed on the wall in the drawing class for example were pictures of the standard subjects—the head of the Buddha, a red-robed swirling demon, a multi-armed goddess—with what looked like an engineering blueprint superimposed on top of each, a scaffolding of lines and angles and measurements dictating exactly how each one should be rendered, prescribing the precise curvature of the Buddha's cheekbone and the exact space between the bracelets on a goddess's arm. A sign perhaps of the darker side of trying to preserve your culture, attempting to capture and bottle something that is by its very nature malleable, that would

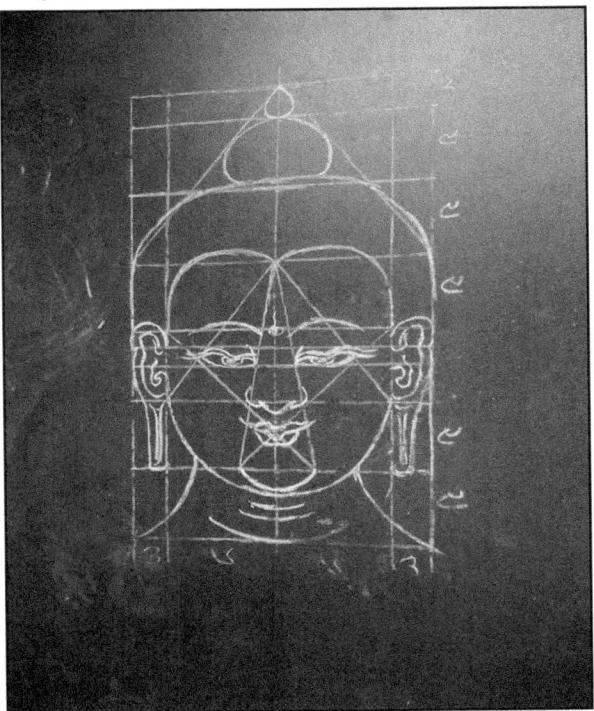

**Painting by numbers**

never have come into existence without an openness to embrace the infinite creativity of human beings and their willingness and curiosity to try new things and create new forms. In Bhutan then the culture that had evolved in those mountains and valleys was being forcibly frozen in time, and not just in the art school. There were also rules enforcing construction of buildings in the traditional Bhutanese style and on civil servants wearing a specific version of Bhutanese dress. I wondered whether the Government might inadvertently be destroying the very source of the beauty it was trying to preserve—its citizens' own creativity. Most foreigners, on the other hand, loved this freezing process and hated the idea of Bhutan being "tainted" by new influences. They lamented how the country had finally permitted television and the Internet to come in back in 1999. A few hundred years ago, a similar mindset would have resisted the influx of Tibetan Buddhism into the country in the first place. And how would those foreigners feel about their own governments back home instructing them how to draw, build, and dress, let alone cutting off their television and broadband connections due to a perceived corrupting influence on the traditional values of their society? Cultural theme-parks were all well and good, so long as you didn't actually have to live in one.

**Thimpu trucking**

Heading out of Thimpu the next morning, slalom-like roads drew us down through the hills to the town of Punakha. We breezed past monasteries, circled around *chortens* (the local shrines), and smiled at the odd ambling monk fingering his prayer beads. I nodded to some other bikers heading our way who were waving to us, before realising that what they were actually doing was signalling for me to pull over and that, unlike our Enfield, their bikes had sirens and lights. I dutifully braked and drew up at the side of the road as a Land Cruiser with blacked out windows drove past, followed by two more motorcycle outriders riding close behind. The car's number plate was "Bhutan 1." I turned to Tashi, who had pulled up just behind us, "Someone important Tashi? Government Minister?"

"Ah, that would be one of the queens."

"Oh, wow!" I paused to think for a second, "But, hang on, *one* of? I thought your handsome king only had a single lady?"

He smiled, "Yes, yes, but his dad, you know, the old king, well he married four sisters."

I turned to Lady R about to make a proposal, but she was already one step ahead of me, "Don't even think about it." She then turned to Tashi, "Actually, she could even be a distant relative of mine. You know, there are quite close ties between aristocracies across the world."

I couldn't help but seize the moment, "Yeah, it's called *in-breeding*." There was an inevitable helmet headbutt from the rear.

# 11
# Shangri Las

A few miles outside of Punakha we came to the wide, sunny valley of Chimi Lhakhang and stopped to stretch our legs. We walked through the fields to reach an old monastery resting peacefully in its centre. Young monks sat in their purple flowing robes outside on the grass chanting from sacred texts beneath their breath. A couple of them were blowing through long brass horns that let out a long, deep, ululation. After stooping through a carved wooden doorway and bowing to a statue of the Buddha, we were led across a small courtyard and entered the inner sanctum, where the jovial elderly Abbot greeted us, "Welcome to Chimi Lhakhang, under the blessings of Lama Drukpa Kinley!"

I shook his hand warmly, "Thank you sir," I paused for a moment, that name sounded familiar, "Err, sorry for asking, but Lama Drukpa Kinley, now is he not also known as the

Divine Madman, the gentleman who was famed for, well, his rather special way of giving blessings and tackling evil?"

The Abbot's eyes lit up, "Oh most certainly, yes! On this very site he subdued the demon of Dochu La using his magic thunderbolt of flaming wisdom!"

I couldn't help but giggle again at just how creative the Bhutanese had been at naming the male member, but luckily, the Abbot took it good-naturedly, "And now, my honoured foreign visitors, let us offer you a blessing from the monastery."

He motioned for me to kneel down in front of a small shrine and started to rummage inside his robes, emerging triumphantly a few seconds later with a large phallus—an ornamental one, I should add. And then, for the first and quite possibly last time in my life, I was tapped and rubbed on both shoulders with a sizeable wooden penis while he wished me long life and prosperity. I then watched benignly as he placed his cock onto Lady R.

**Working the prayer wheels at Chimi Lhakhang**

The Abbot explained to us that people came from miles around to receive this unique blessing that is said to offer a host of benefits to the discerning parishioner. There was ample proof of this as we walked back towards the bike through the neighbouring village, where we discovered the endearingly named "Phallus Handicraft" (very pleasingly right next-door to the "Royal Restaurant-cum-Bar"), which anywhere else in the world would have been classified as a sex shop, given its window display of what appeared to be a selection of wooden dildos in a wide variety of shapes, sizes and finishes.

**Restaurant Cum Bar**

We left Punakhaa and its splendid dzong—the Bhutanese word for castle-monastery, not another term for Drukpa Kinley's protective appendage—early the next morning on what must have been the quietest main road in the world. Although it was the principal, in fact the only, highway running from west to east Bhutan, we hadn't seen another vehicle for miles. We were entering the more remote half of what was already a very remote country. Houses were few and far between, the valleys and hills and forests still beautiful but a little starker, and when the sun drifted behind a cloud, exhibiting a faint air of foreboding, lingering shadows hinted at some potential hidden menace lying somewhere behind the trees. Possibly yetis.

Our destination was Phobjikha, a place isolated even by Bhutan's high standards and one of its legendary hidden valleys. Bhutan's special brand of Buddhism did not start from a clean slate, instead the ideas of the Buddha only gained traction once they had been blended with the existing and rather esoteric cult of Bon, which had long swirled through the mountains and valleys. It was Bon that mixed a whole pantheon of gods, rituals, mystery, and magic into the conventional Buddhist doctrine of a rather straight-laced eight-step path to Nirvana. One of the most intriguing of those additions was that of *beyul*s, hidden, spectacularly beautiful valleys that are said to be used as a kind of spiritual retreat by the enlightened.

The *beyul*s traditionally stay secret thanks to the protection of special deities who throw obstacles into the path of any normal person trying to find them, usually in the form of a fierce blizzard or a marauding snow leopard. The chosen few, however, get decent directions, normally from a magic scroll they've conveniently found at just the right moment hidden beneath a rock or at the bottom of a forest pool, and are then afforded safe passage. We are actually more familiar with the idea of beyuls in the West than we might realise—one of the most renowned among the Bhutanese is known as Shambhala, a name that was corrupted into "Shangri La" by the author James Hilton in his 1933 book, *Lost Horizon*. This tells of a plane crash in the Himalayas and its survivors discovering an Eden-like valley tucked away in the mountains that is inhabited by peace-loving lamas who enjoy remarkable longevity. And there we were on our motorcycle heading towards the real thing, and rather cheekily trying to circumvent the usual entry requirements with a judicious use of Google Maps and Tashi's local knowledge.

The single-track road meandered through a dense coniferous forest, occasionally bringing us out into the open and taking our breath away as layer upon layer of mountain ranges rose up in the distance. We passed the occasional smiling, leathery villager, bent over with a load of wood on their head or brandishing a stick herding a couple of goats, and about once an hour we'd come across another motorised vehicle. Late in the afternoon we crossed a high pass, wobbled unsteadily beneath an immense rocky overhang next to a drop into the void, and then finally picked our way down into Phobjikha Valley. In front of us on either side thickly wooded slopes descended to a wide U-shaped valley that glowed green and yellow in the afternoon light. A semi-circle of Himalayan peaks formed a sentinel-like backdrop. Thin plumes of smoke rose from a couple of wooden houses in the distance. There was no sign of any enlightened beings, but it certainly had a certain *je ne sais quoi*.

By that point the road had become a track, but that fit our surroundings perfectly—a strip of tarmac leading into a *beyul* would seem terribly inappropriate. We rattled our way up the valley for a couple of miles before turning off up a steep and even rougher track to reach our accommodation for the night. It was a basic but neat lodge of wood and stone adorned with a couple of simply magnificent ejaculating members on either side of the main entrance. After unloading, we decided to make use of one of its few amenities—a traditional Bhutanese hot stone bath. It involved proceeding to an outside shed where a trough of water had been heated by tossing large rocks into it that contained a mysterious mineral said to be beneficial to health. The shed was freezing and the bath was boiling, which made for some interesting physical contortions as we tried to get in, and then out, and then in again. After several attempts, we finally managed to settle ourselves more or less comfortably, and Lady R gave a satisfied sigh, "Ah, this is such bliss, the simple rustic life, all one needs really."

While that seemed rather at odds with her silver-spoon-in-the-mouth upbringing, I could not resist leaning in and kissing her, just happy that she was happy. She carried on, "We have food, we have warmth, we have each other, what more would you want?"

She then looked at me with such an expression of peace and contentment that even I managed to forget my own requirements for Internet, central heating, and double lattes. But a darker thought then pushed its way into my mind and, before I knew it, was out into the open, "Well I guess you might also need some other lovers available to be really happy, given your desire for an open relationship?"

Really, what was my problem? But to my credit, I managed to deliver it gently and with a sheepish smile. Maybe it was just the effect of the mineral-infused steam, but Lady R lent forward and kissed me back, "You're all I need baby."

I was then ready to grab an axe and start chopping down some trees to build her that dream house so that we could settle there in Shangri La and live happily ever after.

Instead, though, we got pissed. After a wholesome dinner of rice and cheesy chillies, we began chatting with the young owner of the lodge and his friend, who was visiting from the next village. Together we made up the sum total of the people in the lodge, which perhaps explained our host's hospitality in producing a bottle of Black Mountain spirit for us to enjoy. I guessed it was of Indian origin, like most other products in Bhutan, but as I twisted the bottle round the words *Bhutanese Army Welfare Programme* peered out at me. Our friends explained that the army does a profitable side-line in distilling booze, both for local consumption and for export to India. Which makes it something of a patriotic duty to drink on a regular basis. Except on Tuesdays, of course. By the third glass we'd decided that Black Mountain was most probably a member of the rum family, though perhaps a rather distant cousin.

Lady R snuggled tight in my arms that night and whispered that she loved me. The hidden valley seemed to have brought out the best in both of us. But we were due to move on the next day. Why couldn't we have a breakdown when we actually needed one? I considered creeping out and sabotaging the motorbike in the middle of the night, but then I remembered the yetis.

I vowed to bring Lady R back to Phobjikha one day, but in the meantime we had something else to look forward to, and my stomach was already rumbling. We were headed further eastwards towards Bumthang, a fertile series of valleys that were famous for their orchards and dairies. That was all thanks to one Mr. Fritz, an itinerant Swiss gentleman, who made his home in Bhutan half a century ago and started off what has become a cottage industry producing everything from cheese to sausages to honey to schnapps. The area had essentially become one big farmers' market minus the hipsters. We rode at a faster pace than normal, both due to the promise of those delights, and more prosaically, because Tashi had informed us that one section of the road would only be open until 11 AM. Lady R had another pop at driving, startling a group of yaks that were chewing the cud by the roadside with her gearbox abuse. I tore myself away from worrying about the damage being done to parts of the engine that I didn't know the names of and looked up to marvel at a panorama of green, wooded hillsides and, behind them, layer upon layer of increasingly misty blue mountains.

And then we came to an abrupt halt. I feared the bike had died on us once again, but as I turned back to face the road I saw a rough wooden barricade blocking the way ahead. Beyond it the track that had been trying rather unsuccessfully to live up to its name as the East-West Highway narrowed and cut across the side of a mountain, a cliff on one side and a straight drop to a river on the other. And they were trying to make it a little wider. With the help of quite a lot of dynamite. We covered our ears as an almighty explosion reverberated around the valley and a large section of cliff came tumbling down. Tashi told us that such roadworks are very important in Bhutan and are seen as an essential part of keeping the country together. In a land of mountainous terrain, and with a population scattered across hundreds of remote villages, roads are essential for people to reach schools and hospitals, to trade with one another, and indeed, to feel any kind of national sentiment or loyalty to the central government. And when you only have one main road going from the east to the west of the country, keeping it up and running—or widening it so that two vehicles can actually pass one another—is understandably something of a national priority.

Watching the blasting, I couldn't help but wonder how they set everything up just right so that the rock either fell down or stayed put, as opposed to merely being loosened and then later dropping onto a passing motorcyclist. I had good reason for such musings, as I had come across similar roadworks a few years ago on a road in northern India. When they had finished blasting and we were driving through in single file, a massive lump of rock had toppled onto the jeep right behind me, crushing its roof and fatally injuring one of the passengers. The blow of a whistle brought me back to Bhutan as the workmen signalled that we could ride through. I looked up nervously at the rock face as we rode past, but the turn of my head meant that I inadvertently tilted the bike nearer to the precipice, earning myself a well-timed slap on the helmet from Lady R along with the astute observation that in the end it was going to be my worries themselves that were the death of me, rather than any of them actually coming true.

As we drew closer to Bumthang, we encountered a group of rather merry looking villagers gathered near the roadside talking and laughing, and Tashi signalled for us to pull over. There was a small festival taking place nearby, and we enthusiastically agreed to go and have a look. We traipsed up a hillside to the local monastery to find that everyone there, monks included, was absolutely rolling drunk. The main attraction seemed to be a piece of amateur theatre which involved one individual, wearing a dress and a devil mask, teasing and gesticulating at another whilst brandishing a giant red wooden phallus. Tashi solemnly informed us that was designed to communicate an important moral lesson. What exactly that lesson might be he was, however, unable to expand upon.

## Shangri Las

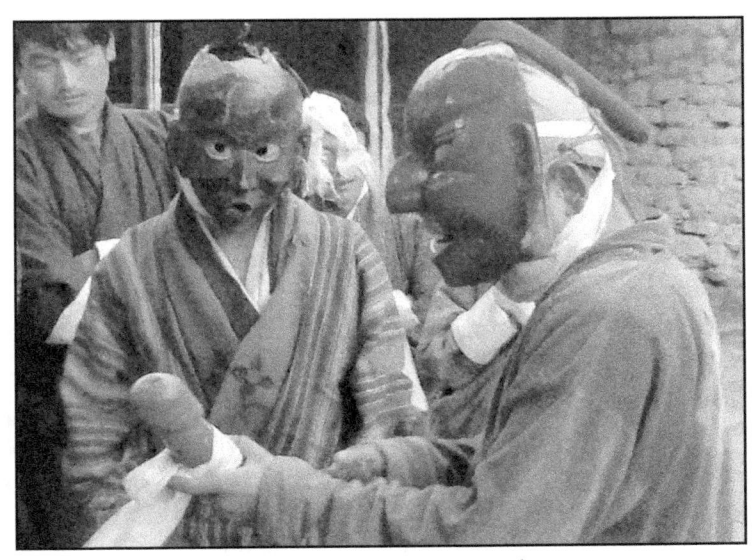

**Amateur dramatics near Bumthang**

There was something I really liked about the Bhutanese, beyond just their open and joyous love for the male genitalia. Yes, there was the politeness and generosity and humility that we had also seen in India and Nepal and that generally made travelling a joy, but in Bhutan it was coupled with a quiet pride in identity and an absence of any colonial hangovers or semi-faked obsequiousness towards foreigners. We were looked in the eye and met openly as equals, they knew who they were and were not afraid to show it. And, to be honest, I thought they had their country a lot better sorted out than pretty much anywhere else I'd ever visited.

When the amateur dramatics finished, we were invited to a small tent for some refreshments and gorged ourselves on exquisite local cheese, herb-infused sausages, and fresh bread. There was no crowding around or hassling or staring, people just came and politely introduced themselves to us (followed by their job, home village, and country) and wished us well, while those interested to interact a little more stayed on for a chat. It was all very genteel and charming, but I should add that each introduction was accompanied by an invitation to down a shot of *arra*, a local spirit that would come in handy if we ever needed to clean out the inside of the engine. It was when I turned from the old lady who I was having a sign language conversation with about the origins of Buddhism (to be fair, she may have been talking about something else on her side, but we were both equally enthusiastic) to check on Lady R that I realised it was probably time to make a move. She had somehow acquired the penis from the play and was standing over two young men and blessing them with it while announcing that they were henceforth honorary citizens of the new queendom that she had decided to establish in the next valley.

Darkness was falling, and the temperature plummeted rapidly. By the time we arrived at our little guesthouse for the night we were both shivering and very glad to see an open fire waiting for us in the lounge. As they served us tea, Tashi asked if we'd like to head out again to see a "traditional naked monks' dance," but we both agreed we'd rather just get to bed. Clearly, we were becoming rather spoiled.

In the farthest corner of already remote Bumthang lies the Tang Valley and, deep within it, the tiny hamlet of Ogyen Choling. The road Tashi had promised would take us there was in reality a stony dried-up river bed running through a dense forest. After the fourth spill, we decided it really wasn't motorcycle-able and so opted to leave the bikes in the middle of nowhere with Sonam to watch over them. Tashi then took over as driver of the pick-up truck, and we crammed ourselves into the cargo bed at the back and clung on for dear life. A few painful miles later we emerged out of the trees into the open. Small patchwork fields separated by low stone walls were spread out either side of a little river that danced its way merrily along, passing a sprinkling of wooden farmhouses and the odd *chorten* here and there. An old chap walking his two oxen raised an arm in greeting. Whether we had arrived today or 500 years ago I could not have imagined it would have looked that much different.

We bumped our way along the valley and, after a couple of wrong turns, found the track that climbed up to the Ogyen Choling compound. There we found a beautiful old monastery in whitewashed stone, looking like it had stood for centuries, set around a cobbled courtyard. The imposing walls and massive wooden doorways gave it the feeling of a medieval fortress. The compound was also home to a substantial manor house, a small museum, and a scattering of outhouses.

We climbed out of the pick-up to greet the owner, who was waiting for us in the courtyard. She was in her early sixties, her small erect frame and tightly tied-back hair softened by a beatifically smiling face and a pair of sparkling brown eyes. Lady R whispered to me that she thought there was something distinctly aristocratic about her, which I suppose is a pretty good bet for anyone who owns all of the land that you can see from their house. After exchanging a few words with Tashi she turned to us, "Please allow me to introduce myself, I am Kunzang Choden." The English was perfect 1950s clipped upper class with a slight Indian twang, which meant I already liked her a lot. She looked at us expectantly as she continued, "So, who might you be and to what do I owe the pleasure of welcoming you to our little paradise?"

I gave a little bow; I wasn't really sure why, "A pleasure to meet you, ma'am, well my name's Andy and this is Lady R and, err, we're just on our way from Delhi to Rangoon actually, so we thought we'd stop in for tea, if that's not too much trouble?"

She immediately broke into a fit of delightful giggles, "Well absolutely. I'd been wondering what was keeping you." She beckoned us to follow her inside, "Now, Rangoon you say, how lovely, so what's all that about?"

As we settled down for tea, I explained how the journey had come about, minus the bit about the mid-life crisis. When I had finished, she nodded approvingly, "Well what a proper adventure; how absolutely marvellous! Now, as you're living in Burma, then maybe you know my good friend, Suu?"

I looked at her uncertainly, "Err, Suu . . . ?"

"Kyi, dear."

"You mean Aung San Suu Kyi?"

She laughed, "Well yes, of course; you do know who she is?"

I smiled, "Yes, certainly, but I'm afraid we're not personally acquainted with her. I think, err, we must go to different pubs."

She laughed and leant over and patted my hand, "Ah, such a pity. I could have given you a gift to deliver," she looked wistfully out of the window, "You know she and Michael would always stay with us when they were down this way."

"Wow, so you knew them well when they were living here?"

She nodded, "Oh yes, very well, I was in Thimpu then, and the king introduced me, of course, when Michael was tutoring the children. Such a lovely couple, and such a pity what happened." Lady R and I both nodded, though I think for different reasons.

Over another cup of tea we found out a little more about Mrs. Choden's younger years. She'd been born in the valley but left at nine, when she became one of the very first Bhutanese to study abroad, which involved riding on horseback for ten days to reach a convent school in India. After completing high school, she had gone on to study in the United States before returning to Bhutan when she graduated, first settling in Thimpu and then later moving back to her home valley where, as Tashi later informed us, the locals refer to her as *Ashi,* or Queen, in recognition of her family tracing a lineage of landowning and religious patronage back at least four centuries. Mrs. Choden was spending her autumn years maintaining the local monastery and trying to ensure the preservation of the traditions of the area. Tashi had told us on the way up that she was also one of Bhutan's most well-known writers. I wasn't quite sure how stiff the competition would be in a country of less than a million people, but I decided to pop the question as she offered us more biscuits, "So Tashi tells us you're also a famous author?"

She smiled and shook her head, "Oh, well, I dabble a little, you know."

"And might we know any of your work?"

"I wouldn't think so, my dears," she paused and giggled again before continuing, "but we can soon remedy that!" She went over to a nearby dresser and pulled open a large drawer, where she rummaged for a minute before pulling out a slim paperback and blowing some dust off the cover,

"There, a little gift to thank you for passing by."

I gratefully took the book she handed me and looked down at the title, curious to see if I was dealing with a writer of romantic novels, political treatises, or geological textbooks. I broke out into a big smile as I read the words *Bhutanese Tales of the Yeti* on the cover. It was a collection of villagers' stories of encounters with the legendary abominable snowman that she had gathered together over the years from across the country and then lovingly edited. I really couldn't think of a more apt gift to receive in a hidden Himalayan valley.

I admit that, much to the amusement of Lady R, I had developed something of a fascination with the legend of the yeti since we started planning the trip. Anyone who has not spent some time in the Himalayas would understandably dismiss stories of a big hairy man-bear roaming the snow-bound mountains as a villager's fairy tale or traveller's yarn, certainly not something to be taken in any way seriously. But on closer examination I had found that there was rather more to it.

Way back in the first century AD, the Roman military commander and natural historian Pliny the Elder had written of an immensely strong man-like animal that could be found in the remote mountains of India and that walked on two legs. Chinese manuscripts from the seventh century tell of large hairy bipeds living in the lands of the snows. Paintings of tall, ape-like creatures dating back several centuries adorn the walls of caves and monasteries at several sites across Bhutan, Nepal, and Tibet. In the nineteenth century, the first accounts started to emerge from western explorers of encountering a yeti-like creature, and by the 1950s, the UK's *Daily Mail* newspaper was funding a dedicated Snowman Expedition to the Himalayas. That was followed by a series of American missions, with the US Government advising their participants that they should not harm any yetis they found, unless it was strictly necessary for self-defence. The list of notable mountaineers who have claimed a yeti sighting is long and distinguished, topped by no less than Edmund Hillary and Tenzing Norgay, the first men to summit Everest. Many Sherpas with extensive mountaineering experience claim the yeti's existence as fact, and a whole host of communities in that vast region, living hundreds of miles apart and having no contact with one another, have their own word for a kind of snow bear or wild man that they live in fear of and say is found only in the highest reaches of the mountains. In Bhutan the belief seemed to extend right up to the highest levels of government, given the ministerial approval that was given in 2001 to create the Sakteng Wildlife Sanctuary in the far east of the country, a 250 square mile area created especially to protect the natural habitat of the yeti.

So, could there be any plausible scientific basis for all these stories and sightings? In 2004, the editor of the prestigious scientific journal *Nature* wrote that, given the recent discovery of Homo floresiensis, a previously unknown diminutive cousin of modern humankind that roamed the Earth until 12,000 years ago, tales of other human-like creatures surviving in remote areas were definitely worthy of investigation. And one has to bear in mind just how remote and largely uninhabited most of the Himalayas is, making it quite feasible that an unknown species, perhaps just a distant cousin of the polar bear that has taken to walking on its hind legs on occasion, could remain undetected. After all, it was only just over a hundred years ago that fantastical legends of an enormous, hairy beast that roamed the central African jungles were, to the shock of scientists, found to be true when the Berlin Natural History Museum received a special delivery from a German soldier in the Congo—the body of a mountain gorilla he'd just shot.

Unfortunately though, we were not above the snow line on the way back from the valley, meaning that the two hours of shaking and rattling in the back of the pick-up truck to return to the bikes were guaranteed to be entirely yeti-free. When we arrived, we found the bikes but no Sonam, despite us having left him there expressly to guard them. Our dashing driver turned up half an hour later as we were enjoying a picnic we'd packed with some of the finest produce of the local orchards and dairies. He was combing his hair and apologised, explaining in broken English that some local ladies who passed by had invited him to join them in "taking water from their well." He accompanied the explanation with a smirk and a wink at Lady R, who immediately blushed and dropped her cheese.

It was either mud or shit, I wasn't quite sure which, but either way it was all over me. The back wheel was spinning out of control and giving me an impromptu shower, which combined with the biting cold and the pitch darkness, was putting me in a rather foul mood. We had set out from Bumthang earlier in the day in warm sunshine to continue our eastwards journey. We crossed a high pass in the mid-afternoon, and the temperature fell as we entered a more desolate landscape with fewer trees and more bare, windswept, rocky hillsides. We were above 3,000 metres, and as the light began to wane so the cold set in and riding became decidedly less fun.

We had reached the remote valley of Ura, and our destination was a homestay in a small settlement that was somewhere out there in the gloom. Exactly where, though, was still open to conjecture. We had left the main road half an hour before and headed down a small track, where Tashi promptly fell off his bike as we hit the first patch of mud and cow dung. I just about managed to stay upright as we slithered along what was, I was increasingly convinced, a road to nowhere. The mud/dung got deeper and eventually had the better of the bike, bogging down the back wheel, which spun furiously providing my impromptu shower but, unfortunately, no traction. Lady R got off and helped Tashi to give me a push, which after several tries suddenly launched me forward as the wheels gripped again. I rocketed away, sharing my shower with my two assistants, but before I could properly enjoy that I saw a dark shape looming up in the middle of the track ahead that turned out to be the back end of a cow. She let out a concerned moo as I braked, shrieked, thrust a foot down to propel myself and the bike sideways, and narrowly slid past her.

The near miss was a positive omen, though, as people always keep their cows close to their homes at night. Sure enough, in another couple of hundred metres a house rose out of the darkness. It was more like a castle really, its three-storey stone edifice topped with a hefty wood and shingle roof, its windows small and shuttered, and a set of broad stone steps leading up to a huge wooden front door. We heard a bolt being drawn back as we approached. The door swung open and bathed us in the soft glow of a hearty fire burning inside. A walnut-faced grandmother with a charming toothless grin mimed for us to come in. We took off our shoes and followed directions through the hall and into the kitchen, where we settled ourselves gratefully around the hearth as her plump, matronly daughter joined us and offered a couple of glasses of warming *arra*, the Bhutanese fire water we'd enjoyed at the village festival a couple of days earlier. Her husband was the valley's *gup*, a kind of local mayor, and was conducting his business from some unseen inner chamber, which meant that every fifteen minutes or so there would be a knock on the front door and a visitor would enter, bow to us, and then disappear into the bowels of the building to make an entreaty to the boss.

We'd been looking forward to the homestay as a way of experiencing Bhutanese rural life first hand, but with the combination of exhaustion, *arra*, and the warmth of the fire, we found ourselves struggling to keep our eyes open. After wolfing down some red rice with pork and chilli, our hostess suggested we call it a night, and we gratefully followed her directions up a steep staircase to a cavernous, draughty room at the top of the house. We wrapped ourselves in several layers of thick woollen blankets, but it was still far from warm. Lady R, who normally insisted on the unacceptability of sleeping while having any kind of bodily contact with another human, announced that I must come and cuddle her to keep her snug. So I fell asleep cosy and smiling with her wrapped in my arms, blessing Bhutan's lack of central heating.

# 12
# Exit the Dragon

I was quite sure it was marijuana. I'd first noticed the distinctive aroma a mile or so back, and it was getting stronger and stronger. At our next stop I decided to broach the subject with Tashi, "So, there was quite a strong smell during that last section; did you notice?"

He nodded, "Ah yeah, sure man, pig's food."

"I'm sorry?"

He smiled, "It's just a plant that grows wild here but has no use for people, so we use it to feed our pigs."

I nodded, "I see, and, err, does it have a name?"

"Hmmm, I think you guys called it pot?"

We certainly did. It turned out that Bhutan, the country which measures its well-being not with Gross National Product but with Gross National Happiness, may also be home to the most contented swine on the planet, as they are a fed on a daily diet of weed. And this food source is presumably under no threat from a local population who feel so well taken care of by the king and the Buddha that artificial stimulants are simply unnecessary. Black Mountain excepted, of course.

We were on the way to the satisfyingly *Lord of the Rings*-sounding town of Mongar, making good progress along the empty road, climbing then descending, tunnelling into dark pine forests, and then emerging out onto open hillsides, with the high mountains sunning themselves in the distance.

**The Bhutanese Himalayas**

I was humming some James Blunt to myself while Lady R tried to explain the finer points of Bhutanese archery to me from the back seat. It was all quite perfect really. Then there was a sharp bang. In a couple of weeks' time that noise would make me immediately assume gunfire, but now in peaceful Bhutan I was correct with my first guess—we'd blown a tyre. It was rather remarkable that it was the first puncture we'd had in all those weeks of riding, especially given the state of the terrain we'd been forcing the bike to go over. But what a blessing that it happened at that moment, as finally we had a use for the pick-up truck, spares, and dashing hunk of a mechanic that we had been lumbered with since crossing the border from India. I pulled up by the roadside and waited for Sonam to catch up in the pick-up. He appeared around the corner a few minutes later and skidded to a halt when he saw us stopped by the roadside. He leaned out of the cab and looked at me quizzically.

"Hey Sonam, little problem I'm afraid, we've blown a tyre."

He grinned at me and then, totally unnecessarily, winked at Lady R,

"Not problem, Sonam fix, Sonam fix!"

"Oh yes!" blurted out Lady R, in what was far too close to her sex voice.

As he got to work, it was with great pleasure that I discovered the spares he'd been carrying along for us were actually for a different bike. It meant that he was basically useless and certainly not the knight in shining armour who could show me up by effortlessly getting us back on the road. On the downside, however, it did mean that we had to get the bike to a mechanic, which meant getting it into the back of the pick-up and transporting it to the next town, not an easy task given it weighed a couple of hundred kilograms. Sonam, Tahsi, and I failed miserably in our attempt to lift it. Plan B saw us standing in the middle of the road for half an hour until a vehicle came along, which we then flagged down. Thankfully, it contained four burly men in skirts. With a mighty group effort, we managed to lift the bike off the ground and into the bed of the pick-up. We lashed it firmly into place, and Lady R and I wedged ourselves into the cab, with me making sure I was planted firmly between her and Casanova.

Fixed up and back on two wheels the next morning, a darker side of the Bhutanese paradise exposed itself when we rounded a corner and found the road engulfed by smoke and were hit by the acrid reek of burning tar. I braked sharply as, in a Dante-esque scene, several blackened figures emerged phantom-like ahead, lurching forward under baskets of rock and barrels of tar. Their faces were covered with dirt, and tattered clothes hung off of gaunt bodies. They were a far cry from the immaculately turned-out Bhutanese that we had grown accustomed to. We pulled up and Tashi told us that they were, in fact, not Bhutanese at all but rather Indians, imported from the badlands of Uttar Pradesh and Bihar that we'd passed through a couple of weeks earlier. They were breaking stones and laying tar for two dollars a day, and with none of the free healthcare, universal education, or benevolent regal concern enjoyed by the Bhutanese around them. The foreman, who was clearly a local, came up and greeted us, "Good morning, sir, madam; we hope you are enjoying our freshly maintained road!"

I smiled at him and stroked a grateful foot along the tarmac, "Oh, we certainly are. Your efforts are very much appreciated," I pointed across to one of the labourers struggling up the bank on the other side of the road under a massive basket of stones, "but I must say that looks like very tough work!"

"Well, these foreign fellows are well used to it by now." He sniffed and waved his hand dismissively in their direction, as though they were not worthy of our concern.

I offered a wry smile, "So all the workers here are Indian?"

He shook his head, "Actually maybe seventy percent, the rest are, well, Bhutanese, but the wrong kind, if you know what I mean." He gave me a knowing wink. I was baffled.

"Err, the wrong kind? How do you mean?"

He sighed, "I mean Nepali. The ones we don't really want." He tutted and turned away to walk back to his crew, barking out instructions as he crossed the road.

As we pulled away I asked Lady R if she understood what the foreman had been talking about. She also sighed but then got underway with one of her Back Seat Briefings. It turned out that Bhutan had an ethnic Nepali minority that had been persecuted since the 1990s, when they started protesting against a new state policy of Bhutanisation. This was a policy that defined "Bhutanese" with the same kind of rigour used to dictate how a picture of the Buddha should look at the art school we'd visited in Thimpu. It was known as *Driglam Namzha* and set out what one should wear and how one should talk, eat, and even bow. And it was imposed on all citizens. Ethnic Nepalis saw this as an affront to their identity and protested. The response from the government was brutal and resulted in many having their citizenship stripped from them or fleeing the country out of fear. The majority headed to Nepal, but just because their ancestors had come from there, it didn't automatically follow that there would be friends or family to give them shelter or that the Nepalese government would welcome hosting them. Over a hundred thousand ended up in squalid refugee camps in the east of the country, where most would spend the next ten or twenty years. Eventually, they were resettled overseas, mostly in the USA, after international pressure on the Bhutanese government to allow their return proved fruitless. Some did stay on in Bhutan after the crackdown but lost most of their rights—it was members of this group that we had seen working alongside the Indians. It seemed Bhutan's concern with Gross National Happiness was firmly switched off the moment you were deemed not to fit into the narrow definition of "national."

That evening, we sat outside a small bar in Bhutan's most easterly town, Trashigang, and enjoyed some Druk beer and a few chicken momos. The settlement hugs the spur of a hill high above a river valley and is home to a couple of thousand people, so something of a metropolis by Bhutanese standards. We got chatting with an Indian teacher sitting at a neighbouring table who was working at a local high school. He explained that it's not just labourers that Bhutan imports from India but also much of its skilled workforce. India is Bhutan's main trading partner, which seems logical given its immense size and the shared border, yet that same logic collapses when applied to China, which presses down along the length of Bhutan from the north in the same way that India pushes up from the south. All trade is prohibited with this northern neighbour, no road crosses their 300 mile border, and the two countries don't even maintain embassies in each other's capitals. In short, the Bhutanese have made a firm decision to jump into India's lap and to all but deny China's existence, perhaps with the fate of Tibet, the Buddhist fiefdom that China forcibly annexed in the 1950s, still forefront in their minds. That made me think of the sharp contrast with what we'd seen in Nepal, a country which, like Bhutan, is squashed in the middle of an Indo-Sino sandwich. Kathmandu instead has chosen not to choose, for fifty years seeking to keep both countries happy and play them off for all it can get, which explains the Chinese bridges and Indian power plants we'd regularly passed while traversing the country. And then there is Burma, which again shares borders with the two giants but has opted to favour China over India. That's mainly because China has historically been happy to do business with the military government, something that India, along with most of the rest of the world, had shied away from. Delhi's reticence has not been helped by reports that groups from India's restive north-east have been able to set up bases just over the border on Burmese territory from which to launch attacks back into India. But all that is changing now as Burma opens up and seeks to reduce Chinese influence, though it remains to be seen what kind of a balance she will be able to strike.

Leaving Trashigang early the next morning our hearts were rather heavy, as that would be our last day in Bhutan. The town marks the point where the highway that traverses the country halts its eastwards path and swings abruptly south to head down to the Indian border. There was, however, still plenty of Bhutan to the east, in fact, its most remote part, but this was accessible only on foot. After several days of walking one would find the Brakpa people, a fascinating nomadic tribe who depend on their yaks for transport, food, and clothing and spend their lives following those shaggy beasts around from pasture to pasture.

Given that it was our last day in the country, I had reconciled myself to the fact that I would leave Bhutan neither having encountered yetis nor Brakpas, but it turned out that I had given up rather too easily. While the yetis remained holed up in the mountains and refusing to show their faces, when we stopped for a tea break in a small village, I spotted a tough-looking, well-weathered man striding down a small dirt track with the kind of strong but light gait that comes from years of walking in the mountains. What was even more noticeable was that his dress didn't fit into either of the two categories that Bhutan had so far offered us—the traditional belted knee-length robe of the majority or the ragged tatters of the road builders. Instead, he was wearing a tunic of what seemed to be yak fur tied around his waist with twine and sporting a wonderful five-pointed fur hat, much like a court jester. The latter confirmed it—he was a living, breathing Brakpa. I had read about their ingenious hats that serve as a miniature umbrella, diverting water down to the end of the points where it can fall to the ground without getting the wearer wet. He eyed me rather suspiciously but seemed to give me the benefit of the doubt as, in response to my wave and greeting, his cracked lips broke into a brief, shy smile. As he turned to look at Lady R, though, he did a double take and started to back away. I whispered to her that her long blonde hair coupled with her height must have had him mistaking her for a yeti. He then disappeared into a tiny wooden shop that we had visited a couple of minutes earlier and found to have precisely six items for sale. For a wandering Brakpa, though, it was presumably the equivalent of a trip to the supermarket.

Like the road that had brought us up from the Indian border when we entered Bhutan, the road back down at the other end of the country left us in no doubt that we were leaving a hidden kingdom. But this time it was done on ten times the scale. We descended mountainside after mountainside on dizzying hairpin roads, twisting and turning so much that we no longer had any idea in which direction we were heading. Low clouds swept across, obscuring the way ahead and behind.

The gods seemed to be making sure we'd never be able to find our way back.

Breaking for lunch in a small village to recover from our giddiness and let our ears pop, I spotted a small kiosk with an IDD sign, indicating that it offered international phone calls. I decided to do something that I had been putting off for the last couple of weeks—place a call through to the Ministry of Foreign Affairs in Burma to see whether there was any news on our request to be granted exceptional permission to cross the closed border with India. The whole trip, of course, hinged on that, and if we didn't get the green light in the next week, then we'd be well and truly high and dry, stranded at India's remotest frontier. The first miracle was that the line actually went through and rang. The second was that, after passing through a couple of people, I managed to reach someone who was familiar with my request. The third was that, instead of telling me it was still under consideration, I was greeted with the magical words: "Yes, Mr. Andy, Minister has now granted you special permission."

I froze, just managing to stop myself from launching into the desperate plea that I had prepared.

"Sir, you are still on the line?"

I hurriedly regained my composure, "Yes, sorry, what? Can you please repeat, did you say 'granted permission'?"

She coughed, "Yes, correct, you can traverse border from India side, also accompanied with your cycle."

I let out an involuntary whoop and punched the air in a most un-British fashion. But then my customary caution returned, and I decided I had better double check, "OK, so I can cross border India to Burma OK, no problem?"

"Correct, sir."

"And I can cross with my cycle that is, err, actually cycle with motor?"

"Correct."

"And of course my partner will be crossing with me; it's OK, yes?"

# Exit the Dragon

She coughed again, "Not correct, sir, one person permission only."

I repeated five different variants of my question to ensure we were understanding each other clearly. Unfortunately, it seemed we were. The Burmese government was taking the unprecedented step of allowing a foreigner and a motorcycle to cross their sealed border with India, but for some unknown political, diplomatic, or psychological reason, they felt that an accompanying passenger was a bridge too far. I politely protested the lack of logic or sense, but she was absolutely resolute.

As I walked slowly back to the shack where Lady R was finishing lunch, I considered how to break the news. I concluded that the very best approach would be to just not say anything. After all, what could we actually do about it anyway, apart from worry? And besides, we had already successfully crossed three borders while being generous with the rules at each one on the issue of vehicle import/export, so it was clear that regulations set by distant capitals were not always enforced on the ground. Though, of course, the India-Burma crossing was rather more conspicuous than the others in that the border was usually closed, and thinking about it, decent communications between capital and border post were actually essential for either of us to cross, as otherwise the local officials simply wouldn't know about the special permission that had been granted for me and my cycle.

The Bhutanese Dragon wasn't quite done with us yet, however. The road and the weather both worsened as we continued southwards and downwards. In one particularly rough section, the road was under construction and had turned into a quagmire of wet mud peppered with football-sized rocks. Lady R dismounted as I started to gingerly guide the bike across. Ahead a digger was perched on the hillside above the road, scraping out earth and stones, which came tumbling down in a mini-avalanche. Tashi, who was riding a few metres behind me, hollered and waved at the digger, which after a minute or so, stopped its work so that it was safe for us to pass. I pushed on forward, both legs outstretched for balance, particularly important given the long and unsecured drop to my right where a cliff descended a couple of hundred meters into a barren valley. I was totally focused as I tried to maintain balance and bearing while judging the depth of the mud ahead and the best path through.

**Deadly digger**

I was, therefore, oblivious to the renewed shouting behind me until a stone bounced off the fuel tank. I looked up and saw that the digger had started work again. Apparently, his pause hadn't been on account of hearing Tashi's pleas or being aware of us at all; he had simply been taking a short break. And traffic was so rare on that stretch that he hadn't bothered to check if anyone was passing below before continuing. An increasing amount of debris was on its way down, and I was a sitting duck, ready to be swept over the cliff edge along with the rest of the surplus material. The only way out was to gun the throttle and go for it, praying that I did not slide right over the edge, which was quite a possibility given the slipperiness of the mud and the narrowness of the road. I spun my right hand round on the throttle and exploded forward, careening wildly from side to side and spraying mud and stones out behind me. The bike tilted alarmingly to the left and right, and my heart missed a beat as one slide brought me to the very edge of the cliff. For a moment there was just thin air in front of me, before I managed to throw my weight the other way and re-orient the front wheel just in time to keep me on the mountain as behind me a shower of earth flew into the abyss. But then I was through, out of range of the digger, and I pulled up shaking, wondering what I had done in a previous life to make large earthmoving equipment take such a dislike to me.

Out of adversity we once again seemed to kindle affection, as Lady R bounded across to me and threw her arms around my neck. When we got going again she decided to shoot a video of us bumping along in commemoration of the fact that, as we had just realised, today was our six-month anniversary. As I focused on the driving, she filmed and pointed out to the prospective future viewer that, while most couples might celebrate such an event with a dinner or a drink, we were clearly cut from different cloth. She then wondered out loud what crazy adventure we might be on at our five-year mark. As far as I could recall, that was the first time she had ever referenced a potentially shared future, and it sent a wave of relief and warmth though my body. If things carried on like that then maybe I'd be able to actively seek her affection and attention a little less. And if I did manage to dial that down, it might just give her the space she needed to come forward of her own accord, instead of getting turned off by feeling I was demanding something.

We continued our descent until just after nightfall, when the road eventually levelled off and straightened out. We pulled over so Tashi could check his phone. He had a number of missed calls and messages from friends concerned for his welfare, as a couple of hours after we had passed that digger, a pick-up truck loaded with passengers had slid in the mud at the same spot and plunged over the cliff edge, plummeting to the valley floor and tragically killing all aboard. It was a very sobering thought, and I felt glad to be out of the mountains for a while. A few miles further on we entered the border town of Samdrup Jognhkar. With its square concrete block buildings and bad fluorescent lighting, it felt a bit like Eastern Europe in the bad old days. And it really didn't look like Bhutan anymore; no, the real Kingdom of the Thunder Dragon was sheltering safely behind the mountains.

# 13
# INTO THE WILD

I was starting to feel that the Indians really just didn't care about their borders. An hour ago, on the Bhutanese side, we'd been courteously checked out of the country with a detailed examination of our papers, some rigorous stamping, and warm handshakes. We'd given Tashi and Sonam a hug (Lady R for just a little too long) and ridden through the border arch into the Indian state of Assam to find absolutely no sign of Indian officialdom on the other side. It seemed they were trusting the Bhutanese not to let any unsavoury characters into their country. Or perhaps they just presumed that there weren't any in Bhutan. We rode up and down and round and round the dusty streets looking for an immigration office. As we did so, it became quite clear that we weren't in Bhutan any longer, with the cows wandering down the streets, the lack of traditional dress, the stares, and the generally less organised but more colourful feel of the street life. I spotted a soldier lounging on a corner with his rifle slung over his shoulder and pulled up. Lady R dismounted to speak to him, "*Namaste*, can you tell us where the immigration office is please?" She gave one of her winning smiles, "We've just crossed from Bhutan."

He wobbled his head and smirked, looking her up and down appreciatively while stroking his formidable moustache but made no sign of replying. Lady R sighed (it should be said that she was not always the most patient of people) and tried again, "Immigration? Passport? Stamp, stamp?"

The soldier finally broke his silence, "You are married, madam?"

"No, I'm not bloody married; now can you please tell me where to go?"

"If you are married, madam, maybe more calm, husband will control."

I intervened at that point, thanking the gentleman for his time while also raising a pacifying hand in Lady R's direction.

We gave up and headed out of town, not knowing what else to do. A couple of miles down the road we spotted a tiny hand-painted wooden sign poking out from behind a tree. I squinted to make it out: "Official Immigration Control." Of all the places. Tucked back from the road stood, or rather leaned, a dilapidated wooden shack. We dismounted and walked over to the door. It was locked. We heard a noise from behind the building and walked round the back to find a middle-aged man down on his hands and knees tending to his vegetable patch. Following a polite enquiry, he reluctantly admitted that he was, indeed, the immigration officer. He dusted himself off and unlocked the shack, where he retrieved an old stamp from the drawer of a 1940s desk, opened our passports without even looking at the identity pages or checking if we had visas, and inked us in. He seemed to care not a jot where we'd come from, where we were going to, or that we were travelling on a motorcycle. There were vegetables to be taken care of, after all. Two minutes later and we were on the road again, officially back in incredible India.

After two weeks in Bhutan being escorted 24/7 with no decisions to make or worries to occupy our minds (bar not riding off a cliff), we were suddenly all alone again, dependent on our wits and heading into the most remote area of India. It was a bit of a sobering and scary thought, but on the other hand, with our minders now gone, we were again free to choose (and lose) our route, pick which hotel to sleep in, and make an informed decision about whether we'd really like to have hot chilli with cheese for dinner again.

**Brotherly love**

We rattled along a freshly gravelled road that cut its way through jungle and rice paddies, raising a spray of small stones up on either side. We were firmly back on the plains now, so there were no ups and downs or hairpin bends to contend with, but we did have to slow every few minutes to weave through steel and barbed wire roadblocks. Each one had a sign mounted on it proclaiming "Army Is Your Friend" which wasn't fully convincing when there were a couple of men with machine guns standing behind it.

Some graffiti on a concrete post by the roadside gave a clue as to the reason for the heavy military presence. It read, "We Demand Free Bodoland—LTF." I didn't know who the LTF were, but that in itself wasn't too surprising—just as the names of many Indian cities that are home to millions remain unknown outside the country, so too do the acronyms of most of its armed rebel groups, of which the country's north-east has more than its fair share. On spotting the slogan, Lady R gave me two sharp taps on the shoulder that, as I now knew well, meant I should stop immediately, regardless of what speed we were travelling at, what other traffic was around, or whether there was an imminent prospect of robbery or death. I screeched to a halt just past the post, and she called out to a middle-aged gentleman squatting at the roadside chewing betel nut, "Excuse me sir, could you possibly tell us who are the LTF?"

He looked at her suspiciously (which I felt was understandable, given that we had just shown up in front of him out of the blue in a heavily militarised zone and asked for his knowledge of a local rebel movement) then spat a stream of bright red liquid onto the ground in front of him, one of the not-so-nice side effects of betel consumption.

"Madam, you are from government?"

Lady R made good use of her dazzling smile once again, "Oh no, no, no, don't worry, just a curious tourist, no government, no police, no journalist, no problem!" She thought for a moment and then added, "We are friends of Bodoland!" I looked around nervously to check no-one had overheard what might be interpreted as a pledge of allegiance to a rebel force attempting to overthrow the Indian State. The old man's face brightened, and he motioned for us to come closer, "LTF is meaning Liberation Tigers Force."

"Oh, how lovely!" Lady R clapped her hands, quite delighted at the prospect of an armed militia in the vicinity, "And what might they be fighting for?"

"Well, we," he checked himself, "I am meaning they, they want, they deserve, their own state in India, free from Assam!"

So it seemed we were actually talking to an LTF cadre, probably best to move on. Lady R was of a different mind, however, "How very exciting! So the same as the United Liberation Front of Assam then?"

His face creased into a frown, "Absolutely not, madam, the ULAF want independence for the whole of Assam from India. They are our sworn enemies, even worse than Indian Army!" He swung his arm up violently in a gesture of defiance as he spoke. I noticed a couple of people at a nearby tea shop pointing at us and muttering to one another. It was time for me to intervene again, "It's been terribly nice talking to you, sir, but now I'm afraid we have to press on. I wish you every success with your, err, endeavours." Lady R looked distinctly annoyed as I pulled her back to the bike.

This was, however, quite a pertinent introduction to north-east India, a hilly and forgotten corner of the vast country where the inhabitants are a smorgasbord of tribes that differ hugely from the plains' peoples in terms of language, religion, appearance, dress, and food. Indeed, many of those tribes wonder how they ever got attached to India in the first place, given they lack pretty much anything in common with the rest of the country. And that includes geography, as the link with the mainland—as people here refer to the rest of India—is tenuous at best. On a map, India seems to be blocked in by Nepal and Bangladesh to the east, but look more closely and you'll see that a narrow strip of Indian territory pushes between them, sometimes only a few miles wide, before emerging out and ballooning into the country's north-east. That strip is the "chicken's neck," the start of which we had passed just outside of Siliguri when we'd emerged from Nepal back into India a couple of weeks before. In the north-east, Delhi is but a distant memory, and Imphal, the main town in the north-eastern state of Manipur, is mind-bogglingly closer to Hong Kong than it is to the Indian capital.

Lady R had by then gotten rebel fever and started Googling furiously from the back seat as we continued on our way. The briefing started soon after, informing me how the LTF and ULAF are but two of many armed groups in Assam campaigning variously for recognition, autonomy, or independence. It was head-spinningly difficult to keep up with her rapid explanations of who wanted what and who was associated with—or opposed to—who, especially as I was simultaneously trying to deal with proper, chaotic traffic after a fortnight's break in Bhutan. What I did manage to grasp was that, ever since Indian independence in 1947, the people of the north-east have resisted what they saw as a colonial occupation by the mainland and have done so mostly violently, via a plethora of armed groups. But those seem to have spent almost as much time splintering and fighting each other, along with running various criminal rackets, as they have on waging the resistance campaign against the mainland. There are now more than seventy militant groups active in the north-east, but the Indian government's response to them hasn't changed much over time, consisting of heavy-handed crackdowns under the auspices of a draconian piece of legislation called the Armed Forces Special Powers Act (another regrettable British legacy). That lets the Army arrest people without warrants, shoot to kill, and generally treat the local population as it sees fit. What there doesn't seem to have been is any serious attempt at dialogue to address the underlying grievances, or initiatives to create jobs and build roads, schools, and hospitals in what is one of the country's poorest and most underdeveloped regions. Thus the main result, apart from hundreds killed, seems to have been a strengthening of the feeling of being under an oppressive occupation by a colonial power.

## Into the Wild

Assam, which we were riding through, is the closest of the north-eastern states to the rest of India, both geographically and culturally, which also means it is the most developed. But it's still had its fair share of violence, with bombings or shootings occurring every couple of months in the last decade. We were closing in on the state capital of Guwahati, which has suffered from some particularly nasty bomb attacks in recent years, though nothing as bad as the areas we'd be heading into after. My worries about that were soon pushed out of my head though as we crossed the mighty Brahmaputra River and I was forced to address the much more immediate concerns of the traffic, fumes, intense heat, and seething mass of humanity that makes up a good old Indian metropolis.

We headed to the nearest Enfield garage for a check-up and service. The bike seemed to be running OK—apart from the puncture in Bhutan, we hadn't had a single mechanical problem while crossing the country—but I didn't want to take any chances. There was going to be enough to worry about from there on without adding concerns about breakdowns, and images of the engine suddenly cutting out as we were trying to escape from AK47-toting rebels were already all too vivid in my imagination.

We decided that we too deserved a decent servicing that night so headed to a five-star hotel. We lapped up the fancy cocktails and a decent bit of steak, but I couldn't quite get my mind off what lay ahead. There was really no good way to get through the north-east, as any route involved very real risks of banditry and being caught up in violence, either at the hands of the various armed groups or of the Indian security forces. But there were at least some routes that avoided going through Nagaland, the most lawless and remote of the seven states, whose inhabitants, the Nagas, were infamous for their headhunting. The first accounts I'd read reassuringly said that this hobby was "only common up to the twentieth century," but later I came across a reference telling me that it was "banned in the 1940s," followed by an article claiming, "a last case was reported in 1969," and finally, that it "may still be practiced in some isolated areas." Lady R was, of course, insisting we take the route that went right through it.

As we strolled around one of Guwahati's pungent spice markets the next morning after breakfast, I sensed she was not in the best of moods, "Baby, you feeling OK?"

"Hmmm." The scowl on her face didn't exactly invite further conversation, but I stupidly decided to persevere, "Something wrong, something I can do?"

"You can stop asking stupid questions like that for a start."

I took a deep breath, "Oh, well, sorry, I was just concerned. I mean hopefully that's like a good thing, right?" I smiled, maybe just a little patronisingly.

She turned to face me, "Look, you need to do this better, OK?"

"Err, do what better?"

"Know when to speak to me and know when I just need to be left alone."

It was a reasonable point, but I decided to take offence at the way it was delivered, "Well maybe that's just a teeny bit princessy? I mean I'm not only here to serve your moods, you know?"

"Well bugger off then." She glared at me. I glared back. We'd gone from zero to teeth-barring in a couple of seconds. I turned on my heel and strolled off purposefully through the stalls without looking back.

It felt worse than before. In my head I was calling her cold, spoilt, insensitive, and much worse. For the first time I realised that right then I actually didn't want her, I wished she wasn't with me, and that all this seemed just too much effort, too much pain for too little reward. I wandered the streets of Guwahati for an hour or so, no longer so worried about bombs. As my anger subsided a little, I felt bad for what I'd said, but I realised that in part it stemmed from a truth I had been trying to deny all along; that as much as Lady R appealed to me for what she was on paper—incredibly smart, curious, interesting, exotic, beautiful—the other sides of her that I seemed to bring out (maybe by those elevated needs for attention and affection)—the aloofness, the coldness—were getting simply too much for me to handle. Perhaps we were simply incompatible. The twelve-year age gap wasn't really helping much either. She was just starting out in the world really, there were a thousand adventures to be had, a thousand people to meet; whereas me, well, I was ready to settle down.

When I arrived back at the hotel in the late morning, I found her sitting on the floor outside the room door. I was on the verge of apologising but then decided against it. Maybe I was ready to destroy this now. We entered the room in silence, packed our things without a word, then went down to the bike and loaded up. As we pulled away I barked over my shoulder, "Can you tell me where we are supposed to be going?"

She snorted, "Well how do I know?"

I shook my head, "You are supposed to be the bloody navigator, for God's sake. How can I read a map and drive at the same time?"

"I didn't look."

I gave a sarcastic laugh, "So just assuming I will take care of everything as usual."

"Screw you."

I felt a surge of adrenaline and anger. I revved the bike hard before bursting into the backstreets of Guwahati, swerving around rickshaws and cows, cutting through tiny gaps in traffic at high speed, and berating my fellow drivers while thumbing the horn. Lady R punched me in the back, "Yeah, go on, bloody kill both of us, you bastard."

I sped up.

I finally slowed down half an hour later, when overtaking a lumbering truck on the highway at speed, I very nearly took us headfirst into a jeep coming the other way. It was too late to pull back behind the truck, and there was only a very narrow space for us to get through. I jerked my legs and arms in and prayed. It was a close call. The racks on the back of the bike, our widest part, hit both the side of the truck and the jeep's wing mirror, but miraculously, we stayed upright.

As dusk fell, signs started appearing warning us to watch out for elephants and rhinos that might be on the road ahead (the tigers, presumably, could take care of themselves). We were entering Kaziranga National Park, nearly 200 square miles of tropical forest, grassland, and marsh. Finally, something to thank the British for, as it was the Viceroy's wife who had established it a hundred years or so ago. Lady R spotted the small turning we were looking for leading up to a wooden gate. I pulled in and our headlight highlighted a plaque reading, "Diphlu River Lodge." I honked the horn, and after a few seconds, a guard appeared and hauled open the gate.

After dismounting, we were escorted up a lantern-lit path to an open-sided reception building and promptly supplied with cold towels and a glass of rum. I was by then consistently ranking hotels based on how quickly I was offered free alcohol at check-in. Our accommodation was a small, self-contained wooden house sitting on stilts and sporting a thatched roof and veranda. Inside it offered polished wooden floors, colourful local fabrics adorning the walls, crisp white sheets, a couple of comfortable armchairs, a small library, and a generous minibar. But the charm and cosiness didn't warm the coldness between us; we went for dinner in the restaurant and ate in silence, then came back and settled into our respective sides of the bed, both refusing to yield.

In the morning, I sat alone on the veranda watching the sun rise over the river as it brought the jungle back to life. A couple of black-necked storks glided over the water, and in the distance a small group of deer appeared from between the trees and started grazing, ears twitching as they looked up every few seconds to watch for predators. After a breakfast of poached eggs and monosyllables, we were back on the road. Tea plantations and bustling small towns slipped by as we continued eastwards, heading towards the Nagaland border. We saw no other foreigners; very few were likely to ever venture that way. We passed through the city of Sivasagar, noted for its temple dedicated to Shiva, the Hindu God of Destruction, and I tried not to see it as an omen of impending doom.

The next day, the villages thinned out and then disappeared altogether. In two hours of riding we passed only a couple of old jeeps. Then the road headed through a lonely tea plantation, and up ahead I saw three people waving. As we got closer I realised they were soldiers, each armed with a sub-machine gun. I pulled up and noted their shoulder patches—they were from the Assam Rifles. The Rifles are a paramilitary force that was originally established by the British to keep these restive border areas and their tribal inhabitants in check. These days they work to counter the various insurgency movements in the area, though they have also been accused of carrying out extrajudicial killings and running extortion rackets, smuggling outfits, and various other nefarious activities, aided by the *carte blanche* of the Armed Forces Special Powers Act tucked into their ammunition belt. I tried to look friendly but not stupid, gullible, or easily rob-able, "*Namaste!*" I smiled and then, for some inexplicable reason, gave a mock salute. They looked decidedly unimpressed.

"Where you go?"

"Oh, we're on our way to Nagaland."

"Why you go?"

"Err, tourism?"

The soldier looked at me incredulously, tilted his head at his colleague, and muttered something in Hindi that led them all to laugh. I decided to change the subject, "So, you're here because there's a security risk or something today?"

He looked at me blankly, "Always security risk."

"Oh, well, but thank goodness you're here to protect us then," I tried another attempt at a smile.

He shook his head, "You are here at own risk."

He motioned for us to move on. I paused for a second, on the verge of asking him what was the point of the army's presence if not to protect the citizenry (plus random foreign tourists) but then thought better of it.

# 14
# Taming the Head-Hunters

Ten miles farther down the road we came to a rickety iron bridge. We clattered over its broken planking and pulled up on the other side, where two battered oil drums and a length of bamboo perched on top of them served to block the road. This then was the border between the states of Assam and Nagaland, and like in Sikkim, we needed to get stamped in, given it was a sensitive area. I dismounted and looked for a sign of life. Some voices drifted across from a small hut by the roadside, so I walked over, poked my head in the doorway, and gave a cheery "Morning!" Two soldiers were slumped on a *charpoy*, a bare bed frame which serves in India for sitting or lying on and doing nothing much in particular. One of them pushed himself to his feet on spotting me and then promptly fell back down again, his revolver tumbling out of its holster onto the floor as he did so. They were clearly rolling drunk. His colleague pointed at me and started shouting, "You! You! What? What?"

**Approaching the Nagaland border**

I tried my best British smile again, "Yes, err, hi, so, we're just crossing into Nagaland, and I believe you gentlemen would want to stamp our passports in order to keep Delhi happy?"

The word *Delhi* seemed to have the desired effect of reminding them that ultimately they answered to a faraway hierarchy, which I might possibly just have some connection with, as one of them slapped his brother in arms on the shoulder, "OK, OK, yes, stamp, stamp."

After some rummaging around, an old dusty stamp pad appeared. I handed over our passports and watched as, tongue sticking out of the corner of his mouth and squinting, he lined up to take aim. He missed on the first go, authorising the table to enter Nagaland instead but came through on the second attempt. I then leaned over to take the passports back, but his hand covered mine, "What you do here?"

"Oh, we're just tourists, spot of sightseeing you know!"

He peered over my shoulder at that point and spotted Lady R outside sitting astride the back of the bike, as opposed to the more demure side-saddle position favoured by Indian ladies. His eyes wandered from her chest down to the bulging bags on the back. I pulled my hand back accompanied by the passports and smiled, "Well, have a lovely day. We really need to get on I'm afraid."

As I climbed back on the bike, both soldiers came out of the hut and leered at us, but it seemed they were a bit too inebriated to formulate a plan that fast, and we were already pulling away when I heard one of them shout for us to hold on. I decided to take a risk and pretend I hadn't heard, just raising my hand in a goodbye wave without turning around and praying not to hear the sound of a weapon being cocked. Thankfully, the road rounded a bend just ahead and we were soon out of sight. I accelerated hard and hoped it wasn't a sign of things to come.

Our surroundings had changed drastically. The road, which back in Assam had been broken tarmac, turned into mud just around the corner from the checkpoint. Dwellings were one storey and thatched huts, as opposed to the sturdy Assamese brick and concrete houses we'd gotten used to over the past couple of days. There were no shops or other indications of commercial activity, and the only signs of any kind of public service or authority were the heavily fortified army camps we passed with billboards declaring "Assam Rifles—Friends of the Hill People" fronted by coils of razor wire and machine gun nests.

Nagaland has a reputation as the wildest part of India's wild north-east. It's inhabited by a collection of warrior tribes who seem to have spent most of history battling one another, as well as the outside world whenever the latter was foolish enough to try to encroach upon their territory. Villages are perched on ridges to facilitate protection and have traditionally exhibited an extreme insularity, often going to war with and even speaking a different language from their neighbours on the next hilltop. The stockades that surround each one would, up until worryingly recently, sport the impaled heads of their unfortunate enemies.

The British, who first encountered the Nagas in the early nineteenth century, considered them too much trouble after the loss of their first few heads (white ones being particularly prized) and subsequently largely left them to their own devices. But during the Second World War, Nagaland unexpectedly took centre stage in the clash between the Allies and the Japanese, as it was there that, after the lightning Japanese advance and corresponding British flight through Burma, the two sides finally properly engaged as the British decided to dig in. It was a vicious and bloody battle, but one that ultimately prevented the Japanese from reaching further westwards into India proper. The Allies prevailed and pushed them back into, and eventually right back across, Burma. Had it gone the other way, the Japanese could well have made it to Delhi and changed the whole outcome of the war. While conflict was ongoing in the area, the Allies managed to co-opt the Nagas to help them out, setting up a kind of sub-contracting arrangement whereby they paid them both to rescue downed Allied pilots and soldiers in distress but also, in a gruesome accommodation to local traditions, to decapitate any Japanese that they might come across.

The jungle was all around us, dense, green, humming, and dripping. Low clouds drifted across the hillside we were fighting up, occasionally parting to throw open vast wooded valleys below. Once in a while a plume of wood smoke curled upwards from a small clearing in the distance, but apart from that, there was no sign of human habitation anymore. However, somewhere out there were the head-hunters, the drug smugglers, the armed rebel groups, and the bandits.

After a couple of hours of this eerie emptiness, a small group of people trudging along the roadside appeared ahead—our first sighting of real-life Nagas. I told myself that finally I could put all the scary legends aside and see that they were just normal, and no doubt friendly, local people going about their daily lives. They didn't make it too easy, however. There were four men and two women, and all carried either a large scythe in their hands or a battered rifle slung over their shoulder. As we drew level with them my smiles and waves were greeted by cold, hard stares, and from one of the gentlemen, the ejection of a mouthful of blood-red betel spit. I accelerated past and then glanced back a hundred metres further on to find them standing motionless in the middle of the road staring after us.

Around the next corner we were forced to slow down again, as another Assam Rifles checkpoint loomed up. This time the soldier on duty flagged us down and instructed me curtly to switch off the engine and called for his superior. A sergeant arrived, a huge bearded and turbaned Sikh, and after a brusque exchange with his minion, approached the bike while carefully eyeing up passengers and luggage. He displayed a slightly fox-like bonhomie and a disturbing habit of licking his lips, "*Namaste*, friends, good to see you here! May I ask where are you going only?"

"Burma."

"Ahahaha, well, oh dear, oh dear, very far, and very dangerous roads, there are bad people around here, you must be careful." He smiled nevertheless, and I wondered if he was including himself.

"We will be, and well, at least it's good to know you're here," I ventured back. But, like his colleagues earlier in the day, he seemed absolutely nonplussed at this assertion.

"So, you have a lot of money with you, yes?"

"No, not at all," I lied, "and our embassy knows exactly where we are," I added for good measure.

He frowned, "Hmmm, long way from your embassy here though."

I nodded back, "Yes, well we have to get along now, it's been a pleasure."

I took a chance once again and started the bike before being told we could leave. He seemed about to stop me but then thought better of it, and I pulled away unimpeded. After we got out of earshot, I mused aloud whether he'd been about to rob us, and Lady R retorted that he was probably just a good soldier doing his duty. Well at least we were talking again.

Two hours on we arrived in Mon, a Wild West-like settlement of shambolic wooden buildings and dirt streets, home to a few thousand people. We were less than ten miles to the west of Burma, but we couldn't cross over there, as there was no road heading that way nor any official border post. One could, however, it was said, just amble over on foot without a problem. The border had hardly any meaning to the Nagas, whose villages and families straddled it. They had little, if any, interaction with either the Indian or Burmese governments, and certainly far less than they did with the various armed groups that were active in the region. The town felt reasonably safe at least, and we received our first nods and smiles as we stopped for samosas and tea.

From Mon we struck out on a narrow track through the jungle to try to find the tiny village of Wanching, where we hoped to spend the night with someone we'd never met. A friend of a friend had once met a Naga lady who lived there and, before the trip, had kindly put us in touch. She'd said that we'd be very welcome to stay and given us the name of the village, along with some rough directions. We'd emailed twenty-four hours before that we would hopefully be there that afternoon but had no idea if she would be too. The village didn't seem to be marked on any map, so we set off without great confidence along what was, for the most part, a heavily waterlogged footpath. It was really hard work, wrestling the bike through the mud and the water. The afternoon was drawing on, and the stress of a day spent mostly on edge was starting to take its toll. There were no people, no huts, just the track, the jungle, and the rapidly sinking sun. Three hours out from Mon, I was seriously considering turning back, when we spotted a pick-up truck parked by the side of the track up ahead and someone standing next to it waving us down. My first thought was army or ambush, but then I realised it was a woman, that she was smiling, and that she wasn't wearing camouflage. As we approached, she started jumping up and down giggling gleefully, "Andy! You made it! Welcome to Nagaland!"

"Mary?"

"Yes, of course, who else?! I'm basically the only one who speaks English between here and Calcutta!"

She broke into a bout of infectious laughter, and I said a silent prayer of thanks.

Mary hopped back in her pick-up with her driver, and we followed them on a rocky side track we never would have found alone. It cut through the jungle for half a mile and then climbed up to a village on a ridge. Small wooden houses lined the main street and were decorated with animal skulls that Mary later told us had in recent years replaced the human ones as a badge of status. There was one much larger, brick house that stood out and where the pick-up turned. We followed it into the courtyard and parked up, thankful to be out of the saddle and in welcoming company. I smiled approvingly at the house as Mary got out of the cab, "Nice place. So looks like you're the richest ones in the village!"

She grinned back, "Ha, well yes, I guess, my father's actually the headman, you know."

"Oh wow, so we should feel well protected then?"

She nodded, "Oh for sure. I mean just so long as my grandfather's not around, he took a few heads back in the day, and you know a white one is extra special!"

I feigned a grimace and signalled towards Lady R, who was trying to extract part of her sodden library from the back of the bike, "Well please tell him that a blonde head would stand out much better than a dark haired one; it can be our little secret."

We followed her into a large outhouse with wooden walls and a dirt floor, where the centrepiece was a massive fireplace that crackled and spat beneath a suspended rack of what seemed to be drying meat. We nodded to a couple of people squatting in the gloom, unsure exactly who they were, and sat down on an old wooden bench. An elderly lady shuffled in with three cups of tea. It all started to feel quite homely. But I couldn't quite get my mind off what she'd said about her grandfather, wondering if it was a joke or not, "So, are there really any head-hunters left up here then?" I ventured, "Lady R has been telling me I'm kind of crazy to think so."

Mary took a sip of her tea and pondered my question, "Well you're both right really, so yes, there are some left, but they're all old men now who took their last heads years ago. I mean nobody's doing it anymore, almost certainly."

Lady R chipped in, sensing victory, "So then, can you please tell Andy that there's really nothing to worry about riding through Nagaland?"

Mary looked at her a little sceptically, "Well, that would not be very honest of me. Chances of getting your head cut off, very slim, yes, but these hills are teeming with groups of men with guns who are after one thing or another. And then there's the Assam Rifles. God, how I wish the mainland would leave us alone."

I thought I'd put in a good word for the oppressor, "But surely the Indian government does do some good, I mean I heard they allocate a fair bit of funding for schools and hospitals and roads and stuff, right?"

She snorted and looked annoyed for the first time since we'd met her, "Oh, they promise that, yes, but as you will have noticed by the state of the roads you've driven on so far, it doesn't quite seem to make its way all the way up here, now does it?"

She had a point, given what we'd seen so far, "So, what happens then?"

"Well, people will tell you it either never arrives, or when it does, then local officials and middle men all take a cut and there ends up being hardly anything left to actually build something with."

I was intrigued, and as our conversation carried on and she told us more about the tragic history of Nagaland and its abuse by a variety of outsiders over the centuries, I started to feel decidedly more sympathetic towards the inhabitants of that lost land.

A variety of people came in and out as we talked, some family, some villagers coming to seek advice from the headman who was settled in an adjoining room, some just to warm themselves round the fire and exchange the latest news and gossip. In essence, the compound seemed to serve as a *de facto* community centre for the village. Everyone who passed by came over to us and shook hands while smiling shyly and, rather refreshingly, giving not even the slightest indication that they might want to take a machete to our necks. The light was fading outside, and as we warmed our hands over the fire, I had an overwhelming sense of our remoteness. I turned back to Mary, "So, I'd make a bet I'm the first Englishman ever to visit this area, right?" Lady R rolled her eyes at my petty bid for fame. Mary laughed, "Oh, so sorry, Andy, actually one of your countrymen was up here just a few months ago staying at a nearby village!"

"Damn him."

"Haha, yes, actually maybe you know him?"

I smiled at this assumption, which we'd found common in remote rural areas, that we would personally know everyone from our own respective country. The most frequent enquiry I received was how David Beckham and the queen were doing and if we wouldn't mind passing on greetings to them on our return.

"Well, I very much doubt it, I'm afraid. There are quite a few of us in England, you know!"

"Sixty-four million, as I recall," shot back Mary, without missing a beat, "but I thought the name *Gordon Ramsey* might just ring a bell?"

I involuntarily spat my mouthful of tea out into the fire, "What? Gordon Ramsey? The famous TV chef?"

"Yes, the very same!"

"What the hell was he doing here?"

"Cooking, of course!"

The surprises kept coming as she pulled an iPad out of her bag and proceeded to show us the TV show where Mr. Ramsey himself was, indeed, sitting around a fire in Nagaland learning tribal cooking techniques. I was utterly devastated.

Our charming host turned out to be quite an encyclopaedia of Naga history and soon had us fully converted to their cause as she explained how things had gone down since the end of the Second World War. The Brits promised the Nagas that, in return for their help against the Japanese, they would make sure Nagaland became independent if the Allies were victorious. But when they won the war and when India itself became independent from Britain in 1947, that promise was conveniently forgotten. In fact, they didn't even get to have their own independent state within the new India; instead they were annexed to Assam. And so, quite understandably, the Nagas protested. That led to attempts at negotiations that lasted for some seven years before the central government got tired of the whole thing and sent in the army, 100,000 strong, to carry out a brutal crackdown. Tens of thousands of Nagas were herded into makeshift concentration camps, where many died from the appalling conditions. But that only strengthened local support for the resistance movement. It took until the early 1960s to reach a settlement in which the Nagas conceded their demand for full independence in return for the promise of being a stand-alone Indian state. But it was not until 1975 that an agreement was signed in which they accepted the Constitution of India and agreed to surrender their arms. That agreement, however, didn't settle everything, as it vaguely stated that more time should be given "to formulate other issues for discussion for final settlement." Today, that final settlement still hasn't come about, more than half a century after the discussions first started. Some Nagas also call into question the legitimacy of those who signed the agreement in their name in the first place. The upshot is that the armed resistance movement to the Indian government continues to this day, and in the meantime, Nagaland remains desperately poor and underdeveloped and largely forgotten by India and the rest of the world. As Mary explained that tragic story, I felt the shadows cast by ignorance and unfamiliarity melting away and wondered how many of the fearsome tales told about the Nagas were due to similar bias from others who'd never actually taken the time to get to know them and hear their side of the story.

"It will save you hours of driving" was something we always wanted to hear, as our bodies were constantly aching from the daily bashing we were giving them on the roads. Mary reckoned that, instead of returning to Mon the way we'd come and then taking the main road onwards through Nagaland to reach the state capital of Kohima, we could instead take a short cut through the hills. It had been raining recently, yes, but apparently, a truck had made it through via the short cut the day before, so she reckoned it would be OK. So we thanked her, said our fond farewells, and made solemn promises of future visits.

At first it was muddy, waterlogged, and slow-going but manageable, and we were confident it would get better further on. The area seemed completely deserted however; it was just thick jungle and not a settlement or trace of human activity in sight. Really not the place for a breakdown as you might be stuck for days without seeing a soul. Or so we thought. As we rounded a tight corner I had to brake sharply to avoid slamming into the back of an Assam Rifles jeep. A group of four soldiers were outside it on the side of the road, rifles levelled at three local men who were lined up against neighbouring tree trunks with their arms tied behind their backs. A number of packages were scattered on the ground beside them. Smugglers being arrested? An extortion racket?

A hit about to go down? God only knew. The soldiers turned at the sound of our engine and looked distinctly surprised. I instinctively took the initiative before they could say anything, "*Namaste*! Morning, gentlemen; hope you're having a good day! Just passing through!"

That took up just enough time to enable us to reach the next corner and disappear out of sight before they had a chance to respond. After a couple more seconds, there was some muffled shouting, but thankfully, no sound of their jeep starting up to pursue us. It seemed they'd decided to finish their business on the roadside instead. I shuddered a little as I wondered what was going to happen next back there.

The conditions deteriorated steadily until they became the worst of the trip, by a large margin. There were huge mounds of mud that we had to ride up, over, and down. In other sections the whole feeble attempt at a track disappeared into water-filled trenches, which we had to gun through as fast as possible to avoid getting stuck, hoping the water didn't get up past our knees. Somehow, the bike kept going, though the engine was wheezing asthmatically and a variety of new and not very healthy clanks and rattles accompanied our progress. We were coated in mud and averaging probably four miles an hour. At that rate we'd never reach our destination by nightfall, and we could only hope it would get better up ahead. It didn't. We were both getting frustrated and worried, and I was pretty exhausted. Lady R tapped me on the shoulder, "OK, we need to stop, I need to rest."

I shook my head vigorously, despite feeling on the verge of collapsing myself, "We don't have time, we only have a couple of hours until nightfall."

She tapped again, more insistently, "You know we're destroying ourselves like this, let's just stop for half an hour."

She was right, but I refused to acknowledge it, "What will actually destroy us is if we're stuck out here in the jungle at nightfall with no shelter and God knows who prowling around."

"OK, bugger you."

I felt a wobble as Lady R did a smart backwards vault, rather impressively dismounting the moving bike and landing on her feet. I hit the brakes and slithered to a halt but didn't turn off the engine, "Get back on the bike!"

"No."

"I'm serious; get back on. I'm pulling away in five seconds."

"Then go. I'm not getting back on. I'll walk."

I stared at her incredulously, "What? You'll walk? On your own? Through the jungle? In the dark?"

"Yes, it's a damn sight better than staying with you."

I felt the blood rushing to my face as I fired back, "You are absolutely crazy. Have you any idea what could happen to you out here?" I was angry; this was ridiculous; we needed to move. I'd had enough; it was time to shout, "Now get on the bloody bike now, you idiot. NOW!" My eyes were blazing, and for a moment, she looked unsure what to do, which was a very rare occurrence. Amazingly, she then sheepishly climbed back on the bike. I couldn't quite believe it. I pulled away fast, before she had a chance to reconsider.

Ahead was yet another water-filled ditch. I gripped the throttle and took it as fast as I could. But it was really deep, and what I'd feared most happened—the engine cut out. The bike was stuck, water up to the fuel tank. We climbed off and spent the next twenty minutes pushing and heaving, trying to free the wheels. Eventually, with a painful sucking sound, they came free of the mud somewhere under the murky water, and we were able to manhandle the bike for the next thirty metres through the rest of the trench and out onto semi-dry land again. We both collapsed on the ground exhausted. It was another ten minutes before I could pull myself up and boot the kickstart. Nothing happened. My second and third attempts were equally ineffectual, and I felt panic starting to set in. We were really screwed. Then Lady R, who'd never once been able to start the bike on her own, stomped over and pushed me manfully aside before kicking it with all her force and pent-up aggression. It fired.

We left the mud behind soon after, but instead of being replaced by tarmac, we now had a rocky moonscape to contend with, covered in huge stones that threw us this way and that as we rocked over them and every few minutes succeeded in toppling us over. Thankfully, our slow speed and the buffer provided by the luggage racks prevented serious injury or us ending up trapped under the bike, but the exertion of repeatedly keeling over, extricating ourselves, and then having to lift a fully-laden Enfield back up again was immense. At the same time our average speed was decreasing even further.

It was around 5PM, and the sun had disappeared below the tree line, casting ominous shadows across our path. The track was showing no signs of getting better. We hadn't passed a village or a single sign of human settlement since leaving Mary's place, some eight hours ago. It seemed inevitable that we were going to still be out in the open when it got dark. Riding across that terrain at night would seem suicidal, but so would stopping and spending the night in the jungle without shelter. I just didn't know what to do; there was a sense of desperation rising inside me and, for the life of me, I couldn't find one consoling thought to temper it with. I was also desperately exhausted and realised that my vision was starting to get hazy. My despair was interrupted by a sharp jab in the back, Lady R's first attempt at communication in the last two hours, "Could that be coming from a village?"

She pointed up ahead, and I realised it wasn't my vision going, the haziness was actually due to smoke drifting across the road in front of us. That could mean one of two things—a bush fire or a settlement. As we rounded the next corner, I uncrossed my fingers and broke into a broad grin at the sight of a small thatched hut up ahead, smoke rising from a hole in its roof.

When we'd first entered Nagaland I'd much preferred to just be alone, but now I could not have been happier to find out that we weren't. The track started to climb, and we saw more huts stretching up to a ridge. A small sign announced that this settlement went by the name of Tamlu. Ahead was a large white wooden church. A couple of other tracks branched off, and I noticed that one of the huts at the intersection had an open front and a counter with some bananas, biscuits, and what looked like a flask of tea standing on it. God bless Tamlu. We pulled up and almost fell off the bike, to the wide-eyed amusement of the rather attractive young lady who was standing behind the counter. Her jet-black hair was tied back in a tidy plait, and she was sporting a "Barcelona 1992 Olympics" T-shirt. We often saw people wearing such surprising shirts, dating from an event that had taken place in Europe or the US at least ten years previously. I thought how fascinating it would be to trace the paths that they had taken to end up there. I smiled at her and pointed at the bananas and biscuits then reached in my pocket for some money. I wished I had learned enough Nagamese to be able to explain our predicament, to at least confirm how many hours it was going to take us to get to the next town and somewhere we could stay for the night. As she handed me my change, I gave a polite nod and smile before gathering up the supplies to take back over to the bike.

"Excuse me, sir, where you from?"

I turned back in surprise. It was really too good to be true, "You speak English?"

She smiled shyly, "Oh a little, I am teacher before, in Sikkim."

"Oh fantastic! Well, I'm British actually. Very nice to meet you!"

She replied with a smile and then made an up and down inspection of me, Lady R, and the bike, all of which were absolutely filthy and looked on the verge of falling apart,

"May I be asking what you are doing here?" She frowned, as though already knowing that no answer I gave could possibly make any real sense.

"Sure, so we're on our way to, hmmm, the town of, what was it, something like, err, Mock-a-Long?"

Lady R kindly rescued me, "Mokokchung, we are on our way to Mokokchung to spend the night. Is it far?"

Our new friend thought for a bit, "Hmm, I am thinking maybe nine hours?"

I froze mid-bite of banana and stared at her in horror. She descended into a fit of giggles and raised her hands towards me, "No, no, wait, wait, maybe I am wrong!" She then called out to a friend across the street. This led, over the next twenty minutes, to a variety of estimates being put forward as various people in the village were consulted. They ranged from four to twelve hours. That kind of uncertainty had unfortunately become a common feature of the trip. Local people would often have very little idea of how long would be needed to travel to the next settlement simply because, unless they were bus or truck drivers, they made such trips so very rarely. Road conditions were so bad that you'd only travel if you had to, and transport options were few and far between. In addition, drive times could vary hugely, depending on the time of year and the weather of the preceding days. But in this case, even if the most optimistic estimate of four hours was right, we were still screwed.

Lady R and I started to argue about what we were going to do. As we got increasingly agitated, I saw our new friend waving towards us, "Please, please, no fight, you sleep with me tonight!"

Well that shut us both up. I turned to her and then amazed myself with how my Britishness persisted, even when it would get me the exact opposite of what I actually wanted, "Oh, that's so very kind if you, but really, we couldn't possibly."

Thankfully, Lady R saved me from myself, "He means we'd love to. Thank you so very much. You're a life saver."

And so, just like that, our predicament was solved. Around the back of the shop we were shown into a small dwelling with a dirt floor and a corrugated iron roof. The main room had a fire pit in the corner, where an elderly lady squatted, sorceress-like, stirring a bubbling cauldron.

"Now, my mother makes you dinner, maybe one hour, you can explore village while waiting?"

That was even better than the Hilton. We thanked her profusely and went out to take a walk along the main street, overjoyed to be free of the bike and the day's stress. We headed up to the church on the hilltop and watched the sun stain the sky a deep orange. I shivered for a moment as I thought how easily we could have still been out there alone in the encroaching darkness. Instead, there in the village we were greeted warmly by everyone we passed, and they all already knew exactly who we were. Nagaland was again feeling a whole lot less scary. I then spotted a handwritten note pinned to the church door:

> *DIRECTIVE—This is for information to all concerned that selling and using of deadly intoxicants, viz. wine, opium, ganga, are strictly prohibited. Any individual or group found dealing with the same will be strictly penalised with a sum of 50,000 Rupees only.*

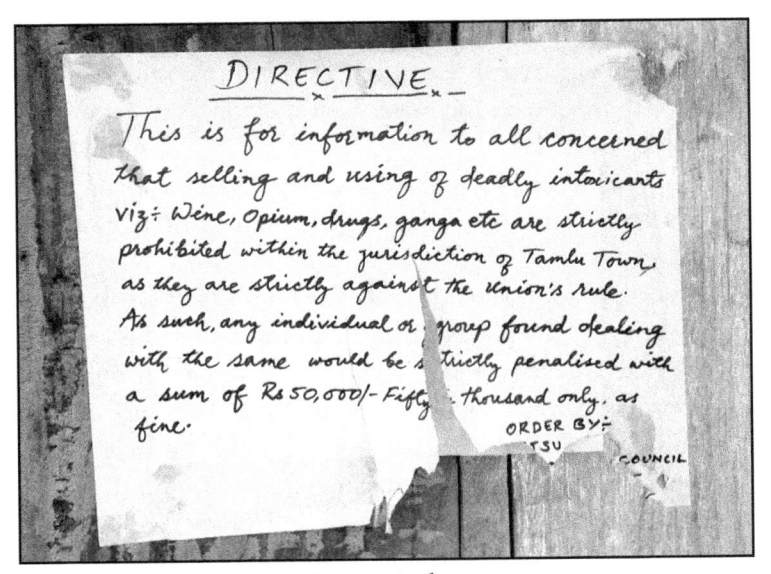

**Keeping it clean**

Well, praise be, there was even law and order up there too.
We arrived back home to the warm glow of the fire and two steaming plates of rice, vegetables, and chicken, though sadly, not accompanied by any wine, opium, or ganga. A

quiet dinner was out of the question however, as it appeared there hadn't been this much entertainment in Tamlu for quite some time. Every couple of minutes people ducked through the door and greeted us with curious laughter. They would then stand for a bit, stare at us and point, and discuss us with our hosts. A couple of children were pushed in and started crying at the sight of Lady R in all her blondeness. Then one old fellow a bit bolder than the rest came and squatted down next to us by the fire. He couldn't have been far short of ninety and was leaning heavily on his stick. His deeply lined face and gnarled hands told of decades of hard outdoor labour. He smiled to reveal his two remaining teeth, both stained dark red by years of betel nut chewing. But he shook my hand with surprising strength as he greeted me, "Good evening, sir; what your country?"

"Oh, you speak English?" Apart from our young host, he was the only other villager so far that we'd been able to converse with, "Well, I'm actually English myself, I must confess."

He slapped me on the knee, "Good, good, very good, may God bless the king!"

"Oh, yes, indeed, well let's hope so, eh?"

His eyes started sparkling a little, "You British come to Nagaland once before..."

"Ah yes, indeed, though that was no-one related to me, I can assure you," I replied quickly, recalling the vicious colonial British raids on Naga villages that I'd read about; the burnings and lootings, before they'd given up in the face of a superior foe.

He shook his head, "British are very good."

"Oh?" I waited for him to continue.

"British agree to give Nagaland independence, but," he paused and let out a deep sigh, "but then the Indians, they occupy us." I nodded sympathetically, and he carried on, "So only British can make India give our land back."

I coughed politely before replying, "Well, you know, our standing in the world is unfortunately not quite what it used to be I'm afraid. I mean in the last years some of the others have got a bit ahead of us really. I suppose we've rather let ourselves go..."

He brushed aside my doubts with a wave of his hand, "Nagas, we are different, you understand? We are not the same as these Indians. And we are poor, they give us nothing in fifty years."

"Yes, I understand that, it's a terrible situation, really..."

He was touching my knee again, "And so, when I hear you come to my village today, I decide to write a letter, a letter you must deliver to your king." He stopped and looked up at me beseechingly. That was something I really had not seen coming,

"Ah, err, OK, well thank you, yes, of course I'd be honoured to do so."

"My letter explains situation here. I know your king very busy, empire so very big. Nagaland, forgotten. But now he will remember. You give my letter and then..." he was grasping my shoulder and looking intently into my eyes, "then I know he will make India give us our freedom."

Even I was getting a bit teary-eyed, what with the passion of his entreaty, the length of his sixty-year struggle to see a free Nagaland, the trust he had in some random white guy delivering a letter to His Majesty, and the obviously rather poor state of media penetration in those parts.

"I promise I will do my best."

He shook my hand, "Thank you, Mr. Gentleman."

As the fire in the corner of the room started to subside, I felt my eyelids growing increasingly heavy and looked forlornly at our hosts. They smiled kindly and ushered us behind a partition, where a basic wooden bedstead stood, stacked with thick woollen blankets, and bid us good night. Within five minutes, I was snuggled under the covers, dimly aware of Lady R gently reprimanding me that the day had undoubtedly proven I really shouldn't fret so much, before I slipped into blissful unconsciousness.

The sound of happy old ladies cackling and the smell of wood smoke served as a rather pleasant alarm clock. We pulled off the blankets and creaked out of bed, bodies stiff and sore. There was no chance of a shower, and our clean clothes were buried in the bags on the back of the bike, which were themselves encrusted in mud and grime. Retrieving them would have involved getting even more dirty, so there really seemed no point, and we instead pulled on the previous day's filthy outfits again. We shuffled back into the main room where the ladies, all immaculately attired, greeted us with a chorus of greetings in a language we didn't understand and motioned us to sit down and wait for tea. The level of hospitality really was becoming quite overwhelming.

After a solid breakfast of rice and fried eggs, I wanted to get moving, as we had no idea what the road ahead was going to be like and how long it would take to finally reach the town we'd been aiming for the day before. I tried to give our hosts some money as a token of our appreciation for everything they'd done and an apology for our abject dirtiness, but they steadfastly refused to accept. As we went out to load up the bike, we found a couple of dozen villagers gathered, swathed in blankets to keep out the morning cold. They smiled and shook our hands and patted our backs, then started whooping as I kicked the engine alive and gave it a couple of theatrical revs. We were told in broken English that we would always have a home there, and I had to wipe a tear from my eye again.

The road was improving, hallelujah. A little mud still, yes, and broken rock in some places, but still a hundred times better than the previous day, and we were getting up to a mind-blowing twenty miles per hour in places. After a couple of hours, we saw some telegraph poles stretched across the horizon, and thirty minutes later, a tarmac road appeared ahead. As we swung onto the asphalt a local bus swept past with the passengers singing "In the name of Jesus, Every knee shall bow" in perfect harmony. It was Sunday, and they were on their way to church—thanks to the American Baptist missionaries who arrived in the late nineteenth century, a good portion of Nagas had converted from headhunting animists into gospel-loving Christians. Things were getting positively tame.

We had survived, but the bike sounded like it was on its last legs. The engine was shaking and rattling like hell, the exhaust was immensely loud, and the steering had developed a death wish, trying to take us off the side of the road at any opportunity. But, bless her, she still carried on. We rumbled through the small villages of the Naga hills, past brightly painted houses interspersed with huge banana plants and lines of villagers in their Sunday best heading off to the morning service. The benign, bucolic nature of it all was like passing into a different world. I started to take Lady R's advice and laugh at myself and my fears. Then we stopped for lunch at a roadside eatery, and I picked up a copy of the *Nagaland Post*, which took the smile right off my face again. No cosy lifestyle features in this Sunday edition, it was, instead, made up in its entirety of stories of banditry, bombings, and badasses, most of which were located in places we would soon be passing on our way to the Burmese border.

**Sobering news**

In Mokokchung we found a mechanic's shop and presented the bike for inspection. The boss took it for a quick spin and returned shaking his head. He then set about it with a spanner and a hammer. After twenty minutes, he sighed, wiped his brow, and told us we needed to get a proper service as soon as possible, but that we should be good for the next hundred miles. We pushed on and by sunset reached the outskirts of Kohima, the state capital. The town had a degree of infamy amongst Second World War buffs as the scene of one of the conflict's bloodiest encounters in the Eastern Theatre. The Battle of the Tennis Court, as it had become known, makes it sound like it was a rambling *Boys Own* adventure, some plucky young chaps going at one another with sporting equipment over Pimm's and only a few bruises to show for their trouble, but the reality had been far more gruesome. It was in Kohima that the British dug in after the Japanese had chased them westwards out of Burma. They then fought a bloody hand-to-hand battle over five days, centred on the Deputy Commissioner's bungalow or rather, to be more precise, his tennis court. Eventually, the Brits prevailed and overcame the Japanese, chasing them all the way back through Burma and cutting a road through the jungle as they did so; the very one which would, hopefully, enable our own passage through to Rangoon. The losses suffered in the epic battle were set in stone in a war cemetery on the edge of town that we passed on our way in, its archway bearing the inscription:

*"When You Go Home,*
*Tell Them Of Us And Say,*
*For Your Tomorrow,*
*We Gave Our Today."*

# 15
# Bombs and Bikers

Kohima, home to around 100,000 people, is sprawled across a series of ridges that we made our way up and down as we looked for somewhere to stay for the night. After being turned away from several establishments that should have been glad to have us, we eventually found a musty old guest house that had a bed free. It was rather damp, dirty and poorly lit, but it did have a hot shower and a bed and that was all we really cared about right now.

Back in the village, Mary had given us a number to call to contact the Naga Chiefs, an Enfield motorcycle club based in the town, and so the next morning I did exactly that.

"Hello?"

"Yes, hi, my name is Andy, and I got your number from Mary in . . . " I was immediately interrupted by the voice on the other end of the line,

"And you're riding a Bullet from Delhi to Rangoon, you crazy bloody bastard! Yes my man, we've been expecting you!"

**The Naga Chiefs' wheels**

There really was something to be said for this bush telegraph thing. We were immediately invited over to their clubhouse and workshop on the other side of town, where four of the Chiefs welcomed us warmly. We sat down for *chai* and regaled them with our adventures so far while their mechanic got to work on the bike. It was rather satisfying how incredulous they were when we recounted the route we'd taken over the past two days; they were simply unable to believe that any bike could possibly make it through. We asked them what the club got up to and, bracing ourselves for tales of drunken mayhem and protection rackets, were pleasantly surprised to hear that most of their time was spent doing charity runs to deliver medicines to remote villages and raising funds to build new schools and hospitals. In Nagaland, it seemed, it was the motorcycle gangs who took care of you and the police who struck fear into your heart.

Once we had been fully serviced, the Chiefs kindly escorted us to the start of the Highway of Sorrows, that mournful road that had been mentioned to us by the kindly Indian diplomat way back in Rangoon. I turned to the nearest Chief as we pulled over to say our goodbyes, "So, we've heard a few rumours about this next stretch of road, but we should be OK, right?"

**The Naga Chiefs**

He whistled softly, "Ah man, well, to be honest, it isn't so safe."

"Right. So, there are often, what, ambushes, hold ups?"

He nodded, "Yeah, last one was last night in fact, two buses taken at gunpoint, all passengers robbed. But only the driver got shot."

"Oh well, that doesn't sound so bad then!" chipped in Lady R, visibly perking up.

Just outside the Kohima city limits we crossed the state line and passed from Nagaland into Manipur. It would be about a three-hour journey down the Highway to reach Imphal, the state capital. The road surface was at least decent, so we could move at a decent clip, but there were lots of tight corners, which meant setting up an ambush would be rather simple. There was also very, very little other traffic, which didn't really help me feel more secure. Suddenly, I heard a siren up ahead. As I started to slow down, an armoured personnel carrier appeared around the corner hurtling down the road the other way with the top half of a soldier peeking out of its turret. He was sporting a leather flying cap and goggles and screaming at the top of his voice for us to pull off the road. I swerved to the side as they swept past. A car with government number plates was following close behind them. As it sunk in that we had just witnessed the level of security public officials felt they needed to travel along that road, I recalled the advice we'd gotten from the authorities back in Delhi on having an armed escort. Well, it was too late now.

But we continued unhindered for the next couple of hours, and then the road straightened up as we came out of the hills and started to pass through a few villages. The presence of people and a clear view of the way ahead was reassuring, and as dusk fell, we safely reached the outskirts of Imphal and I breathed a sigh of relief. Imphal, however, was not exactly a haven of tranquillity. There had been bombings and shootings every couple of weeks recently as the Indian Army battled it out with a plethora of insurgency groups and criminal gangs that used the place as a base. We'd been told to make sure we arrived before sunset, go straight to our hotel, lock ourselves in, and leave town early in the morning. Sounded good to me.

I ignored the incessant horning and shouting behind me at first as we made our way towards the centre, but it just went on and on. Finally, I shot a look backwards over my shoulder and saw that there were two other Enfields close behind, two guys on each. I shouted back at them, doing my best impression of an authoritative tone, "Hey! What? What the hell do you want?"

One of the bikes came alongside us, "You are Mr. Andy, yes?"

Surely this couldn't be happening, "Ah, yes, actually I am, but sorry, who are you?"

"Oh, we are Royal Riders Motorcycle Club of Imphal, and we come to escort you into town, give you security!"

I laughed in surprise and gave them a thumbs up as I went through an emotional 180-degree turn. Two more bikes joined us at the next intersection, saluting me as they drew alongside. It seemed the Naga Chiefs had passed the word down the line to Imphal's finest (and only) biker club that we were on the way, and so they'd ridden out to pick us up, God bless them. We roared through the streets brimming with confidence as the traffic parted to let our posse through. When we arrived at our hotel, our new friends waited in the lobby for us to check in, the other guests eyeing them suspiciously and presumably wondering if we were staying there under duress. The guys then asked us if we'd like to go around town with them that evening. We recalled the warnings about staying locked up during the night hours, but well, that didn't take into account having your very own local biker gang escort now, did it?

It was also the night of Diwali, which made things rather more interesting. Diwali is the Indian festival of lights and a couple of decades ago was a gentle, candle-lit celebration of the victory of light over darkness and good over evil. Now though, it's a fearsome, all-out firework fest, where anyone and everyone lets off firecrackers and rockets for the whole night. When you are located somewhere that's plagued by bombings and shootings, this makes it rather difficult to know which are the good bangs and which are the bad ones.

We cruised through the streets, now eight Enfields in total, our combined engines making a low, loud, head-turning growl. As explosions went off around us and we tried to convince ourselves they were all of a celebratory nature, we passed sandbagged machine gun posts and armoured personnel carriers on the prowl. An army foot patrol had four young men spread-eagled against a wall, guns trained on them. It had the distinct feel of a city under occupation.

**Security patrol**

We stopped off at the Royal Riders' clubhouse and met some of the other boys, many of whom were ex-cons or drug dealers whose reformed passion was the Enfield Bullet. They were gentlemen to a fault, and like the Naga Chiefs, their main club activity seemed to be charity, getting medical supplies into remote villages and filling the void left by the failed state. As we chatted over a few beers, they asked if we'd like to come to a festival, and we quickly agreed. I was expecting a fairly feisty collection of bikers, rock bands, and copious amounts of cider. So I was rather bemused when fifteen minutes later we rolled up at the entrance to the Ninth Annual Manipur Food Festival. We parked up and, perhaps uniquely for any food festival in the world, had to pass through metal detectors, get a thorough pat down, and then follow two soldiers with submachine guns to the entrance of the main tent. Our biker friends looked quite unperturbed, though, and told us that level of security at public events was quite the norm in Manipur.

We had a walk around, stopping at various stalls, each hosted by a different ethnic group. *Naga* is actually just a rather convenient word to amalgamate many of the tribes in the region, and there we had the chance to meet Ao, Konyak, Angami, Tangkhul, Mao, and probably many more, but the strength of the local fire water served up at the Mao stall unfortunately erased my memory of any of the names that came after. There was a stage in the centre of the tent, and a procession of amateur singers and musicians stepped up to get their fifteen minutes of fame. By that point I was leaning rather heavily on Lady R as I tried to get my vision back.

"Hey Andy!" Eddy, the cheekiest of the Riders, was tugging at my sleeve.

"Yes?"

"You like the music, man?"

"Oh, it's marvellous really, very much enjoyable."

"You play yourself, right?"

"Oh, I strum a little guitar on occasion, but you know, just for fun. I try not to inflict it on anyone else." Lady R nodded sagely.

"Oh well, now's your chance, man! You're up next"

I looked at him blankly, "What?"

"You're next, man. I volunteered you to go perform. Hey, it'll be fun, we love that white man's music here!"

Had I been any less drunk, I would have feigned injury, a sudden voice impediment, or the loss of a close family member, but my brain was a bit too foggy for that, and so before I knew it I was being dragged up onto the stage. I was plonked on a stool to loud applause, and a guitar was thrust into my arms. I looked out into the crowd and forced a smile. It seemed there was nothing else for it,

"Well, good evening ladies and gentlemen, this one is dedicated to my beautiful lady wife."

I saw Lady R smile and blush as I launched into a just-about-passable rendition of Adele's *Someone Like You*. It seemed to go down OK, and there was a decent round of applause at the end, so I rose and made several bows. I was starting to quite enjoy myself and prepared to follow up with a splash of Bon Jovi when someone gently escorted me off the stage.

**Serenading the Food Festival**

My thirty-eighth birthday, really not a very pleasant thought to wake up to, but at least I was going to be spending it trying to cross the officially closed India-Burma border on a motorcycle, as opposed to buying a sports car or starting a ridiculous relationship with a totally unsuitable woman who was years younger than me. Hang on a minute. Lady R kindly brought me breakfast in bed, and we cuddled together for a bit and laughed nervously about the day ahead. She, of course, was still blissfully unaware that the Burmese government had only granted permission to one of us to cross the border. It was really make or break time for our whole adventure, and I was going to need all the birthday luck I could get.

Finding we had a rear wheel puncture before we even left the hotel did not seem a very good omen. I did what any self-respecting man would do in such a situation and called someone else to help. Within five minutes, one of the Royal Riders was with us and making arrangements to have it fixed. Twenty minutes later, we were good to go. It was an ominous reminder, though, that the external help that saved us from our technical ineptitude would, in a matter of hours, be a thing of the past. In India, Nepal, and Bhutan, where Enfields are ubiquitous, a skilled mechanic is never that far away and spare parts are on offer in every small town, so we were never really that far from help whenever we broke down, no matter how much of a pain it had been some of the time. But in Burma we'd have the only Enfield in the country, so we were going to be pretty much buggered if it stopped working.

For the moment, though, it was time to enjoy our last dose of Indian biker camaraderie as ten Royal Riders escorted us majestically through town. We passed a cow munching through a mound of rubbish by the roadside, nothing new in itself, but this one was sporting a garland of bright orange flowers, something I'd never seen before. On enquiring as to why this might be, I was informed that it was not only my birthday but also, and rather more importantly, Holy Cow Day.

At the outskirts of the city, we pulled over for hugs and firm handshakes and then we were on our own again, hearts beating fast. The Riders had told us that the final stretch of thirty miles or so to the border was notorious bandit and smuggler country. But it started out on the flat, with everything looking pretty normal as we hummed along through small towns and peaceful fields with a fair bit of other traffic. I had just started to relax a little when the road narrowed and we started climbing into the hills. In a couple of minutes, all signs of human activity and other traffic had completely melted away. A large sign loomed up by the roadside which we stopped to read:

*1. You Are Advised and Cautioned Not to Pay Any Money to Anyone in Uniform or Underground Groups.
2. If Any Persons Found or Caught Doing So Will be Prosecuted as Per Law.
3. If You Are Being Forced and Harassed You May Contact The Following Numbers:*

It then listed two local mobile phone numbers. That sounded like inspired advice—if we got held up and money was demanded, we'd just tell our persecutors about this very sign, and if they carried on insisting, why, I would simply take out my phone and call the police while they stood there pointing their guns at us. I couldn't see what could possibly go wrong.

We continued upwards, nervous as hell and wallets at the ready, twisting and turning on the narrow tarmac road, thick jungle all around us. Occasionally we overtook an Indian army truck, with troops eyeing us suspiciously from the back, rifles cradled on their knees. Half way to the border the road passed an Assam Rifles camp, shrouded in razor wire and guarded by sentries, a wooden placard strung to the fence proclaiming they were "Bringing Peace to the Hill People." A couple of soldiers and a few oil drums blocked the road ahead. As we pulled up, one of the soldiers came up with his palm outstretched towards us, "No, no, no. Must turn around. This way only Burma."

I gave my politest, most diplomatic smile, "Yes we know. We are on our way there."

He snorted and shook his head, "No, not possible, nobody can."

I reached inside my jacket and pulled out the muddy, greasy, crumpled letter from the Burmese Ministry of Foreign Affairs that gave us permission to cross the border. They'd emailed that to me a few days back, and although I'd been quite delighted at the time, I then realised that the fact that it was written in Burmese meant it might be rather useless until we actually reached the other side of the border. The officer looked at the paper as I explained it was a special permission to cross and pointed to the Burmese government crest at the top, which at least had the name of the country written in English. He frowned and shook his head, "I am not sure about this; it is first time."

I nodded sympathetically, "Yes, absolutely, I understand, but really this says we have exceptional leave from the Burmese government to cross, and well, I'm sure you wouldn't want to cause a diplomatic incident by blocking us now, would you?"

He looked uncertain for a second, opened his mouth then closed it again, and finally handed the paper back, "OK you continue and ask at next roadblock; they decide."

After another forty-five minutes, we reached the outskirts of the frontier town of Moreh and were flagged down again by the army. I confidently tried the same line but this time was laughed at, "Nobody can cross; border is closed!"

I nodded sympathetically, "Yes, but as I said, we have a special permission, so long as you let us out, then the Burmese will let us in, no problem!"

"Is not possible."

I felt the adrenaline starting to pump inside me. God, we were so close; all that effort, it was not going to be for nothing; this one solider wasn't going to stop me now. So, bugger diplomacy, it was time for some bare-faced deceit, "I understand that normally no, but this time yes. We have confirmation from your Foreign Minister, who we met in Delhi."

He eyed our dirty selves and our decrepit bike up and down doubtfully; we clearly didn't look like any kind of VIPs he'd ever seen. But then it seemed he decided to err on the side of caution. He spat some betel nut out of the side of his mouth and waved his hand at me dismissively, "Well, if you want to make more trouble for yourself, OK, you go into town and Special Branch will deal with you . . . They are telling you same same, I guarantee," he paused and smiled sarcastically, "Only they will be asking more questions and keeping you there until you are giving good answers."

"That sounds perfect," I replied, already planning my upcoming denial of everything I'd just said, "So, where can we find them?"

He snorted, "They're Special Branch; they will find you."

Rather than a bustling border town, buzzing with trucks and trade, Moreh turned out to be a small and rather shambolic outpost of grubby streets and shabby shops. We stopped outside a teashop, ordered a brew, and waited to be found. Within five minutes, a rather shifty looking skinny chap in jeans, a dirty T-shirt, and sandals sauntered up and asked us to come with him. I asked for some ID, which he flashed at me with a sigh and an eye roll. After taking us to a small shop to photocopy our passports, he led us up a side road into a police compound and pointed towards a run-down office. We went in and sat down on a wooden bench next to a table covered in papers, waiting for something to happen. A few minutes later the door opened, "*Namaste*! I am Kunal!"

An amply-proportioned middle-aged man dressed from head to toe in khaki and sporting a freshly-waxed moustache stood in the doorway smiling at us, while mopping his forehead with a handkerchief,

"Welcome, welcome to my office! An honour to have foreign visitors here down in this backwater!"

We greeted him warmly, relieved to be in the company of someone who seemed to be friendly, hospitable, and so far, showing no intentions of putting us in jail. He sat down behind his desk and leaned over towards us, clasping his hands together, "So, what brings you here, friends?"

I took a deep breath; this really was the final showdown, "Well, we're on our way to Burma, and we're well aware the border is normally closed, but you see, we already have a special permission from the Burmese to come in." I produced the crumpled letter once again. "So all you need to do really is just let us out, I mean hopefully that might not be too much trouble?" I thought of adding a suggestion that we could possibly "facilitate" his assistance in some way but decided it was better to leave that as a final option. Kunal stroked his moustache and frowned as he considered what I had just said, "Let's have some tea."

Well, at least it wasn't a straight no. He rang an old-fashioned brass bell that was sitting on his desk, and after a couple of moments, a boy of maybe seven arrived with a tray of glasses brimming with sweet, milky *chai*. We sat and sipped while Kunal questioned us about our trip, appearing to be genuinely interested in the places we'd passed through and the adventures that had befallen us. He explained that he used to be based in the state capital of Imphal, where we'd just come from, but had been posted in Moreh for a year or two and was very much missing his family. I felt the best option then was to become good friends with this man, and there is no better way to do that in India than asking about family. Three quarters of an hour later, as we concluded a discussion about potentially suitable university courses for his third niece, I ventured to try my hand at the main order of business again, "So, for the border crossing, what do you think we should do?"

He looked confused for a few seconds, as though he'd completely forgotten why we were there,

"Oh yes, right, OK, hmm, a fine question." He thought for a moment or two, and then his face brightened, "Tell you what, I'll send a couple of the boys down to the Burmese border post to tell them about you and that letter, and we'll see what they say!"

I broke out into an extremely broad grin, "That sounds like a fantastic idea. Thank you so much!"

He picked up the phone and barked some instructions, "OK, all is well, they are popping down there now only." He considered for a second and then continued, "Thing is those damn Burmese really don't speak much English; leads to a lot of problems."

I looked at him in surprise, it seemed unbelievable that guards on either side of an international border, and a very sensitive one at that, were unable to converse with one another in a common language, "Oh, wow, but OK, I guess generally relations between you and the Burmese are OK?"

Kunal laughed dryly and shook his head, "Oh no, I wouldn't say that, no I wouldn't say that at all. They are, well, a little tricky you know?"

This was sounding rather interesting, "Ah really, how so?"

At that moment the phone rang, and Kunal raised a hand as he answered and then spent a few minutes talking in Hindi to who I presumed was one of his superiors in Imphal, given his very respectful tone and frequent use of the honorific *ji*. After he'd finished up, he replaced the receiver and took a sip of tea, "Now, where were we? Ah yes, the tricky buggers over the border. Well, as you will be being aware, we have a problem here with a few fighting groups, guerrilla types and such. They are going around robbing and shooting while pretending they are freedom fighters." I nodded sympathetically, and he continued, "And the damn Burmese, they shelter them, they let them put up over there, and then these bloody boys sneak back over the border and raid into India, then scuttling back to Burma again before we can catch them. Not a damned thing we can do about it!"

I had another ten questions lined up, but before I could get started, there was a knock on the door and a breathless teenager poked his head into the room. Kunal raised his chin in enquiry, and the youth replied by grinning and giving a thumbs up.

"Well my goodness!" he exclaimed as he clapped his hands together, "it seems you're in luck!" He pondered for a few seconds, "but very probably they are not understanding what we are asking and will turn you back."

He dusted off his stamp, in any case, and smacked it down reassuringly on our passports, officially checking us out of India. He then shook our hands and told us to follow two of his men on their motorbike, who would take us down to the border post. We mounted up and rode behind our escorts to the edge of town, where we were promptly stopped at an army roadblock. A robust, stern looking gentleman in camouflage rose from behind his sandbags and approached us. I rummaged for my passport, praying that we were not going to get halted by the very last person in India that we had to deal with. But he waved for me to stop what I was doing with a smile, "No, no, photo, photo!"

I breathed a sigh of relief, laughed and stopped to pose for a selfie.

We were riding through deserted no-man's land, not in India nor in Burma. Our escorts suddenly swerved across to the other side of the road and motioned for us to do the same. I was confused for a second, given the lack of any other traffic, but then realised that, of course, in Burma they drive on the other side of the road, and so halfway across no man's land, we needed to follow decent diplomatic protocol and do the same. We came around a final corner and there it was in front of us. And it was just how borders should be—a narrow iron bridge extending across a river and on the other side, patrolling up and down with a rifle slung over his shoulder, a lone, olive-clad Burmese soldier. A glittering golden pagoda rose out of the jungle in the distance behind him. Our escorts pulled up and reached over to shake our hands, grinning broadly, "Goodbye and good luck; we are hoping you get in!"

I laughed, "Thanks! Well if they say no, then we might be seeing you again quite soon!"

He shook his head vigorously, "Oh no sir, not possible, you already leave India now. Need new visa if want to come back and must be getting from embassy only."

I had not really thought about that until then. So, if the Burmese held good on their promise to not let Lady R in, then she really would be in a bit of a pickle, stuck on the bridge between two countries forever. That was going to take some explaining to her family.

# 16
## THE GOLDEN LAND

As we got half way across the bridge, the soldier on the other side stopped pacing and turned to look at us, stony faced. His hand was now on the barrel of the rifle that was hanging off of his shoulder, as though in preparation to level it at us. I got ready to brake and raise my hands, but he suddenly snapped his legs together and swooped his other hand up in a smart salute. I couldn't help but immediately reciprocate, accompanied by an ear to ear grin. We clattered onto Burmese soil, and I pulled up and turned off the engine. The soldier was a couple of metres away, still standing to attention. Then I heard a voice from my other side, "Ah, Mr. Benfield I presume? We have been expecting you. Welcome to Burma!"

An immigration officer in an immaculate white shirt and trousers had emerged from a small wooden building a few metres away that I hadn't spotted before and was now approaching us beaming with an outstretched arm. I greeted him warmly, determined to bond as quickly and firmly as possible with the man who held our immediate future and, indeed, the success of our whole adventure in his hands. He asked us to follow him to his office.

**Finally ... Burma!**

The room was dimly lit, and every available surface was covered in piles of papers that were in turn covered in dust. The teak floor creaked and groaned as we made our way over to two worn leather armchairs that he directed us to sit down on in front of a heavy wooden desk, where a number of dossiers were laid out, each neatly bound with a length of string.

"So, now, Mr. Benfield, as you may know, I have received the official notification DE54782, err . . . ", he consulted one of the dossiers, " . . . slash, 3, yes, that's it, slash 3, from the Ministry of Foreign Affairs in Nay Pyi Taw just last Tuesday." He looked at me expectantly, and I nodded and smiled. He then carefully opened the dossier to quote the contents:

> *"This is alerting to the arrival of one Special Alien and giving exceptional permission to waive usual prohibition on border crossing."*

He read a little further then frowned in apparent concern. I crossed my fingers. He coughed, "Please give me a minute. Would you care for some tea while I check this?"

We readily agreed, and a pot and cups promptly appeared, this time it was the refreshing Chinese green variety beloved of Burma, instead of the sweet milky *chai* of India. As we sipped away, our friend worked methodically through the dossiers on his desk while talking to himself under his breath, checking, well, we weren't quite sure what. No doubt the special instruction from his bosses in the capital and the fact that we were the first foreigners to cross the border were making him especially careful. Normally he'd only be dealing with Indian traders, whose permissions would be limited to day visits to the border town.

Several other officials appeared at intervals, coming to shake our hands and then indulging in earnest conversations with our friend. After an hour or so, I was starting to doze off, when a polite cough from across the desk roused me, "Mr. Andy, all is in order for you."

I was immediately wide awake again, "Oh, really? Well, wonderful, thank you so much!"

But he looked apologetic as he continued, "All is in order for you, yes . . . I am afraid, however, not for your companion."

The smile froze on my face, and I decided to feign ignorance, "I'm sorry; how do you mean?"

He coughed politely, "Well, you see, we only have permission for one person and one motorcycle. But today we have two people and one motorcycle. So this is not OK. Only one person and one motorcycle will enter Burma."

I nodded before I started my objection, "Ah yes I see your point, but she is my, err, wife, and therefore, in fact, we are one person in the eyes of the law of our country, you see, inseparable in the eyes of God," I paused then quickly added, "and Buddha."

Lady R nodded empathically, and amazingly, he seemed to give my line of spurious reasoning serious consideration as he steepled his fingers and looked up at the ceiling. After a few moments, he let out a sigh, "Well, yes, I suppose I can understand."

I got up to shake his hand, "Great! So, we're good. Thank you so much for your help!"

He raised his palm towards me, "No, no, no, I mean I do see your point in theory, but it is not my opinion that counts. I will need to call my superiors in Nay Pyi Taw."

I sat back down deflated. I couldn't imagine any way Nay Pyi Taw were going to change the firm line they'd given me on the phone just a few days before. I started wondering if they had a tent Lady R could use on the bridge.

He got up and walked over to where an old rotary-dial Bakelite telephone sat on a table on top of a specially placed lace doily. He took out his handkerchief and carefully wiped the receiver down before laboriously dialling the number of the Ministry. After a minute or so, he turned to us and smiled, "Telephone connection not so good in Burma."

Thank God.

"Let me try again."

He hung and up and re-dialled. That time he did, unfortunately, get through and spoke briskly in Burmese to someone for a couple of minutes before hanging up and turning back to us, "I'm afraid the person I need to speak is not reachable in Nay Pyi Taw right now; he has gone out of station." He took a deep breath, and I could see the battle going on behind his eyes, between traditional Burmese hospitality and bureaucratic rigour. Finally, he sighed and smiled, "Well, in such cases I suppose I might justify making an ad hoc ruling on the ground . . . " I nodded vigorously, keen to encourage more decentralised decision-making in the new Burma. "And of course, you are an Englishman and a gentleman." I nodded even more vigorously and held my breath as he hesitated again, "OK, OK, you are both welcome to enter our country."

I let out an impromptu whoop and jumped up to hug him in a distinctly ungentlemanly manner, "But," he continued, once I had let him go, "should Nay Pyi Taw later advise that this is not the proper decision, then we will, of course, need to arrange deportation."

I gulped and nodded again, "Yes, of course, naturally."

I immediately decided that we needed to put as much distance between ourselves and our friend and his colleagues as fast as possible. Meanwhile, Lady R beamed at me, followed by an I-told-you-not-to-worry-too-much-you-idiot expression, which I was really tempted to wipe off her face by telling her what they'd said to me on the phone a few days previously. I then thought better of it, especially given we were still in the immigration office.

With our passports now proudly displaying their final stamp, I reached out to shake hands with our saviour, "Thank you so, so much. So may we go now?"

He beamed back, "My pleasure, and yes, absolutely. The policemen will now show you to your hotel for the night."

That was the exact opposite of what I wanted. But he insisted it would not be safe for us to travel onwards in the dark, and so we dutifully saddled up and followed our two police chaperones on their moped along a narrow road through the jungle. On arriving at the dilapidated lime-green block that had optimistically been labelled a hotel, we thanked our escorts, who informed us they'd be very, very close by should we need anything.

After showering and changing into fresh clothes, it was time to go find some birthday dinner. As we were about to exit the compound, I spotted the two policemen sitting at a tea shop across the road, so we decided to slip out the back way instead. Tamu was really a small village that seemed to be about fifty years back in time from the Indian side. The streets

He shook his head vigorously, "Ah no, this only warm up, then we go to party!"

Lady R picked this moment to chime in, "Oh how lovely, well it's Andy's birthday this evening, so you simply must invite us too!"

Our friend was suitably encouraged, "Oh, you will be most welcome. You are not minding some jungle walking, no?"

Lady R gave one of her little claps, "Oh no, I just love walking in the jungle at night!"

I shook my head at her in disbelief; only a couple of hours ago we were being told about the Indian militant groups that had bases in the immediate vicinity, and now she wanted to go roaming around in the bushes after dark with a bunch of complete strangers. However, the final straw was yet to come, "So, how far is it?" asked Lady R excitedly.

"Hmm, well maybe twenty minutes' walking, then cross the river in small boat to India, then maybe twenty more minutes."

I intervened, "Sorry, so you mean cross the border illegally?"

He winked at me, "Oh yes sir, is only way!"

It being my birthday, I was eventually able to prevail and convince Lady R that we really should head back to the hotel rather than out on another adventure, especially one that put at risk the crowning achievement of the trip. To make it up to her, when we arrived a little tipsily at the lobby half an hour later, I picked up a guitar that was propped against the reception desk and treated her to a slightly off-key performance of a couple of country and western classics before bedtime, which to her credit, she quite convincingly pretended to enjoy.

Fish soup for breakfast takes a little getting used to. *Mohinga*, as it's known, is the Burmese morning staple, and thrown in with the fish are some rice noodles, garlic, lemongrass, and ginger for good measure. We were in an open-fronted tea-shop, ubiquitous across the country, sitting astride tiny plastic stools, being warmed by the morning sun as we slurped our breakfast broth. Though the Burmese are no different in stature from any of their neighbouring countrymen, for some reason, tea-shop furniture always consists of stools that stand maybe fifty centimetres above the ground set around tables just a few centimetres higher. It makes them look for all the world like dolls' houses frequented by giants. But as one of the very few legitimate places of social gathering in a country that has in the past banned more than four people meeting at once in order to contain any potential opposition, tea shops have had a serious role. They've acted as a hub for undercover political activism, a place where, under the guise of having a drink with a friend, you could actually be spreading news and hatching plans with the people on the next table, while of course, always keeping an eye out for the man reading the paper in the corner, knowing he could well be a government spy.

A line of young, barefooted Buddhist monks passed us as they made their morning procession along the streets, chanting softly with their alms bowls cradled in front of them. Buddhism is central to traditional Burmese notions of identity, and the military had often justified their rule by claiming they were safeguarding the country's main religion from external threats. So when the revered monks themselves started complaining, the army had a problem. That's exactly what happened in 2007, when the Generals decided to remove fuel subsidies, which led to prices shooting up and mass protests across the country, protests that, crucially, the monks joined, presenting a powerful symbol of dissent at the front of the crowds with their alms bowls turned upside down. They also announced they were going to stop providing religious services to the soldiers. While the military did manage to eventually suppress the protests, they realised they were going to have to change tack in future, as their claims to legitimacy were under serious threat. A page had been turned in Burmese history, and it was the start of a long path of opening up, which would eventually culminate in democratic elections.

It would have been all too easy to just spend the whole day there at the teashop watching the gentle Burmese world go by, but that deportation comment was still ringing in my ears and I wanted to start making tracks. The final leg of the journey we hadn't really prepared at all in terms of routes, distances, or where we might stay for the night; it had been such a distant and unlikely prospect to make it that far that it didn't seem to warrant our attention before the trip. What we did know was that Rangoon was a few days to the south east. Back at the hotel, Lady R informed me that there was only one road out of town, unless we wanted to go back into India, so the first bit was easy enough. As we packed up the bike, I looked around for signs of our minders, but they seemed to have melted away during the night. We were thus able to slip out of town unobserved, and I started to relax a little as we left the last pagoda on the outskirts behind us. But around the next corner, just before a small bridge, a police checkpoint appeared and we were waved down. I pulled over and reached for our documents, prepared at best for a lengthy explanation, if they didn't know who we were, or to be detained, if they did, as I feared by now our friend in immigration would have reached Nay Pyi Taw. The policeman waved back my hand holding our passports, "No need, we know who you are, Mr. Andy."

I smiled and braced for it, "Yes, that's right, so is there something we can do for you, officer?"

"Yes, you give us what we want."

Either that meant Lady R or it meant a bribe. I decided to gamble on the latter, "I think I understand what you mean," I reached into my pocket for my wallet, but he looked puzzled as I drew it out and pointed to the mobile phone in his hand instead, "Photo, photo!"

I looked at him in surprise, "You just want a photo with us?"

"Yes, most certainly!" I shook my head in relieved disbelief, "It would be the least we could do." We arranged ourselves around the bike with him while he shot a couple of selfies, grinning manically. After a hearty handshake, he wished us a safe journey and we were allowed to carry on. We'd made it out of Tamu and hopefully with each passing mile would pass a little further into obscurity.

As in Nepal and Bhutan, a number of signs proudly informed us that the road we were on was a gift from the Indian Border Roads Organisation. The Indians had also supplied some rather delightful road safety signs, a little more racy than their western counterparts, including "Go Gently Round my Curves," "After Whisky Driving Risky," and the simply outrageous "Stop Nagging and Let Him Drive."

**After Whisky, Driving Risky**

The road was also refreshingly clear of other traffic, just the occasional bullock cart or bicycle, a world apart from the crazy buses and trucks on the other side of the border. There were, however, a lot of rivers, and we crossed dozens of iron and wood bridges that the Indians hadn't been kind enough to work on. Some were relatively benign, if still very old, while others were quite terrifying as they creaked and sagged alarmingly with the planking jolting up and down under our wheels as we gingerly made our way across.

## The Golden Land

Burmese has its own script, and English signs are rare (beyond the Indian road safety ones), so a placard proclaiming the "Office of the Thado Literature and Culture Committee" easily caught our eyes. Curiosity got the better of us, and we decided to stop for a look. I pulled in and killed the engine, and we dismounted and strolled over towards the porch of a large, rambling old house. A young lady dressed in a floral skirt and crisp cream blouse stepped out and smiled at us, "Oh hello! Welcome! Tea?"

I gave in immediately, "Well, good morning! That's awfully kind of you, please, don't mind if we do!"

She nodded and ushered us inside to a large open room with a variety of paintings and certificates on the walls and two large sofas set around a coffee table covered in books and pamphlets, where we were motioned to sit down. A young man and an older lady emerged from an adjoining room, giggling as they eyed us up and down. I thought I'd better break the ice, "I'm afraid this is terribly rude of us, but well, we saw your sign outside, and I'm afraid we don't really know who the Thado, I mean, presumably, err, you, are, so we thought we'd better pop in and find out."

**Office of the Thado Literature and Culture Committee**

The older lady grinned warmly as she came to sit down opposite us and gave me a grandmotherly pat on the knee, "Yes, yes, and so you should! We are Thado, and we are proud! Actually, we are a tribe, and a Christian tribe, just like you."

We'd got used to the assumption that all white people were Christians and, if it helped with local bonding, then, well, praise Jesus. Lady R's adventure antenna was up, and I could see she was dying to get started on a thorough interrogation. If we were really lucky then they'd also be involved in an armed resistance movement. She leaned in, "Oh, I see, and so Thado are just found around here?"

Grandmother tutted, "No, no, no my dear. Thado we are all across north-east India as well as a little in Burma but, you know, we are neither Indian or Burmese," she looked from Lady R to me with a sparkling but firm gaze, "We are the one and only Thado, own language, own tradition!"

Her face then folded into a frown, "But we have many problems."

I nodded with concern and took a sip of tea, "I'm sorry to hear that. Is it the government?"

I got another slap on the knee as she replied triumphantly, "It's you, the British!"

Oh God, here we went again, was there no group we hadn't abused in Asia at some point in the past?

I bowed my head, "My sincere apologies, madam."

She cackled adorably, "Well, some time back now, you know, we made uprising against you in India in, hmmm, maybe 1917, because you want us to go and fight your war far away in Europe."

I really had to cringe at that. And to think these days we went around the world preaching about human rights. I shook my head, "That really is bad, well, I can totally understand why you took up arms."

She nodded, "Ah yes, but you were too strong for us. And nowadays same story, but different people. Now it's the Burmese and the Indians who oppress us . . . " she gestured towards the direction of the border and then tailed off. The young man next to her took her hand and then piped up, "So, yes, here we are, last bastion of the Thado, trying to keep our people and traditions alive!"

He reached across and handed me a small pamphlet, "Here you are, sir; this can teach you further aspects of our culture that we are trying to preserve."

I took it eagerly, "Well thank you, I shall certainly read it with great interest," I smiled at him, "And may I say you speak really excellent English. I guess the schools around here must be pretty good!"

He laughed, "Oh, no sir, this is thanks to KL only."

"I'm sorry?"

"KL, Kuala Lumpur; you know it?"

I looked at him in slight confusion, "Right, yes, I am familiar with the city but, sorry, what is the connection?"

He in turn looked at me like I was a bit slow, "Well we all go to work there in Malaysia of course!"

That seemed rather far-fetched given our location. But he then explained that many of the young people from that and neighbouring villages followed a long and dangerous route to get to Malaysia illegally, first overland to the Burmese coast and then onwards by ship. If they managed it, then they looked for work, which was, by definition, against the law, given they had no papers or permits and thus opened them to both abuse from their employers and detention or worse by the authorities. If they could avoid both of those, they'd spend a couple of years in KL, save far more money than they could hope for in a decade of working in Burma, then head back home again to help their families. Here was the darker side of globalisation.

We made a sizeable donation to the Office of the Thado Literature and Culture Committee as we left, and my heart went out to yet another lost and forgotten group of people struggling to maintain their identity and basic freedoms in a world of much bigger fish that continually threatened their very existence.

# 17
# POLICE STATE

A sign ahead announced we were crossing the Tropic of Cancer, which in the absence of any other writing we could read, at least reassured us that we were heading in the right direction—south. By lunch time we were drawing into the bustling market town of Kale. We passed a number of large, opulent houses that rather stood out from their more modest neighbours. Lady R latched onto the anomaly, and ten minutes of Googling later, she whacked the back of my helmet to tell me she had something interesting to say. She'd discovered that the root cause of the unexpected displays of wealth was, rather bizarrely, the poor regulation of Indian pharmacies. That meant that, for a little tea money, one could easily obtain prescription medication on the other side of the border without a real prescription. And that included pills for treating a cold; more precisely those that contain pseudoephedrine, which just happens to also be the main ingredient for making methamphetamine, a drug that's become increasingly popular in South East Asia in recent years. Some enterprising people in Kale were, allegedly, organising to buy the pills in India, smuggle them across the border into Burma (where you couldn't find them for love nor money), and then transport them to jungle labs in the lawless borderlands of the country's far east. There they'd be turned into meth and then run into the lucrative markets of Thailand and China. Being such a vital ingredient, and one that could only be sourced in India, the little pills magically jump ten times in value once they have been spirited across the border. That can, evidently, buy you an awful lot of neo-gothic columns, mirrored blue windows, and tasteful marble cladding.

**The Tropic of Cancer**

While the popularity of meth and the lucrative smuggling route are fairly new phenomena, narcotics are nothing new to Burma, something for which we can, once again, blame the British. It was the erstwhile colonial power that introduced opium into the country, setting up a monopoly supply business under its own administration. Today, only Afghanistan produces more each year. And it's not likely to slow down any time soon, given the economic rationale—growing the poppies whose sap produces it is simply more lucrative than farming other crops, bringing in around twenty times as much cash for a farmer as rice would, for example.

This profit-generating potential has also made the drug trade a pivotal part of the country's long-running civil strife. For half a century Burma has been riven not only by military rule but also by conflict with various ethnic groups living on its peripheries seeking independence from the central government. At the start of the Second World War the country was being ruled as a British colony. After the Japanese invaded in 1942 and made rapid inroads into the heartlands, the Burmese made a pact with them, promising to help them beat the British and open the way for a Japanese advance towards India. In return, Japan agreed to leave Burma a free and independent country after the war. But the non-Burmese, the multiple ethnic groups that lived in the highlands on the peripheries of Burma, went the other way. They promised to help the British fight the Japanese and their Burmese allies in return for future British support for independence for their respective regions. The hill peoples certainly kept their side of the bargain. Their knowledge of those wild lands and their toughness as fighters were crucial in overpowering and eventually pushing the Japanese out of Burma. But London conveniently forgot all about their own promises when the war ended.

Deserted by the British, their struggles for independence continued, and drug trafficking provided a handy source of financing for it. In Shan State, in the east of the country, a popular armed resistance movement sprouted up in the 1960s and grew by financing itself through a ten percent tax on opium production. After a while, though, the revolutionaries realised that it wasn't really sustainable and worried about the devastating effect promoting opium growth was having on the people for whose freedoms they were fighting. The problem was that it would take a bit of time to establish alternative sources of funding, plus it seemed a bit of a waste to just destroy all the existing crop.

The Shan, therefore, came up with a novel plan—offer the US, the main ultimate customer of the heroin that their crop was refined into, the opportunity to buy all the opium then growing in the areas under Shan control. The Americans were then welcome to burn it or do whatever they liked. The Shan would promise not to grow any more, and the Americans could come in and check whenever they wanted. With the money from the sale the Shan would be able to support their movement for a bit, plus finance a crop substitution effort. An added bonus was that the Shans' detractors would no longer be able to brand them as narco-terrorists. Sadly though, the Americans said no, claiming this whole resistance struggle business was just a cover up for being drug kingpins, as opposed to a genuine bid for self-determination.

I knew a bit about all that thanks to an obscure documentary produced by two intrepid filmmakers who had spent some thirty years visiting Shan state and exploring the opium trade there. It was a documentary I had watched because one of those filmmakers was Adrian Cowell, one of the six plucky Oxbridge chaps who'd been the first to drive from London to Singapore via Burma in 1955.

We found a lovely little terrace outside a café overlooking the town's main intersection and its clock tower. As we were tucking into some tea leaf salad, a local staple with a rather pleasing mild narcotic effect, a jovial, portly gentleman in a grimy T-shirt and *longyi* sauntered over and beamed at us. I gave him a nod, and he gave me a gap-toothed grin in return,

"Please finish to eat, and then you come with me."

It seemed we'd attracted the attention of the local crazy. I raised my fork and pointed it in his direction with an attempt at gravitas, "That's very kind of you, but I'm afraid we are rather busy after lunch."

He chortled, "Ah, but no-one too busy for Burmese police."

I lowered my cutlery as I felt the nerves of the day before coming back, but I decided to play dumb in any case and forced a smile, "Oh I see, you're from the police? Well a pleasure to meet you. How can we help you?"

He grinned again and licked his lips, "I am here to escort you to your hotel for the night. As a foreigner, you are our honoured guest in Burma."

While I wanted no more contact with the authorities than absolutely necessary, refusing his offer would arouse suspicion, so I didn't see we really had much choice. We finished up and then followed him on his moped through the backstreets of town to what was, no doubt, a formerly quite impressive hotel. It was dog-eared and damp now, but it was also not the police station, which was a relief, as I had considered that the whole escort business might have just been a ruse to get us to come quietly to the lock-up. We checked in and went up to the room for a siesta.

After an hour or so, I crept back down the stairs and peeked around the corner into the lobby to check that our friend had gone. Alas, no, there he was, spread over an over-stuffed cracked leather sofa ensconced in a newspaper. Whether his continued presence was for protection or observation purposes I wasn't really sure, but I certainly didn't like it. At no point, however, had he said that we had to stay there or must remain under his supervision. It seemed to me, therefore, that it was definitely time to do a runner. I snuck back up to the room and advised Lady R of my plan, and as I anticipated, she took little convincing to add fleeing from the law to her list of notable life achievements. We shouldered our still-packed bags and headed down the back stairs. I quickly loaded up the bike and then pushed it out onto the street to avoid signalling our unscheduled departure. Five minutes later, we were leaving the outskirts of town, sniggering like schoolchildren.

A wide, slow-flowing green river slid past to our right, cliffs rose up to our left, and in front of us we faced a road that was more potholes than tarmac. A couple of hours from Kale, we were by then out of reach of the policeman but also sadly past the furthest reaches of the Indian Border Roads Organisation. We jolted into the village of Kalewa, where a number of boats were drawn up on a sandbank at the side of the Chindwin River, one of the country's principal watercourses that joins up with the Irrawaddy farther south. With the successful border crossing and escape from the police under our belts, we were feeling rather jaunty and decided it might be quite fun, and not entirely cheating, to hoist the bike onto one of the boats and have a nice little rest for a day or so as we floated further south instead of riding. We drew up at the river bank and then walked from vessel to vessel motioning enthusiastically at the bike, the boat, and the river in impeccable sign language. But before we could secure a firm passage, a moped appeared carrying yet another local policeman. Word clearly travelled fast in those parts. We were politely but firmly told that boating was absolutely out of the question and that we'd instead, surprise, surprise, be accompanied to the hotel where we would be staying for the night.

**Boats at Kalewa**

We were taken up a steep dirt track to a corrugated iron roofed guest house. Someone was roused from underneath a blanket to sign us in. They showed us to a room with a bare, cracked concrete floor and walls that may have once been dark green but were now faded and peeling, stained with mud, betel nut juice, what might have been blood, and a couple of other totally unidentifiable substances. Some chicken wire over a hole in the wall served as a window and gave us a beautiful view directly onto the smoke-belching diesel generator that stood right outside. There was just room enough for a single bed, which consisted of a rusting iron bedstead with a thin, stained yellow mattress on top. A group of mosquitoes hummed around the bare bulb that hung down forlornly on a tired electric wire from the centre of the ceiling. And that was pretty much it. Apart from the shared bathroom, which appeared never to have been cleaned and where the shower was doubling as the toilet. The stench didn't seem to put off the cockroaches however.

As dawn broke the next day, we were already loaded up and heading out of the door, anxious to be free of the digs and the police. We left town via a long bridge over the river as the morning mist swirled across the water below and continued our journey southward. We'd read that some western aid agencies had committed a few years back to tarmac the whole stretch from Kalewa down to Monywa, the regional capital and our planned stop for the night, and so we were looking forward to a nice easy ride through some picturesque countryside. But it seemed they had been delayed in their work or else the money had been siphoned off somewhere along the way, as this was a road that could not have seen any improvements since at least the 1980s. After a couple of miles, asphalt had become an endangered species, appearing only as small isolated islands every once in a while that were best avoided in order to at least maintain some consistency of surface under the wheels.

**Road conditions**

The surroundings were at least breathtaking. Rice paddies stretched back from the road for half a mile or so, before the land swept upwards into thickly forested hills, rolling off towards the Indian border. There was no other traffic to speak of, just the odd bullock cart driven by a straw-hatted farmer or a young lady guiding her goats along in the morning breeze. Without exception, they, as well as the people out tending the fields, turned at the sound of our engine before their faces lit up in surprise and we were offered warm smiles and enthusiastic waves. This incessant welcoming and good cheer was starting to put us both in a seriously good mood, despite the atrocious road conditions.

Just how damn nice the average Burmese villager is was solidly demonstrated when we rounded a corner and the track abruptly disappeared into a long, wide, muddy, watery trench. It looked quite capable of swallowing the bike whole, and there was no way round. I pulled over and started to roll up my trousers in preparation for an exploratory wade. But at that moment a local farmer sucking on a huge dark green cheroot appeared from a neighbouring field, hoe balanced on one shoulder. He surmised the situation in a couple of seconds then raised a hand to me to indicate that I should stay where I was. He then removed his flip flops, hauled up his *longyi*, and plunged into the trench. It seemed not too deep at first, but after a couple more metres he went in up to his thighs and let out a loud guffaw, turning to us and shaking his head. He backtracked a bit and tried another route, which ended in similar circumstances. Several identical misadventures followed. He eventually found the shallowest path through the mire and then turned and gave us a thumbs up. I fired her up and carefully followed his route through, slithering rather wildly but avoiding going under. When we reached the other side, he smiled and nodded in satisfaction then gave us a wink, shouldered his hoe again, and continued on his way.

**A battery-powered pedestrian**

A couple of hours later, we pulled up at one of the very few tea houses along the route. The young patroness, dressed in a spotless yellow *htamein*, the Burmese figure-hugging sarong, and blessed with a shimmering sheet of long black hair adorned with a sprig of jasmine, greeted us with her baby on her hip, pointing out to him the two strange white animals, who he then goggled with huge liquid brown eyes. She started to enquire via sign language where we had come from and where we were heading. Once she'd understood, she paused for a second to think then pointed at me with a big smile, "You, hero! You James Bond!"

Well, I didn't like to deny it. We were certainly a far cry from that first day back at the Taj Mahal, when the waiter had asked us where we were off to and we'd felt embarrassed to tell him of our intentions, given how ridiculously ambitious they sounded. Now we really had a story to tell, even in sign language. We had made it across several thousand miles, crossed five international borders, and hell, might even get all the way to Rangoon.

**Rush hour**

The road onwards to Monywa at least had variety. The mud was behind us, and instead, the surface had changed to loose, fist-sized rocks. It was slow going and unstable, and there was the constant risk of a puncture. Stoically, though, the bike soldiered on—maybe she'd just become more resilient, toughened up a bit, got all the breakdowns out of her system—and ten hours after we'd set out from Kalewa, we finally hit the tarmac on the outskirts of Monywa.

The town sits on the banks of the Chindwin and is a major trade centre for the region. We read that it was particularly renowned for its blankets, which seemed a little surprising, given that the temperature was thirty-eight degrees Celsius at 4PM. Wikipedia also helpfully informed us that "Very few tourists visit Monywa as its facilities are limited." We got ready for another uncomfortable night, but as we were roaming around town looking for shelter, we passed a small lake and spotted a sign for the "Win Unity Resort." I started to raise my hopes a little, as surely the use of the word *Resort* meant at least a clear distinction between the roles of shower and toilet. And how very right I was. We turned off the main road and into heaven. Greeting us was an oasis of immaculately manicured tropical gardens where a series of large, red-roofed villas had been built, each with a raised terrace facing towards the lake. The place looked like it had just opened, and on approaching reception, we were told that we could take any villa we liked, as they didn't actually have any other guests.

I took a delicious hot shower and watched the mud and dust disappear down the shiny chrome plug hole then wrapped myself in a fluffy white dressing grown, pulled a bottle of wine out of the minibar, and adjourned to the terrace. As Lady R sorted herself out, I went back to reception and bought some cigarettes. Neither of us had smoked for a couple of weeks, after both agreeing to try to quit, but well, with the hardest part of the journey behind us, our last border crossing done, and most importantly, my first decent glass of Shiraz in over a month in my hand, I decided to allow myself just a little one. Or two. I returned to the terrace of the room, splayed myself into an armchair, took a sip of wine, lit up one of Burma's finest Red Rubies, and closed my eyes. As I was savouring a feeling of quite sublime bliss, I suddenly felt the cigarette being pulled out of my hand. I opened my eyes to find Lady R standing over me in the process of treading my smoke into the floor. She looked annoyed, "What are you doing? We agreed to stop smoking! Do you have absolutely no willpower?"

"Jesus, I'm just having a cigarette after a hard day, OK? Cut me some slack."

As I said it, I felt it unlikely that she would, and I was instantly proven right. "God you just can't do what you say, can you?"

That was right on the mark, but I felt perhaps it was best addressed with some light humour. That message, however, which departed safely and in a timely manner from my brain, unfortunately didn't make it to my lips before being hijacked by pride and defensiveness, and instead I managed to go with, "I'll smoke whenever I goddam want to, and you will not tell me what to do."

I glared at her as I pulled another cigarette from the packet and brought it to my lips. I had to give it to her, she was quick—before I could bring up the lighter she had swiped across with her hand, knocking that one from my mouth too and accidentally clipping my face at the same time. I shot up out of the chair, "Oh, so we're moving into domestic violence now are we? You need to hit me to get your point across?"

I felt pathetic, even as I blurted it out, and she understandably looked at me with disdain, "You are so damn melodramatic."

She turned around and started to walk down towards the lake. I bawled after her, "Yeah, that's it, just run away."

Which was fairly hypocritical given my past behaviour. She thrust her middle finger up over her head in response. As I lit up my third cigarette and took a healthy gulp of wine, I wondered just how much I really cared anymore.

In marked contrast to our relationship, the road was definitely getting easier. From Monywa, it was easy, flat byways through baked scrubland, past monasteries and tea shops, processions of schoolchildren and smiling ladies carrying a variety of loads on their heads. We crossed the wide, glimmering Irrawaddy River and then arrived at Burma's top tourist attraction. The town of Bagan was the seat of royalty from the ninth to the thirteenth centuries. From there the rulers governed a kingdom that, for the first time, unified the regions that would subsequently become modern Burma. And they were certainly committed Buddhists, constructing some 10,000 temples, pagodas, and monasteries in the area, of which around 2,000 survive today and are what bring in the tourists. There is a strong tradition in Burma of "making merit," earning your good fortune and your place in the afterlife by carrying out altruistic deeds, such as building pagodas or donating to monks. It is also sometimes done to compensate for past sins, an approach that can open the door to only committing such sins in the first place because you know the karmic slate can be wiped clean afterwards with, for example, a good spate of temple building. I pondered that when Lady R told me that Bagan's original name translates as "The City that Tramples on Enemies."

Even Marco Polo visited Bagan, describing it as "one of the finest sights in the world." Though 700 years had passed since he'd passed by, it was still looking pretty impressive. More or less wherever one looked the spire of a dark orange stone temple rose up from the scrubland. They ranged from the small—enclosing a single Buddha statue—to the huge—with several tiers that rose up step-like, each a little smaller than the one below, surmounted by a massive dome and housing multiple chambers, statues, and paintings. Bagan used to be a whole city, not just places of worship, but the rest of it had been built of wood rather than stone and so had long since rotted away into the dust. Today the temples were the only remaining witness to the once mighty civilisation that they had formed a part of.

**Temples of Bagan**

Like our arrival in Pokhara, back in Nepal, we were abruptly transported from being travellers to tourists, as people tried to sell us postcards, act as our guides, or entice us into their restaurant with a promise of a free bottle of beer. The upside was that we blended in perfectly, we weren't the centre of attention for once, and not a single policeman showed up to kindly offer us an escort to our accommodation for the night. We were comfortably settled into the hotel bar that evening when a middle-aged American couple sitting nearby greeted us, "So, how y'all enjoying your holiday in Burma?"

"Oh, very nicely, thank you," I replied, thinking that our definitions of "holiday" were probably rather different, "How about you?"

The man frowned a little, "Well to be honest, it's OK, but you know the pool here in the hotel, really, they need to make it cooler; it's kinda a pain in the ass. We keep tellin' 'em but nothing gets done."

Our definitions of "big pain in the ass" were probably rather different.

I nodded sympathetically, "I'm so sorry to hear that; anything else that's caused you trouble?"

He nodded firmly, "Yep, for a start, these damn street dogs you see around, ya know? Some of them look absolutely disgusting, teeming with fleas I'll bet. And when we were in Rangoon, it's like the whole city had this sorta, well, spicy smell?" he shook his head and took a swig of his imported beer, "But the worst thing is, sweet as they seem, most of these damn people just can't speak proper English!"

I smiled and bit my lip, "I should think you must be looking forward to getting home?"

He brought his glass down onto the bar enthusiastically, "Oh, you bet ya, it's cool to see it once, but we'll be mighty glad to leave the third world behind us, to tell you the truth."

He pointed his cigar at me, "So, which tour company are you guys travelling with?"

I smiled, "Oh us? None actually; we just rode our motorcycle here from Delhi."

He laughed and reached over to pat me on the back, "Haha, good one! Man, I wonder if anyone's actually ever done that? I doubt it though. Damn, they'd have to be crazy!"

I smiled and nodded in agreement.

# 18
# THE FINAL STRETCH

Over the centuries, Burma's rulers have had a tradition of shifting their capital in order to make a new start, gain better protection from their enemies, or simply because their astrologer told them to do so. The latter was said to be the main reason behind the most recent move in 2005, when the generals upped sticks from Rangoon, which is still the country's main metropolitan hub, and declared Nay Pyi Taw would be the new capital. There was some military rationale behind it too, as Nay Pyi Taw, in the centre of the country, would have them better placed to keep watch over all its corners, as opposed to Rangoon, which sits way down south by the coast.

There was only one small problem at the time they hatched that plan—Nay Pyi Taw did not actually exist, it was just a patch of jungle. And so they built their brand-new home from scratch. That allowed them to install military order and precision in all aspects of urban planning, as well as to add on handy extras, such as roads that could double as runways and a network of underground tunnels and bunkers. Building work was carried out mainly by their friends, the Chinese, for the cool reported sum of $5bn. As for the name, it means Abode of Kings, presumably an attempt at a legitimacy-enhancing link with Burma's erstwhile monarchs (who had, of course, been ousted some time back by the British).

That day we were on our way to see it for ourselves, but first we had to pass through Meiktila, a town that sits pretty much right in the middle of the country. It was, unfortunately, chiefly famous for two days of anti-Muslim rioting that had occurred a while back and left at least forty people dead. As we had heard elsewhere in the country, the Muslims and Buddhists in Meiktila used to rub along just fine, but more recently, sinister forces had been at work portraying all non-Buddhists as unpatriotic and spreading rumours that they were breeding fast and would soon take over the country. Such rumours could, of course, serve to provide an excuse in future for a military claw-back of power in the name of maintaining social cohesion, should the current democratic experiment be felt to be getting out of hand.

Some locals had felt that the reaction in the overseas media after the Meiktila killings was unfair, one-sided, and an example of foreigners meddling in things they just didn't understand. Despite the overwhelming warmth and hospitality of the Burmese, buried in their DNA is, quite understandably, the legacy of British oppression followed by a half century of military rule that often highlighted the threat foreigners could pose to the country and thus justified the need for the army to stay in control. As we drove through the outskirts of town looking for a place to eat, we noticed a few stares that seemed less than friendly and then a couple of shouts with accompanying dismissive hand gestures that appeared to indicate we were less than welcome. That was the first time that we'd felt like anything less than honoured guests in the country, and it was certainly unnerving. We quickly found a restaurant that was well back from the road where we could take our lunch unobserved.

From Meiktila we were treated, for the first time since the first day of our trip, to a perfectly smooth, multi-lane, and completely empty road. It had been built to connect Rangoon, in the far south of the country, to Nay Pyi Taw, almost 250 miles to the north, and then Mandalay, another 200 miles further up. We were joining it mid-way between the last two and heading south. As with the highway from Delhi to the Taj Mahal, the philosophy seemed to have been "build it and they will come." But they certainly hadn't yet. For the first half hour it was quite a joy to cruise along at sixty miles an hour, not a pothole or other vehicle in site, on a lovely wide, straight stretch of tarmac. But it soon got a little boring, and we realised that weaving through bullock carts, mud, stray chickens, and surprise army checkpoints were really all part of the fun.

Two hours later, we perked up as we reached the exit for Nay Pyi Taw. It was another wide empty road that led us towards the city, although there wasn't really any city as such in sight—no high rises in the distance, no growing throng of people and traffic and noise. In India it would pass for a national park. A series of far flung "zones"—residential, governmental, hotel, diplomatic, military—separated by wide expanses of wasteland were linked by six-, eight-, and even ten-lane highways. The place certainly had room to grow, which seemed to be the idea, as it was hoped that businesses, foreign embassies, maybe even normal people would soon see the charms and advantages of the new capital and move up there to join the civil servants and soldiers, who seemed to be the only inhabitants so far. There was not a soul on the streets and it was distinctly eerie, surely the world's most deserted capital. We swept down the highway to the hotel zone, passing precisely one bicycle and one bullock cart on the way. A lone street sweeper in a bamboo hat moved slowly across the lanes with a broom in hand, methodically sweeping each square centimetre of tarmac. We passed signs to the main, in fact the only, tourist attractions—a replica of Rangoon's Shwedagon Pagoda, a Water Fountain Park boasting a nightly light show, the "National Herbal Park," and a zoo advertising, rather incongruously in that weather, its very own colony of penguins.

"You know, if we continue on the main highway, we could be in Rangoon by nightfall."

It seemed unreal, even as I said it over breakfast. It was probably the first time I had dared to voice our destination as anything more than a vague possibility.

Lady R frowned, "This is the wrong way to finish an adventure."

"How do you mean?"

"I mean an easy run on a sterile highway that could be just about anywhere."

I saw her point, "Well, you know there is one other possibility..."

"Continue to China?" She positively beamed across the table at me.

"Err, no, sweetie, either the bike or I would fall apart just at the thought."

She frowned, "Hmmm, I need to trade in both for younger models, clearly. So?"

I smiled, "Well, I was going to say that there's an old road we could take from near here that runs all the way down to Rangoon. It'd be much rougher, of course, and take longer, and no doubt it's full of potholes and wandering livestock and..."

She slapped her hand on the table, "We're doing it."

It was like travelling through a magic portal as we swung off the empty highway on the outskirts of Nay Pyi Taw, followed a small, rutted track for a few hundred metres and then, rounding a corner, found the real Burma suddenly restored. A couple of tea shops by the side of the road were busy with their morning trade, men in *longyis* sitting on small plastic stools outside sipping sweet milky brews. A gnarled old oak tree housed an elaborate shrine to the local *nat*, or spirit, providing insurance against misfortune. A 1950s bus tooted its horn as it rumbled past, and an old lady carrying a bundle of vegetables on her head while puffing on a long dark green cheroot took it out of her mouth for a second and gave us a delightful, toothless smile.

**Fruit seller**

We zig-zagged happily along, around children on bicycles in their green and white uniforms heading off to school, little boys herding water buffalo, and the odd belching, beaten up old truck. Then suddenly there were some men with guns blocking the way ahead. We were waved down and signalled to turn off the engine. One of the troops approached us with his rifle slung over his shoulder, "Mr. Andy?"

"Err, wow, yes, but how on earth did you know?"

"We are the Army; we know everything!" he smiled and then beckoned to his colleague and pointed to our number plate. A list was produced, and the plate checked against it.

"Don't worry, we keep good track of you."

It certainly seemed they did. I peered over and saw that our number plate was on a very short list of foreign registered vehicles that were allowed to be in the country, ours being the only motorcycle. On request, I signed in a dusty ledger, committing to God knows what, then braced for the word *deportation*. But it didn't come, and they, instead, wished us a smooth onward passage. It looked like we were almost home and dry.

A few hours later as darkness fell, the headlight attracted a swarm of flying bugs that smacked into my eyes and mouth. It was making driving increasingly difficult, but having learned nothing from the last couple of months, we decided to push on, regardless, with another bash at night driving. A truck turned onto the road up ahead without catching sight of another motorcycle in front of us. The rider swerved but was going too fast to avoid a collision and, with a sickening screech, crashed into the side of the truck and was thrown into the middle of the road as bits of bike were scattered across the tarmac. I braked hard and pulled up next to his motionless body. Lady R jumped off and started frantically waving her arms to alert the traffic behind to stop. A small crowd quickly gathered, and someone called an ambulance as the rider moved a little and started to groan. We waited until the medics turned up and put him on a stretcher, bloodied but conscious. I turned to Lady R, and without needing to say anything, we agreed it was time to stop for the night.

On the outskirts of the small town of Bago we found a little hotel that had a room available. As we hauled the bags off the bike, it seemed barely believable that it would be the last time we'd do it. After checking in, we collapsed into lounge chairs on the veranda, ordered some wine, and I lit up a cigarette.

"So, it's nearly over?" I smiled at Lady R, and she nodded her head in return, "Well, we could still continue to China..."

I laughed, "Maybe next time, baby."

"Hmmm, you're really going to be too old pretty soon."

I took a drag on my cigarette and eyed her suspiciously, "For adventure?"

"Well, for just about everything, I'd say."

"Ha, well it's been quite a ride, hasn't it?"

"Yes, it certainly has," she took a sip of her wine, "but all good things come to an end."

She lowered her gaze and started to circle her finger round the rim of her glass, "But really, it's been amazing, you've been amazing, and I think the trip has taught us a lot."

I nodded in agreement, "Like the complete unreliability of the Enfield motorcycle and my blatant lack of essential maintenance skills, for example."

She laughed, but drily, "Yes, all that, of course. But I mean also about us."

I looked her in the eye, "Well I guess, like the bike, we've had our issues, our breakdowns, but somehow we got through, and we're still going, stronger through adversity, and now cruising right to the finish line, no?"

But I didn't really believe any of it, and for once, I was already welcoming the directness I knew I'd get in response, the fact that she was not afraid of saying what I seemingly couldn't. It only took a couple of seconds to come. She sighed, "I, well, I guess I don't know that we are, and we are not fixable with a couple of priests and a rock, you know. We have to be our own mechanics. And do you think we're really capable of that?"

I opened my mouth to reply and then closed it again.

At sunrise next morning we were already loading up the bike, one final time, stuffing a rucksack into each side of the metal frame on the back then wrapping bungee cords around tight to keep them in place. I checked the petrol and the brake fluid and gave the tyres a kick, as I had nearly every morning for the last two months. We were good to go. I thought of last night's conversation. Perhaps it was just a blip; maybe all would be forgotten once we got home and realised what we'd done together, what we'd achieved.

As we hit the road there was a light mist over the paddy fields, giving the surrounding countryside an ethereal air. It was just after 7AM, so the roads were pretty clear. A sign announced we were only thirty miles from Rangoon. How impossible it had seemed when we pulled away from the guest house in Delhi—that we could get all the way to Rangoon just by following the tarmac (well rock, dirt, and mud), mile by mile, day by day. Now it was twenty miles left. Now ten. The traffic started to increase, a gathering hubbub of buses, trucks and small cars setting out for the big city. Five. Two.

"We're crossing the city limits!" I shouted out to Lady R. She wrapped her arms around me and gave me a lovely squeeze.

"My God, we've actually made it, Andy!"

"We bloody well have!" I let out a long toot on the horn, then thought for a moment, "But you know it's always right near home that accidents happen."

She rapped me sharply on the helmet, "Oh, will you never learn not to worry so much!" I laughed before she added, "But of course what we're doing right now is actually illegal."

She was right and I'd completely forgotten. For the first time in eight weeks of riding we were in an area where motorcycling was, in fact, against the law. Rangoon, unlike the rest of the country, prohibits motorcycles within the city limits. The reasons for that are disputed, but range from a story about a general having seen the state of Hanoi in Vietnam with its swarms of bikes and vowing that Rangoon would never end up like that, to a motorcyclist having made a gun sign at another general's daughter when her motorcade forced him to pull over in the city, and a blanket ban having been introduced as a result, citing security concerns. We were chancing it in any case and counting on our letter from the Foreign Ministry to see us through any trouble. It really would be more than a little frustrating to be arrested so close to our goal.

As the only bike on the road we attracted even more attention than usual, two strange foreigners on a loaded-up, and by then, very beaten-up Royal Enfield Bullet with foreign licence plates rumbling through the morning traffic. People started shouting from buses and giving us the thumbs up, taxi drivers honked and pulled aside to let us through, and at one traffic light an old Burmese lady hobbled up and, with a beautiful worn smile, draped a small garland of jasmine flowers around Lady R's neck.

And then there she was, her immense golden dome rising up ahead, topped by a glimmering spire that was encrusted with precious stones—the Shwedagon Pagoda, Burma's holiest site and one that was delightfully described by the English traveller Ralph Fitch in the sixteenth century as "the fairest place, as I suppose, that doe bee in all the worlde." We nodded respectfully to the grand old dame and then rumbled on past the sparkling waters of Kandawgyi Lake, overtaking a line of pink-robed, shaven-headed nuns out on their morning alms round. The roads narrowed as we drew into downtown, riding past street sellers hawking everything from betel nut to fried fish to lottery tickets on broken pavements beneath crumbling old colonial buildings.

There was the sign, Shwe Bontha Street, our home. We turned in and drove slowly down before pulling up outside the building that I'd walked away from in so much trepidation two months before. I killed the engine for the last time. A mix of exhilaration and relief swept over me as Lady R curled her arms around me and banged the front of her helmet lightly into the back of mine.

Delhi seemed a world away, and yet we'd somehow just connected it with Rangoon. We'd driven 4,000 miles, passed through four countries, endured God knows how many breakdowns, and had more than our fill of men with guns. But we'd made it. We'd ridden to Rangoon. I turned to Lady R, who was looking exactly how I felt, happily stunned,

"My God, it seems we've just gone and bloody done it, darling!"

She grinned back at me, "You see, I told you it wouldn't be that difficult. Absolutely nothing to worry about really."

# 19
# BURMA AND BUST

The next morning I woke early and waited for my brain to boot up and tell me where we were. To remember which place we were aiming for today, what dangers might lie ahead, how far we still had to go. But no, today there was nowhere to get to, nothing to chase, nothing to worry about. My eyes adjusted to the morning light of our apartment. I moved a little and groaned; my whole body was stiff, particularly my hands from so many hours gripping the handlebars and also, to be honest, my arse, which had taken the brunt of the bumping, shaking, and juddering. I leaned over to cuddle Lady R and instead found a note on the pillow saying she'd gone for a run. I shook my head at the ridiculous energy of the youth.

I thought back to the last time I'd woken up in this bed, full of anticipation and nerves, a thousand questions churning through my head about the trip ahead. Well a good deal of what I'd worried about had actually come to pass—the atrocious roads, the men with guns, the epic mechanical failures. But I suppose that what I hadn't counted on was that we would never really be alone. Had we been forced to rely solely on our own mettle then we undoubtedly wouldn't have made it. But instead, from Delhi all the way to Rangoon, we'd been helped and rescued and taken in by everyone from priests to biker gangs to local farmers. We'd faced our share of danger, true, but the overwhelming feeling of the places we'd passed through was one of welcome and hospitality, and the more remote the place the warmer that welcome had been.

This was certainly the most adventurous thing I'd ever done, and I was confident I'd be dining out on the stories for quite some time. In fact, we'd already been contacted by a couple of newspapers and magazines asking us to write features for them. And, even more remarkably, I'd had a call from the Indian Ambassador's office asking if I'd like to come over to his residence for a whiskey and a chat about what was going on at the India-Burma border. Well, don't mind if I do, Your Excellency. So maybe the mid-life crisis had been assuaged for now.

I stretched and forced myself up, realising I couldn't leave the bike out on the street much longer, given its kind were banned in the city. I threw on a pair of shorts and a T-shirt and went downstairs to move it into a nearby garage. I flicked on the ignition and went to kick it alive. Nothing. A second attempt fared no better, and I then noticed that the dial showed the battery was dead. I climbed off and glanced down at the front wheel and saw that the tyre was also completely flat. It seemed the old girl had just hung on until Rangoon before giving up the ghost.

Lady R arrived home very sweaty a couple of hours later after what had clearly been an epic return to two-legged travel. She pointed out to the street, "I see the bike's still out there. I thought you were going to move it?"

I threw her a towel, "Yeah, I tried, but it was dead, kaput, so I had to get a mechanic over, he's only just left."

"Ah, OK." She mopped her brow then pulled at her hair a little and bit her lip, "Hey, look, I think we need to talk."

I could feel myself starting to tremble a little. I averted my gaze, took a deep breath, and then turned back to her, "You're wanting to tell me that it's not just the trip that's over, aren't you?"

She sighed deeply, "Well, OK, if you put it like that, directly, then yes, I am. And I think you know it, well, we both know it really, don't we?" She spoke softly and reached out to touch my arm as she attempted a half smile. She looked more gentle and approachable and loveable than ever.

Would I protest or break down or accuse her of having used me for a free adventure? But no, I suddenly realised that just as I'd had an imaginary, overly negative, vision of the trip before we set out, so too I'd had an overly positive one of the relationship between me and Lady R. Just as the trip on paper looked terrifying, so Lady R on paper looked like my perfect partner. I'd thought the adventure would provide the glue that was needed to finally seal things. And true, there were moments where wonder or achievement or adversity had certainly brought us closer together. But overall the heightened understanding of each other that such closeness had yielded had made us more aware of our differences and incompatibilities, as opposed to the reasons why we should be together.

I could still reel off a list of positive and endearing attributes about her and about how we complemented one another, but that was no longer enough. I realised I had filled in the gaps between us before with an optimistic imagination that the searing light of two months on the road had exposed as wishful thinking. This would perhaps be fixable if we had the tools and knowledge for the job, but we seemed to be sorely lacking in that department, and unfortunately, there was no capable garage to hand things over to. We'd returned home now, back to the apartment we shared, back to the same life, but both with a different, clearer perspective on the other and on us as a couple.

I raised my head to look her in the eye, "I always wondered where the Highway of Sorrows would eventually take us, and well, I guess now I know."

She averted her gaze. There was no need to say any more. My backpack was still next to the door, not yet unpacked. I walked slowly over and hauled it onto my shoulder. As I opened the front door I remembered the ring that I'd had tucked in my wallet since buying it in Bhutan. I looked around to Lady R but she had her back turned now. I placed it gently on the side table by the door without saying anything. I left the apartment and headed downstairs and climbed onto the bike. I was alone this time as I fired her up and pulled out into the street, off to find a place to stay for the night, and then only God, Buddha, or Ganesh knew what. It was Burma and Bust.

## *Also from Road Dog Publications*

### *Motorcycles, Life, and . . .* [1,2] *by Brent Allen*
Sit down at a table and talk motorcycles, life and . . . (fill in the blank) with award winning riding instructor and creator of the popular "Howzit Done?" video series, Brent "Capt. Crash" Allen. Here are his thoughts about riding and life and how they combine told in a lighthearted tone.

### *The Elemental Motorcyclist* [1,2] *by Brent Allen*
Brent's second book offers more insights into life and riding and how they go together. This volume, while still told in the author's typical easy-going tone, gets down to more specifics about being a better rider.

### *A Short Ride in the Jungle* [1,2] *by Antonia Bolingbroke-Kent*
A young woman tackles the famed Ho Chi Minh Trail alone on a diminutive pink Honda Cub armed only with her love of Southeast Asia and its people, and her wits.

### *Bonneville Go or Bust* [1,2] *by Zoë Cano*
A true story with a difference. Zoe had no experience for such a mammoth adventure of a lifetime but goes all out to make her dream come true to travel solo across the lesser known roads of the American continent on a classic motorcycle.

*I loved reading this book. She has a way of putting you right into the scene. It was like riding on the back seat and experiencing this adventure along with Zoe.* —★★★★ Amazon Review

### *Southern Escapades* [1,2] *by Zoë Cano*
As an encore to her cross country trip, Zoë rides along the tropical Gulf of Mexico & Atlantic Coast in Florida, through the forgotten back roads of Alabama and Georgia. This adventure uncovers the many hidden gems of lesser known places in these beautiful Southern states.

*. . . Zoe has once again interested and entertained me with her American adventures. Her insightful prose is a delight to read and makes me want to visit the same places.* —★★★★★ Amazon Review

# *Also from Road Dog Publications*

## *Chilli, Skulls & Tequila* [1,2] *by Zoë Cano*
Zoë takes to four wheels this time for an adventure south of the border in Baja. The extra set of wheels does nothing to diminish the "adventure" of this journey as Zoë travels to unique, out-of-the-way places tucked into Baja's forgotten corners.

## *Hellbent for Paradise* [1,2] *by Zoë Cano*
The inspiring—and often nail-biting—tale of Zoë's exploits roaming the jaw-dropping natural wonders of New Zealand on a mission to find her own paradise.

## *Beads in the Headlight* [1] *by Isabel Dyson*
A British couple tackle riding from Alaska to Tierra del Fuego two-up on a 31 year-old BMW "airhead." Join them on this epic journey across two continents.

*A great blend of travel, motorcycling, determination, and humor.*—★★★★★ Amazon Review

## *Chasing America* [1,2] *by Tracy Farr*
Tracy Farr sets off on multiple legs of a motorcycle ride to the four corners of America in search of the essence of the land and its people.

## *In Search of Greener Grass* [1] *by Graham Field*
With game show winnings and his KLR 650, Graham sets out solo for Mongolia and beyond. Foreword by Ted Simon

## *Eureka* [1] *by Graham Field*
Graham sets out on a journey to Kazakhstan only to realize his contrived goal is not making him happy. He has a "Eureka!" moment and turns around and begins to enjoy the ride as the ride itself becomes the destination.

## *Different Natures* [1] *by Graham Field*
The story of two early journeys Graham made while living in the US, one north to Alaska and the other south through Mexico. Follow along as Graham tells the stories in his own unique way.

## *Also from Road Dog Publications*

### *Thoughts on the Road*[1,2] *by Michael Fitterling*
The Editor of Vintage Japanese Motorcycle Magazine, ponders his experiences with motorcycles & riding and how they've intersected and influenced his life.

### *Northeast by Northwest*[1,2] *by Michael Fitterling*
The author finds two motorcycle journeys of immense help staving off depression and the other effects of stress. Along the way, he discovers the beauty of North America and the kindness of its people.

> *. . . one of the most captivating stories I have read in a long time. Truly a MUST read!!*—★★★★★ Amazon Review

### *Hit the Road, Jac!*[1,2] *by Jacqui Furneaux*
At 50, Jacqui leaves her home and family, buys a motorcycle in India, and begins a seven-year journey with no particular plan and along the way comes to terms with herself and her family—both adventure and introspection

### *Asphalt & Dirt*[1,2] *by Aaron Heinrich*
A compilation of profiles of both famous figures in the motorcycle industry and relatively unknown people who ride, dispelling the myth of the stereotypical "biker" image.

### *A Tale of Two Dusters & Other Stories*[1,2] *by Kirk Swanick*
In this collection of tales, Kirk Swanick tells of growing up a gear head behind both the wheels of muscle cars and the handlebars of motorcycles and describes the joys and trials of riding

### *Man in the Saddle*[1,2] *by Paul van Hoof*
Aboard an old 1975 Moto Guzzi V7 Paul starts out from Alaska for Ushaia. Along the way there are many twists and turns, some which change his life forever. English translation from the original Dutch

Distributed by: NBN national book network

Road Dog PUBLICATIONS
www.roaddogpub.com

Also available for [1] Kindle from amazon.com & [2] Nook from bn.com

CPSIA information can be obtained
at www.ICGtesting.com
Printed in the USA
BVHW090949280219
541422BV00019B/363/P